Must Be a Mistake: A Small Town Romance

Timber Falls, Volume 2

Fiona West

Published by Tempest and Kite, 2020.

This is a work of fiction. Similarities to real people, places, or events are entirely coincidental.

MUST BE A MISTAKE: A SMALL TOWN ROMANCE

First edition. June 9, 2020.

Copyright © 2020 Fiona West.

Written by Fiona West.

PROLOGUE

ELEVEN YEARS AGO

It was unseasonably warm for June . . . The heat didn't usually descend until the Fourth of July, but Ainsley was using the cheap fans her new sister-in-law had gotten for the bridesmaids in earnest. The summer insects sang and the birds chirped and hopped in the stand of trees that separated them from the main road. The shade was all taken, but with her fair skin, she needed to get out of the sun or she'd burn. She never had figured out a way to tan in her sixteen years—she went from paper white to lobster red within minutes. She looked around and spotted Kyle Durand alone under an ancient maple tree at the edge of the church property. He drove her and Daniel, her best friend, home from school most days, after they got out of orchestra rehearsals.

She strolled over to him, cake in hand, trying to be casual. Kyle was leaving for college in a few days; he'd be gone a long time. Even on summer break, she already missed seeing him every day. She was fairly sure he never thought about her. Of course, she'd probably see him on breaks, but he'd want to see his family, too. He'd become such a fixture in her life, and she didn't know when that had happened. He was just a guy—a handsome, older guy—who took her home from school some-times. But now he was leaving. All the way to California.

"Trade you," she said, picking her way through the grass carefully, since she'd already kicked off her pinching, shiny high-heeled shoes.

"What?"

"I'll trade you a spot in the shade for my piece of cake. It's the last chocolate one . . ."

"I like vanilla cake," he replied with a straight face. "Didn't you put on sunscreen?"

"No, Kyle Durand, I didn't. I didn't put on *sunscreen* before I was part of an *indoor wedding . . .*" *Kyle Ridiculous Durand.*

"An indoor wedding with an outdoor component," he pointed out, as he unbuttoned his dress shirt sleeves and proceeded to roll up them up.

How did he get arms like that when all she ever saw him do was run? *He must do push-ups, too, probably shirtless.*

"Here," he said, scooting over, half out of the dappled shade. "We can share."

She sat down gratefully; a breeze had kicked up, but it wasn't cooling her enough. "I only brought one fork . . . you take it."

"I'll go get my own fork in a minute. Just eat your half first."

"So you're just going to watch me eat? That's not weird or anything . . ."

"Who says I'm looking at you?" Kyle said, glancing at the crowd of their family and friends. "At least the wedding wasn't too long."

That's an odd thing to say.

"I've always thought the true test of a wedding shouldn't be how long it was, but how happy the people are afterward. I mean, it's kind of silly, isn't it? How we pour all this time and energy and money into the first day of a marriage, when really, what matters is the day-to-day for the rest of their lives." She took a big stab at the cake and shoved it into her mouth to keep herself from talking; she was probably embarrassing herself with her brain dump, philosophizing about marriage with Kyle Amazing Durand . . . Her mouth and her brain both skipped like a scratched record when Kyle's thumb gently swiped the corner of her mouth.

"Sorry," he mumbled. "You had a . . . you had frosting on your face."

"Oh. Okay." She watched wide-eyed as he stuck his thumb in his mouth and sucked off the frosting. The frosting that had been near her mouth was now in Kyle's mouth. That was far too much mouth-thinking for two people who were just friends. It was also the hottest thing she'd ever seen. She sat frozen, her face beet red, sweating through her loaner lavender bridesmaid dress.

She passed the cake to him clumsily. "Here, you can have the rest. I should . . . I should go see if . . . I think someone said something about group pictures—"

"Ainsley?"

"Yes?" She was already up off the grass, dusting off her backside. She probably shouldn't have sat down in the first place . . .

Kyle was watching her like he was waiting for her to answer a question he hadn't asked. Then suddenly, his expression shuttered. "Nothing. I was just . . . never mind. If I don't see you before I go, have a good fall."

"Yes, you too. We'll see you at Thanksgiving, I'm sure."

"Yeah, planning on it."

"Okay then." Her mother was indeed calling her over for pictures; a lucky coincidence, since she'd been lying earlier. When she turned to look over her shoulder, he was staring after her, the cake untouched.

CHAPTER ONE

AINSLEY SIGHED AS HER first graders lined up for library; Cooper Durand was still in the Naughty Chair. She didn't refer to it that way in front of her students, of course. She called it the Think It Over Chair. A place for them to take a deep breath, regain their self-control in a safe area. But that didn't change its stripes: it was a Naughty Chair. And Cooper certainly belonged there: she'd caught him peeing on a tree at recess instead of getting the pass to go inside. She'd happened to see him out her window today as she was eating lunch alone in her room, and she nearly choked on her chicken salad sandwich. She'd asked Mrs. Talbot, the recess lady, to watch out for him, but recess was a pretty hectic place as it was, and Mrs. Talbot's eyesight wasn't what it used to be. This was the only instance she knew about, but there could've been more. A *lot* more. The kids got a morning and afternoon recess . . . She sighed again and reached a hand toward him.

"Cooper, come lead the line with me, please." The boy bounded up and trotted over to the head of the group. She held his hand as the class meandered down the hall, looking less like a line and more like a dodecahedron. "What did you do that you shouldn't have done?"

"Pee on the tree when you were looking."

"So close," she said, schooling her face into a stern but kind look. "Try again."

"Pee on the tree."

"Better. And what did you *not* do that you *should've* done?"

"Get the pass from Mrs. Talbot." He looked up at her, genuinely frustrated. "But Kacie and Fran always get it first and they take too long! Recess is over by the time they come back."

"Well, they're not supposed to go together anyway, so I'll talk to Mrs. Talbot, okay?" She squeezed his hand, and he gave her a semi-toothless grin.

"Thanks, Miss Buchanan." He paused. "Don't worry, I peed on a different one every day, so one wouldn't grow taller. Uncle Kyle says urine is a good fertilizer."

"Yes, well . . . that's a relief. Also, maybe don't listen to everything Uncle Kyle says."

"Why not?" He was whispering because they'd reached the closed library doors.

"Because little boys don't need to know the agricultural applications for urine," she whispered back, turning to smile at the librarian, CJ. "See you later, Buchanan's Bunch." She had sixty-two math manipulatives calling her that weren't going to cut out and laminate themselves. She'd have a talk with Uncle Kyle later . . . if she could get him to talk to her at all. *Whatever.* Lots of other fish in the sea. Less grunty, broody fish. Well, *some* other fish in the sea. More like a lake, really. And at that moment, it was feeling downright puddle-ish. She'd been on four dates with Todd Glazer . . . all of which were boring. When he'd called for a fifth, she'd let him down gently.

Ainsley blitzed through the afternoon math lesson and ended up with time to spare—everything this time of year was just a review of kindergarten—so they read *Lily's Big Day* by Kevin Henkes again. Her students never got tired of hearing a story about a child (well, a mouse child) who wanted desperately to be her teacher's flower girl, who wanted to be special to the people she loved. It was so delightfully relatable to them.

Posey raised her hand. "Are you going to get married, Miss Buchanan?"

"Yes, I think so. Someday." She smiled at the kids, who were beaming at her. "Do you think I'd pick one of you to be my flower person?"

"No," the kids chorused, giggling. *Oh good; they actually listened to the story.*

When she walked her gaggle of skipping, yawning, babbling students out to the buses, Kyle Durand was there to pick up Cooper, who broke ranks to run to him. Kyle Hot Stuff Durand, with his tousled brown hair, so dark it was almost black. His stormy brown eyes, the physique that showcased the benefits of daily exercise. He greeted his nephew too quietly for her to hear over the melee of students. The boy nodded, then shook his head, apparently reconsidering his first answer to whatever question he'd asked. Kyle looked up and caught her gaze. "He had a rough day?"

There was a momentary stand-off: he stared at her as though he were waiting for her to come to him or shout her answer across the hoards still pairing student with caregiver or mode of transportation. She crossed her arms and stared right back. With half a grin, he sauntered over to her slowly as if she didn't have another ten kids waiting for her to put them on the bus. *What the heck is so funny?*

"In the future, I'd appreciate it if you encouraged Cooper to keep his tree-watering activities confined to your own yard."

His eyes snapped to the boy in horror. "You *didn't*."

"I had a good reason!" Cooper shouted.

Dr. Durand ran a hand down his face. "It won't happen again. Sorry."

"Well, I'm satisfied with the time he's served in the Think It Over Chair, but I wanted to make someone at home aware of the . . . issue."

"Sure, yes. I will pass the message on to Philip. Sorry about that; I just figured it's the kind of thing the boy should know, in case of a zombie apocalypse."

Ainsley smiled in spite of herself. "A what?"

"Zombie apocalypse," Kyle said, his brown eyes somber despite his ridiculous statement. How he kept a straight face, she'd never know. "We've gotta prepare the kids for what's coming. As an educator, you play a key role, I'm surprised you don't know all about it."

"Thank you for your time, Dr. Durand," Ainsley said, still smiling, walking backward, leading the line toward the rest of the buses. "See you Monday."

"Only if the zombies don't attack first," he called back, and several teachers around them stopped to stare. Ainsley didn't let herself laugh until she turned to put Damon, Denver, and Heaven on bus number 6.

CHAPTER TWO

KYLE SLAMMED HIS TRUCK door. What had gotten into him? Her shirt, that's what. She was wearing that blouse he liked, the dark-blue see-through one with the rainbow trout on it. How she managed to make rainbow trout look cute and hot at the same time, he hadn't been able to figure out. And he had spent considerable time thinking about it—while doing his laundry, at family dinners, working at the hospital . . . He felt a bit bad about that last one. But when he wasn't working, he didn't feel bad thinking about Ainsley. He was a good multitasker. He'd been doing it for years anyway. If he hadn't gone to that dumb wedding, he wouldn't have this problem.

"Are we going home or what?" Cooper called from the back seat. Kyle slid on his sunglasses and muttered under his breath about brothers and their unreasonable expectations. He'd agreed to pick up his nephew right after Philip had his second baby, and now, it was somehow expected he'd do it every day. If he didn't get to see Ainsley, he'd have pawned Coop off on his mom weeks ago.

"Of course we are."

"Then why are we just sitting here? I'm hungry."

"You're always hungry. It's amazing your dad has any money at all."

"I'm a growing boy. That's what Mom says." That did sound like Claire. Besides, the kid wasn't overweight. No one could figure out where he put it all; his belly was like a black hole.

Kyle started the truck and turned onto the main road. The buses had already left. Ainsley had gone back inside. He'd realized something, engaged in a silent battle of wills over something as simple as a short conference. She was never going to come to him. Though he'd never said it out loud, that's what he'd been waiting for, all this time. Waiting for her to see him, waiting for her to figure out why he tagged along with his brother as often as possible. But it wasn't going to happen . . . so what were his other options? During that short walk across the concrete pickup area, he'd weighed them: 1.) Give up. But if his infatuation with her had lasted this long, he didn't think it would die just because he wanted it to, just because he was scared. It was like a raccoon in a koi pond; it just kept coming back. He suspected that his autism was playing a role in his fascination with her, but he couldn't be sure. 2.) Keep waiting. That hadn't worked so far. 3.) Go after her. It wasn't like he hadn't thought of it. He had, of course he had. But it wasn't his style; he'd never needed to before. In high school and college, he'd had plenty of women who'd made their interest clear, most of them with dollar signs over their eyes like cartoon characters. It was widely known that his family was fairly well-off; his trust from Grandpa Tank had allowed him to have a nice down payment for his house.

But that wasn't Ainsley. Two years younger than him, she'd never been part of his circle of friends. And if she had liked him, she had too much self-respect to be overt about her feelings. So today, he'd flirted with her. At least he thought he had.

She'd smiled. That was a good start. *Phase One: Win Ainsley's Attention.* As mad as he was at himself for getting into this without a solid plan, at least he hadn't completely screwed up.

Now I just need a Phase Two . . .

"SO, COOP," PHILIP STARTED, passing the mashed potatoes down the table to Kyle, "how was your day?" Claire had expected Kyle to stay as usual; dinner was his payment for picking up Cooper. Since he started his shifts at 7 p.m., picking him up at 3:30 wasn't bad, and he did get a free meal out of it.

"Miss Buchanan's getting married."

Kyle stopped chewing his steak. "What did you say?"

"That's wonderful," Claire cooed, tossing her straight red hair. "Who's she marrying?"

Cooper shrugged, poking at the sautéed green beans on his plate.

Wonderful? thought Kyle. *That's the worst news I've ever heard. Also, is that little sneak trying to divert attention from Tree-Peeing Gate?*

"She didn't say?" Claire probed.

Cooper shook his head, and Kyle turned to his sister-in-law.

"You're the queen of Timber Falls gossip, why haven't I heard about this?"

"I hadn't heard a thing, but most of my gossip channels are hospital-related."

"Why the sudden interest?" His brother Philip smirked. "Is the most eligible bachelor in Timber Falls ready to settle down?"

Kyle flipped him off by rubbing his eye with his middle finger, and Philip returned the gesture.

"Quit it," Claire warned, getting up to retrieve her infant daughter from her bedroom down the hall. "He's six, not an idiot."

"Can I go play the tablet?" Cooper asked, and Philip nodded.

"Still haven't heard an answer," he added, directing a pointed look at Kyle, who'd given up eating altogether.

"It's not sudden, and you know it."

"Seems like you missed your chance, bud."

Kyle worried his lower lip between his fingers. "You think?"

Philip shrugged. "That's what the six-year-old scuttlebutt would indicate."

"Who could she even be dating? Wouldn't we have heard something about it before now? Daniel hasn't said anything. He keeps tabs on her." Kyle got to his feet. Pacing would work, pacing would help. He could think better if he was moving. Better to panic while moving than to panic while sitting still.

"Friendship isn't exactly the same as keeping tabs, but okay." His brother pointed with his fork. "Internet. Could've met him on the internet, I hear that's the thing now."

"Okay, Grandpa."

Philip threw his arms out. "I'm practically a millennial!"

"No, you're not." He paused. "You don't think she's back with Dean, do you?"

"Dean moved to Portland."

"Dean belongs in Portland."

"Yes, Dean does belong in Portland. Weirdo."

"Remember when he dyed his hair black?"

"Weirdo."

"Who's a weirdo?" asked Claire, flopping back down at the table with Hannah in her arms.

"Dean Hoppsteader."

"Didn't he move to Portland?" Claire picked up her fork to resume eating, but Hannah couldn't stay latched. Her high-pitched cries tugged at Kyle's heartstrings, but he tried not to let it show. Infant cries were one of the few things that made him teary if he was already on edge.

He coughed, pivoting to give Claire some privacy as she tried to adjust her hold on Hannah. "We have lactation consultants at the hospital, you know."

Claire snorted. "I don't need a lactation consultant."

"I'm just saying. If you did, we have them."

His sister-in-law enunciated her words patronizingly. "I have done this before with Coop. I don't need a lactation consultant; they're the same breasts I had then."

"But not the same baby," her husband added gently, reaching over to rub her back.

"Don't touch," Claire said without looking up, still trying to get Hannah to latch, and Kyle felt momentary sympathy for his brother.

"I've got to get to work. Thanks for dinner, Claire."

"Thanks for picking up Cooper, Kyle. I should be able to do it myself soon, I've just been so exhausted, and Hannah's still nursing a lot . . ."

"Don't worry about it," he said, waving her off. "I don't mind." He paused at the threshold of the open front door. "Also, Ainsley caught him peeing on a tree at school. Bye." Kyle shut the door behind him before he could hear their reaction. He felt only slightly guilty for throwing Coop under the bus, since he had given him the idea.

He whipped out his phone as he got in the car. Daniel. His brother would know, he'd been best friends with her since middle school.

Kyle: Is Ainsley engaged?

Daniel: Don't think so. Why?

Kyle: Heard a rumor.

Daniel: Pretty sure she would've told me or Winnie . . .

Kyle: Probably just a rumor.

Kyle: Don't tell her I said anything.

Daniel: But come to think of it, she has been on a few dates with some guy she met on an app, so I could be wrong.

So maybe it is true. That was upsetting for two reasons: she'd been dating someone, and she'd debased herself by using one of those terrible apps. He appreciated Daniel's insights into the situation, even though he was annoyed with him in general right now. It felt like every time he came home and wanted to chill in his own living room, his brother and his brother's fiancée had beaten him to it. At least he was working nights now; the house was quieter during the day. Kyle liked quiet. Kyle missed quiet. He didn't regret letting Daniel move into his house, but he could be a little . . .

"A little much," Kyle grumbled aloud as he started his car.

CHAPTER THREE

KYLE WAS BURNING THROUGH the crowd of patients in the waiting room today. He'd already seen a little girl with a high fever, sewn up an accidental hacksaw injury, removed a Lego from a preschooler's nostril, and sent a woman coughing up blood to get a CT scan, and it was only nine in the morning.

"What's next?"

Trevor Harper, his favorite nurse, had the next patient ready for him. "Possible broken wrist. She fell off a chair."

"Ouch."

"Yeah. All other vitals were normal. Exam room 3."

"Thank you." Kyle knocked on the door.

"Come in." It sounded like a man's voice that answered him. He half wished they still used paper charts; at least then he could check and make sure he was getting the patient's gender right. He opened the door. A woman in her early fifties with honey-blonde hair sat on the exam table, her legs swaying as she kicked her feet. She cradled her right arm against her chest. A young man with the same shade of hair stood anxiously next to the exam table.

"Mrs. Carpenter?"

She turned her head to look at him, but didn't answer. Her body language was stiff; she clearly didn't recognize him. Given that his mother had known her for years, her aloof gaze surprised him.

"Mom," the man nudged. "Say hello to the doctor." He turned to Kyle, clearly frustrated. "I'm sorry, she seems to be a little . . . out of it, at the moment."

Kyle's mind started cranking. Maybe there was more to this than met the eye?

"That's all right. Crash, right? Kyle Durand." Kyle offered his hand, and the man shook it firmly. That wasn't the man's real name; he'd been in some kind of reckless aircraft incident that had earned him the nickname years ago.

"Yes, I remember you and your family. How are you?"

"Better than you, sounds like. Were you with your mother when she fell?" Kyle sat down and opened her chart on the screen.

"No, the household staff called me. I was at work." He ran a hand through his hair, and Kyle noticed he was sweating right through his Brooks Brothers dress shirt. He scanned her file: no history of cancer, high blood pressure, high cholesterol, surgeries of any kind . . .

"Sorry, is this correct? This paperwork?"

Crash reddened. "I don't know. She filled out some of it, but she's been pretty confused."

"Okay. That's all right, we'll just work with what we've got." Kyle sauntered over to the sink and scrubbed his hands thoroughly.

"Carter," she whispered, "can we go home now?"

"Not yet," he replied gently, rubbing her back. "Dr. Durand's going to look at your arm first."

"How long have we been here?" she asked, looking around the spare exam room with a sigh. "I didn't get the spider. I don't want it to get away; I think it was a brown recluse."

"Mrs. Carpenter, can you tell me what happened when you fell?" He suspected she'd hit her head, but he started with the basics. He shined a light into her right eye, and she lifted a hand to block it, squinting.

"Do you mind?" she asked. "That's really bright."

"Mom, you have to let him examine you," Crash said, pulling her hand down.

Kyle put down his light. He was going to have to try another tactic with her, despite the seats filling up in the waiting area.

"I'm sorry, Willow, I didn't introduce myself very well. I'm Kyle Durand. You know my mother, Farrah?"

Her eyes lit up. "Yes, Farrah cuts my hair. She has for twenty-five years. No one mixes color like Farrah."

"That's her," he agreed. "Ever since you moved to Timber Falls, you've been coming to her, haven't you?"

"That's right." She paused. "You're her son?"

"Yes, I'm her second-oldest son. Same as your twins, Chase and Christopher."

"Where is Chase?" she asked. "I haven't seen him lately."

"Chase is in rehab, Mom . . . remember? We went to see him last weekend?"

"Oh, that's right . . ." She turned to Crash again. "Can we go now? I don't care for this place."

"Pretty soon," Crash promised, and when he looked back at Kyle, he saw the deep frustration in the younger man.

"Tell me about your accident, Willow."

"Accident?"

"Yes, you fell off a chair, right?"

"It rolled right out from under me . . ."

Crash looked stunned. "You stood on a chair with *wheels*?"

"There was a spider up in the corner. I asked the staff to kill it for me, but they said it was too high up. I'm taller than they are, so I thought I could get it, but I guess . . ." She rubbed her wrist with regret in her voice. "I guess not."

"Does your wrist hurt?"

"Yes."

"May I examine it? I promise I'll be very gentle."

Willow gave him a skeptical side-eye, but she offered him her arm. He took her hand as if to shake it, then tipped her hand up, watching for her reaction. She bit her lip, but said nothing.

"Does that hurt, Mrs. Carpenter?"

"A little bit . . ."

He gripped her thumb gently, telescoping it in toward her wrist, and he heard her breath catch. Willow pulled her hand back, and he let go of her. He suspected she had a scaphoid fracture, which was common in this type of fall, but he'd need another minute to check two more things . . . She eyed him with mistrust, giving him an injured look. But more than that, she was wearing all her emotions on her sleeve. This woman was the head of the Ladies' Auxiliary of Linn and Marion Counties. She hosted benefits and organized the Christmas bazaar, and he'd never seen her flustered, let alone hurt. This was more than physical pain on her carefully made-up face.

"Willow, I'm sorry if I hurt you. Let's go ahead and do some X-rays and see what it looks like inside, okay? That won't hurt at all." He paused. He wanted more information. An idea occurred to him . . . It was maybe a little deceptive, but he didn't think she really wanted to cooperate at the moment. "May I look at your hair, Willow? I'd like to see if Farrah did a good job the last time she dyed it . . ."

"Of course," she said, tipping her head down for him to see better. He combed his fingers through her hair, looking for blood, contusions, bumps, anything to indicate she'd taken a blow to the head . . . but her scalp looked perfect aside from some light dandruff. He tipped it lightly from side to side to see if she complained of pain, but she just smiled at him. Despite his mind being firmly at work, he smiled back. He wanted her at ease.

"Do you have a headache?"

"No, not right now."

"Have you had any alcohol to drink today?"

"I think I had a glass of wine with my lunch."

"And what did you have for lunch?" It was a test. He didn't want to be right. He wanted so badly to be wrong. He wanted Mrs. Carpenter to just have poor balance from a lack of exercise and too much alcohol. He wanted that to be what had lowered her inhibitions enough to stand on a rolling chair.

"Um . . ."

Crash pulled out his phone. "I can call the staff and ask . . ." Kyle gave him a little head shake.

"Willow, what did you have for breakfast?"

"She always—"

Crash finally shut up when he saw Kyle's stern look.

"I always have eggs and half a grapefruit for breakfast."

"Is that right?" Kyle said conversationally, but he looked to Crash, who gave him a slight nod to confirm the information.

"And what were you trying to do on the chair?"

"I don't . . ." She swallowed hard. "I don't remember."

"Okay. Wait here for just a minute, I'm going to talk to your son outside. You can use your phone if you want; there's free Wi-Fi in the hospital. The password is 'santiamhealth.'" Another test, and perhaps not a very fair one. But he wanted to know how her short-term memory was being affected. "Carter and I will be right back."

The younger man followed him out into the hall, his expression grim.

"Has this happened before?"

"Has she fallen before? No. But there's been other little things . . . Last month, she was making a cup of tea, and she grabbed the handle of the kettle with her hand, even though it's not insulated. She's had that teakettle since I was in high school. She should know better."

"Okay. Any other recent instances of 'she should've known better'?" Thankfully, Kyle had a good memory; he'd put this into the chart later . . . He wasn't allowed to use his phone, annoyingly. He understood the reason for the rule, but he still resented it. He would never misuse the information or allow it to fall into the wrong hands.

"Yeah. Yes, she was . . . she was in the garage, and she was trying to find a box of books that she gave away to the library last week."

"New books or old books?"

"Old. Super old, like I'm not sure they'd even want them in that condition. Textbooks from her college days and stuff."

"Okay." That last question was purely selfish; their friend Starla had been receiving anonymous donations of recent bestsellers at the Rachel Rutherford Memorial Library, and they were all curious as to who was sending them. This ruled her out as the book fairy; Kyle agreed with Starla that the mystery needed to be solved.

"Well, here's what I'd like to do. We're going to go ahead and do the X-ray today and see what's happening with her wrist, but I'd also like to refer you to a neurologist."

He stiffened. "Is it that serious?"

"That kind of increased risk taking, paired with forgetfulness and some of the other things I've observed just now? It's not good. I'm not ready to make any kind of guess yet as to what kind of illness it is, but . . ." He sighed. "If she didn't hit her head, then there's a few other reasons why she might be having trouble cognitively, none of them good."

Crash just stared at him, then his gaze fell to the tile. "I see."

"Where's your dad?"

"He's in Tokyo this week. Then he'll be in Australia for a while . . . then I'm not sure."

"Are there any family members living with your mother right now? It might be better if she wasn't alone . . . even given the presence of the staff."

His gaze was still trained on the floor, and Kyle thought he might have tears in his eyes. "Chase is in rehab, and Christopher's living in New York."

"Okay. Well, it doesn't have to be decided today, but the four of you should talk about ways to keep your mom safe. She got lucky this time. If she'd hit her head on something on the way down, it might've been a very different story."

"Okay. I see. Yes, I will . . . investigate."

Kyle pulled a card out of his wallet. "When you get stuck in the wheels of bureaucracy, shoot me a text or an email, and I'll see what I can do to help." Carter wasn't a kid, but he was the youngest in his family. He shouldn't be the one dealing with this. But he'd met Mr. Carpenter before, and he wasn't the kind of person who was going to reschedule his work trip to accommodate someone else. Kyle wasn't judging it; it was just a fact.

He could see down the hall to the waiting room. It was standing room only.

"I've got to keep moving. Sorry."

"That's okay," Crash said, rousing from his quiet moment. He shook Kyle's hand firmly. "I appreciate your time. I'll follow up with you soon."

"Please do."

Too bad it would constitute a HIPAA violation for him to tell his mom to be extra understanding while making small talk with Willow the next time she came in. Few would expect a woman so young to have Alzheimer's.

CHAPTER FOUR

KYLE GOT UP EARLY ON Friday morning; normally, he might give himself a break and do VR boxing or go to the gym, but today, he had a mission. Today, he started Phase Two: Win Ainsley's Time. He often saw her running when he was out in the morning. She never appeared to notice, but then again, she ran with headphones on, blasting music, against the advice of every running blog ever. He didn't like it when she ran through the woods; anyone might be waiting for her around a corner, any kind of creep.

Luck was on his side today, and she came trotting down the stairs of her apartment building and out into the street . . . but she wasn't alone. His brother's fiancée, Winnie, was running, too, but was already falling behind. Ainsley turned around to tease her, and he waved. She waved back with a shy smile; she was too far away for him to clearly see her left hand. He'd thought to join her, but this wasn't going to work . . . She already had a running buddy today. He followed them until they went into the park, then turned back toward his own house.

Rats. He'd just have to find a moment to speak to her another day. Where could he do it that wouldn't seem obvious? A neon-pink flyer on a telephone pole caught his eye as he passed it:

TOWN MEETING FRIDAY 7:00 P.M.
Discussion on how to save the historic covered bridge in Manfield
Park, how you can participate in the Fall Carnival at Franklin
Elementary, and other upcoming notable events.

Kyle took a picture of the flyer with his phone. If a school event was being discussed, chances were good that Ainsley would be there. His mom was always bugging him to come to those things anyway. *Two birds? Meet my stone.*

COUNCILMAN ROGERS STOOD up from behind the long folding table they'd placed for him horizontally at the VA hall. "Good evening, fellow Timberites." Kyle pretended to cough so he wouldn't let out a snort at the moniker. His mom glared at him, well versed in the ways men covered their tracks. Maggie sat on his other side, immersed in a fantasy book thick enough to kill a man if it fell on him.

"What book is that?" Kyle whispered.

"Terry Pratchett," she said, not looking up.

"Is it . . . good?" He didn't know how to talk to his sister anymore.

"Yes."

"Is she your favorite author?"

Maggie glared at him over the top of her glasses. "*Sir* Terry Pratchett is one of the best fantasy writers of the modern era. His Discworld series has forty-one books, of which I have read twenty-five. There is no one like him."

"Gotcha. So it's just a midlist thing . . . kind of an under-the-radar, indie thing," Kyle mumbled under the councilman's droning. Maggie rolled her eyes at him, but turned back to her book with a smile. He elbowed Maggie and she elbowed him back. He did it again.

"Stop it," his mother hissed under her breath. Kyle looked up. Councilwoman Park on the end was staring at him, and he resolved to get himself together. He'd hoped to at least get to *see* Ainsley, if not sit next to her, but she didn't appear to be here . . . Sigh. At least there would be cookies at the end. He'd gone for a run today. He could have at least one. He was still thinking about what kind of cookie he'd get when Maggie stood up next to him. Reflexively, he stood up too, even before he realized that someone was edging down the row.

"Excuse me, sorry," Ainsley whispered as she passed, and it took all his self-control not to reach out and steady her at her hips. She was always so . . . wobbly. She should really be doing some balance and strength training with her morning runs. She only had until thirty before her bone mass would start depleting.

I must be insane to care about the bone mass of a woman I'm not even dating.

But what if she falls and breaks something? his mind argued back. *That's expensive, not to mention the potential for complications like blood clots, bones not set correctly . . . Teachers don't make a lot of money.*

She flopped into a chair four seats down, and Kyle leaned forward under the auspices of scratching his ankle. Ainsley was wearing a skirt with black and white stripes in wide slashes, shorter at the front than at the back, and a black cardigan over a white T-shirt. It was tight across her chest, and he made himself look away. That was the polite thing to do.

Of course, the really polite thing to do would be to just ask her out instead of following her all over town. He crossed his arms and sat back in his chair. What was so hard about it? He'd gone to medical school at Stanford, for heaven's sake. It couldn't be harder than that. *Just ask the question, just walk up to her and say, "Ainsley, would you like to get lunch sometime?"*

"Dr. Durand?" His father and his brother were both absent; that meant Councilwoman Park was talking to him. Everyone was looking at him.

He sat up. "Yes?"

"Would you be willing to provide care at the emergency medical care station during the Turkey Trot in November?"

He nodded. "Yes, that'd be fine. And I can ask the hospital about donating supplies as well."

"Great."

He'd been hoping to run, but this was okay, too. He could run the Bunny Run in the spring or go up to Portland to run the marathon. Plus, maybe Ainsley would get a blister or something, and he'd have to touch her gently and comfort her. *This is getting out of hand . . .*

"Hey"—he nudged his sister—"you want to work the booth with me?"

"Absolutely not."

"Aw, come on. It'll be fun. You can give the lollipops and stickers to the kids who fall down."

"No, thank you."

Maggie was only here because their mother had made her come. She had little interest in town life and no interest in medicine. It wasn't even a fraction, it was a negative integer. In a family that already had three doctors and a physical therapist in it, folks tended to view that as surprising. So far, the only things that interested her were fantasy novels, video games, and cosplay. He imagined she'd have her own Etsy shop before too much longer, selling capes. Kyle frowned; it was hard enough getting to know his sister when she was so much younger than he was. He used to wish they were more alike; now he just wished he understood her better.

"Mags," he whispered again.

"What?" she asked, exasperated.

"What kind of cookie are you going to get?"

"Kyle. Leave me alone."

"But I'm a grown-up. I can't get away with reading at the town meeting."

"And that's my problem why?"

His mother elbowed him, and Kyle resigned himself to listening to the meeting.

"The Save Our Bridge campaign kicks off tonight, and all the proceeds go directly to saving the Manfield bridge. The county seems to think that it's a hazard, but if we can raise the money, they'll allow us to retrofit it and save this piece of Timber Falls history. We've made T-shirts to create awareness, so let us know what size you'd like, and it's twenty-five dollars apiece." Councilman Rogers held up the shirt, which had "S.O.B." printed on it in block letters. No picture of the bridge, no mention of the campaign.

"We'll take a break now; make sure to sign up when you grab one of Esther Kirschbaum's peanut butter cookies."

Kyle edged past his mother, who was talking to Mrs. Price on her other side, toward the center aisle. Ainsley was involved in a conversation with Jennie Wallace, and he took the opportunity to look her up and down, just because he loved looking at her. But his gaze caught on her forearm; that was a nasty scratch. *How did she do that? Does she own an animal?* He eavesdropped as he tried to figure out which chocolate chip cookie had the most chips.

"What'd you do to your arm?"

Ainsley shrugged. "Build accident."

"Are you still doing that?" Jennie asked. "Geez, I thought you'd have given that up ages ago."

"It's for a good cause. I like spending time with my dad. He likes building. And I'm good at it."

"Well," said Jennie, "you're coming out with us on Saturday." Ainsley started to shake her head, but Jennie spoke over her nonverbal objection. "Yes, you are. You never do anything. You keep to yourself too much."

"Just because I'm not with you and the other girls in town doesn't mean I'm alone."

"Committees do not count as a social life."

"And yet, they keep me very busy . . ."

Kyle cleared his throat, which was too full of cookie, and reached for a cup of water. Jennie, attuned as she was to every single male in her vicinity, turned to him.

"Do my eyes deceive me, or is Kyle Durand attending a town function voluntarily?"

He gave her a polite nod. "I heard there were cookies and inappropriate T-shirts, and I couldn't miss that." He glanced at Ainsley's left hand: no ring. Maybe it was getting sized. No tan line, either, though. But if it was very new, there wouldn't be. Or she could be allergic to certain metals.

She smirked at him, but Jennie cocked her head.

"T-shirts? What?"

Kyle glanced at Ainsley; he sometimes struggled with non-verbals, but the obvious twinkle in her eye told him she'd gotten the joke.

"Never mind." Councilman Rogers was coming back up to the front. "You ladies have a good evening."

"Wait, Kyle." Jennie touched his arm. He didn't care for casual touching, and he knew his face was probably broadcasting that. "Ainsley and I are going to go get a drink tomorrow night at Annie's. Why don't you come out with us?"

Usually, work was a convenient excuse not to get dragged to social activities. This time, he was available, but he had zero interest in going to a loud, smelly bar, especially when he saw Ainsley shift her weight and look away uncomfortably. *Why is she uncomfortable? Probably afraid that she'd be a third wheel while Jennie flirts with me all night. Not an unlikely scenario.*

"I can't. Sorry." Councilman Park was clearing his throat up front. Kyle hurried back to his seat, and his mother patted his knee approvingly. "What was that for?"

"You're talking to young women."

"So?"

"So I want more grandkids. That's step one."

"More? You've still got Mags in the house. Just cool your jets, lady."

"Ugh. No one says that," Maggie said, shifting away from him so that their shoulders weren't touching, as if disgusted by being associated with him in any way.

"Radical, Mags. Neato."

"You're the worst." But she was smiling, and Kyle grinned back at her. His mother passed him a clipboard.

"What's this?"

"Sign-ups for the events you've been ignoring."

Councilman Park was still talking. "There is a single clipboard coming around with several different sign-up sheets, for those interested. There's one for the Turkey Trot, one for the Habitat for Humanity build that's happening in Stayton—that's an ongoing project—and one for the bridge committee. All participants on the committee get a free T-shirt." *Is that how Ainsley got that nasty scratch?* It fit with the rest of the discussion he'd overheard between her and Jennie. *Building. A good cause.* He looked it over. Yeah, it was kind of a long drive, but it was only half a day, and he had Saturdays off this month. He unhooked the pen from the top of the clipboard and signed up for the build.

It was only once he'd passed the clipboard that he remembered that he knew less than nothing about construction, and he'd failed to put down his contact info for the Turkey Trot.

CHAPTER FIVE

AFTER SCHOOL, AS WAS her habit, Ainsley walked Aiden and Emily to the Rachel Rutherford Memorial Library in the center of town. Starla hadn't asked her to, but she knew it made her friend feel better to have an adult with them, and besides, they were sweet kids.

"Big plans tonight, guys?"

"No." Aiden sulked. "Got my tablet taken away again."

"How come?"

"Because he hit me!" Emily supplied, indignant.

"Oh, I see. And Mom didn't like that, huh?"

"No, Dad didn't. He said I can't hit girls." *Well, at least Charlie is doing something right. Now if he'd just decide that cheating wasn't okay, either . . .* He was forever nagging Starla to quit her job at the library, and it bugged the heck out of Ainsley. He just wanted her without income, said they didn't need it (unlikely). Said she didn't keep the house clean enough (downright dirty lies). Said he missed her too much (gag).

"Well, he's right. Hitting's not a good solution to your problems. You've gotta learn to talk it out." She reached out to ruffle Aiden's hair, but he ducked to the side, protecting it with one hand. They approached the library, and she recognized most of the cars in the parking lot: Starla's gray Traverse, Mavis

Johnson's Jeep, and Farrah Durand's Mini Cooper. Each car fit its owner so well, now that she thought about it. Farrah was all about style, Mavis was a practical, four-wheel drive kind of lady, and Starla . . . Starla drove a Traverse because Charlie thought it was good advertising for the dealership. As far as she could tell, Starla did a lot of things simply because she didn't want to make waves. She was trying so hard to make her marriage work . . . it didn't seem fair to Ainsley that Charlie couldn't at least meet her partway. Keeping it in his pants would be a good start. Ainsley caught Aiden's profile in her peripheral vision; every day, he looked more like Charlie. Charlie was handsome in a classic, 1950s sort of way . . . He'd always looked great in a letterman's jacket. Dazzling smile that he knew how to use. Muscular. Even now, she couldn't imagine him gaining that pudge that some men did around the time they hit thirty. He spent a lot of time at the gym. It probably didn't hurt that his particular gym was in Salem, where no one from town would see him hitting on other women.

Ainsley huffed her dissatisfaction aloud. *Enough.* She'd told Starla that she'd support her if she wanted to stay married, until she said she wanted to do otherwise. The kids dispersed as soon as they got inside the building, each to their own favorite part of the library. They were clearly at home here: Emily tossed her coat on the floor near a cart full of books to be reshelved, claiming a stool, and Aiden kicked off his shoes as soon as he reached the bank of computers near the big windows that overlooked the parking lot.

"Nice try," Starla said, not looking up from her computer at the center of the library.

"What?" Aiden said, turning to her warily.

"No screens. Your dad said."

"What?" Aiden screeched, and Mavis Johnson gave him a quelling look from the reference section. He blushed fiercely before stomping over to Starla's desk. They proceeded with their argument in hushed, annoyed tones.

"Dad said no *tablet*, not no *screens*."

Starla kept her cool in a way that Ainsley admired. "Would you like to read his text message? He sent it this morning, right after you hit your sister . . ."

"I barely even tapped her, he's totally overreacting!"

"Aiden."

"Mom, you weren't there, he's not being fair! He only saw what I did, he never punishes her! She was poking me for like twenty minutes before I hit her!"

"What your dad says goes, kiddo. I'm sorry. You can talk to him about it if you'd like to use my phone." She unlocked the device and held it out to him, but he spun on his heel and stomped back over to where his backpack lay. Slinging it over his shoulder, he made his way to the far corner of the building, where the beanbag chairs were. He whipped out a worn copy of *Ember* and began to read. If it was possible to read vindictively, Aiden had it down pat: he insisted on rereading the same book over and over, in part because he knew it drove his mother crazy.

Speaking of things that made Starla crazy . . .

"Your book fairy make her drop last night?" Ainsley asked, sitting on the edge of the desk.

"Yes, but I missed her again. She knew I was waiting for her." Starla pounded one dainty fist into her open hand, a move that might have been threatening coming from someone else.

She shook her head, and a little of her straight, shiny brown hair slid out of its ponytail. "I had a sandwich and everything, all set to spend the evening in my car. Then I fell asleep reading. Woke up at eleven thirty and drove home." Her friend wasn't as short as she was, but somehow, she just seemed . . . breakable. She was much thinner too, a fact Ainsley didn't resent; with her glasses and nerdy style, Starla had a girl-next-door cuteness that everyone admired. Basically, she and Charlie could both be movie stars if they ever decided to move to California. Happily for her, Starla was stuck here.

Ainsley chuckled. "You're really committed to outing this donor. What did she leave this time?"

"The new David Baldacci, some hot new romances, and a stack of kids' chapter books, all brand new with the labels still on them. Got them at Powell's." She grunted angrily. "Why would they do this to me? Who is this person? What is their objective? I hate mysteries. They're the only thing I don't read. It's crazy-making."

"*Do this to you?* They're being nice, Star." A hulking shadow fell over the info desk, and Ainsley pivoted to see her cousin Sawyer standing next to her. "Hi there!" she greeted, giving him a squeeze around his plaid flannel middle. They were cousins, yes, but he felt more like a brother she just didn't see as often. Being a single mom, Aunt Rhea had needed more from the Buchanans than some extended relatives, so Sawyer and his sister, Paige, had been over to play often. "You're looking extra hermit-y today. You need a haircut."

"Got one scheduled for a little later." Sawyer usually only came into town once a week, and he seemed to take personal pride in seeing as few people as possible when he did so. He gave her a rare, indulgent smile, then turned his attention to Starla. The two stared at each other for a long moment until Sawyer cleared his throat.

"Got my holds?"

"Oh," she said. "Right. Yes, just . . . just let me . . . ah." She pulled out a stack of novels with a rubber band around them from under the desk and handed them over. It seemed to Ainsley that the transfer took longer than it should . . . Was Starla blushing? Sawyer was pretty good-looking: he had that chiseled mountain-man look happening.

"What were y'all talking about?" He'd lived down south until he was six or seven, and he still had a bit of a twang and that unfortunate word in his vocabulary which pegged him immediately as "not from around here."

"The book fairy."

He rolled his eyes. "This again."

"Yes, this again. This forever. This until the mystery is solved and she comes forward to be rewarded. Nice would be letting me thank her and bake her brownies. I hate random acts of kindness. They are the worst."

"You only hate them because you think you're the only one who should get to do them," Sawyer mused.

"No, Ainsley can do them, too. Timber Falls would fall apart without her." She turned to her, giving Ainsley a look over her glasses. "I know you bought Halley Grant's winter coat last year."

Ainsley shifted uncomfortably. "You know Mr. Grant has depression; he's been out of work a long time. It's not her fault. And a purple coat in her size with a fox on it—her *favorite* animal—just fell into my cart while I was at Walmart. Can I help that, Starla? Huh? Can I?"

Starla just laughed quietly, shaking her head again. "You're the next Hattie, you know." At the mention of the town's unofficial mayor, Ainsley cackled.

"I don't have the clout to be the next Hattie."

"Why do you think it's a her?" Sawyer's deep voice startled Ainsley. Then again, her cousin was kind of that way: he was too used to being alone.

"Why do I think who's a her? Hattie?"

"No, your book fairy. How did you gender her?"

Starla shrugged one shoulder. "It's mostly romance. Hardly any thrillers in the mix. Sometimes we get some women's fiction, I guess I just assumed . . ."

He nodded sagely. "I see. So you made broad assumptions based on stereotypes."

She steepled her fingers, leaning forward. "Who do *you* think the book fairy is?"

"Don't know, don't care." He set down his stack of books. "And neither should you."

"Doesn't it bother you?" Starla hissed, pulling the stack toward her indignantly. "Not knowing?"

Sawyer crossed his arms. "Nope. I like a good mystery. Knowing the end isn't all it's cracked up to be." That statement made Ainsley's heart hurt more than a little. Sawyer's life wasn't turning out quite the way he'd planned it lately, and she felt terrible for him. Her mom and Aunt Rhea were always saying how he was doing fine *considering*, but she knew from their whispered kitchen conversations that stopped abruptly when she entered the room that they were worried about him.

Starla rolled her eyes. "Of course you do. You practically live to defy convention. You *are* a mystery."

"I'll take that as a compliment." He grinned, reclaiming his stack. "See you next Thursday."

"With shorter hair, hopefully," Starla said, nudging her tortoiseshell glasses back up her nose with a smile.

His gaze lingered on Starla as he backed toward the door, and Ainsley raised an eyebrow at him. Did her cousin have a crush on the hot librarian? If so, she felt honor bound to disapprove . . . as long as Starla was married to Charlie, anyway. As if he read it in her glare, Sawyer broke his stare and turned for the door, then blasted out without looking back.

"Kyle signed up to build on Saturday," Starla said, and it took Ainsley a moment to register the change in conversation.

"Kyle who?" she asked, picking up the stack of response cards to sort them.

"What do you mean, Kyle who? Kyle Durand."

"No, he didn't," Ainsley laughed. Starla looked at her over her glasses. "He did?"

Starla nodded. "Right here." She handed her the sign-up sheet that had been passed around at the town meeting. He'd signed up all right, but she couldn't imagine that he'd meant to. She knew Kyle. Kyle and his pretty hands did not do tools unless they were scalpels and stethoscopes. This did not make sense. Surely he had meant to sign up for the Turkey Trot; she often saw him out running. It was an honest error.

"I'll call him," Ainsley said, holding out her hand for the paper. "It must be a mistake."

Her friend smiled as she handed it over, then went back to looking through the other sign-ups.

"What?"

"Someone said he was joking with you outside the school the other week."

Ainsley's shields went up. "I was doing my job. Cooper had been . . . struggling to obey the recess rules." She wasn't going to out the kid; she knew how rumors could get out of hand in a small town. She'd had personal experience with that, and it hurt worse than a rusty nail through the shoe at the Habitat construction site and the tetanus shot that followed it. She knew that one from experience, too. "I *had* to talk to Kyle."

"You don't have Claire's number? Or Philip's?"

"Of course I do. They came to Back to School night."

"Your phone's broken, then? That's a bummer."

Ainsley lifted an eyebrow at her friend. "No, my phone's fine, what are you—oh."

"Yes. Oh."

She waved away her friend's teasing like she was a seagull after her peanut butter sandwich. "He was right there. It was convenient. Also, it was actually him who'd inadvertently contributed to the misbehavior, so . . ." Ainsley trailed off when she saw that Starla wasn't convinced in the slightest. "Whatever. Think whatever you want. I'm going to go call him now. As part of my *organizational responsibilities*."

"Good," Starla purred. "Then he'll have your number in case he has construction questions on a Friday night and you have to go with him to a movie that might help clarify the responsibilities. And eat ice cream afterward. And go back to his place."

She leaned forward. "Look, every other unmarried woman in this town may be clamoring for Kyle Durand's attention, but

I'm not. He'd never be interested in me. And he's already got my number, so joke's on you." Ainsley blew her bangs off her forehead as she left the room and ducked outside into the crisp fall evening.

She was still annoyed with Starla when Kyle answered. "Hello?"

"Hi. So we got back all the sign-up sheets from the town meeting, and you'd indicated that you were interested in building with us this weekend, so naturally that didn't seem right, so I thought I'd just call and see which sheet you actually meant to sign up for and then I can direct you to the correct person for information. I'm guessing that it's the Turkey Trot, but I didn't want to assume, even though someone said you'd kindly signed up to help us with the first aid booth." She took a breath. "Oh, and this is Ainsley, by the way."

"Which Ainsley?" he asked, deadpan.

Why was he always giving her such a hard time, for heaven's sake?

"There's only one Ainsley," she huffed, blowing at her bangs again.

"That's the truth," he mumbled, and she noted the rueful timbre of his voice.

"What is that supposed to mean?"

"Nothing. I didn't sign up on the wrong sheet. I'd like to help build. When's the training?"

It took Ainsley a full five seconds to process this information, and Kyle grunted. "Ainsley? You there?"

"Yes," she croaked, then forcefully cleared her throat. "Yes, I'm here. Just show up at the build on Saturday, and we'll give you your orientation."

"Do I need a . . . hammer or something?"

Don't laugh, don't laugh. "No, we'll provide the tools."

The relief in his voice was obvious. "Good."

"You have the address?"

He muttered something she couldn't hear, then spoke up. "Can I get it again?"

"Sure," she said. "548 Parrot Lane, Stayton."

"Got it."

"Okay, great. Great. Just come around 7:45 and we'll get you started."

"See you then."

Weirdest. Phone. Call. Ever.

CHAPTER SIX

"MAKEUP."

Ainsley passed her father his Daily Buzz coffee. She preferred Cuppa Joe, but Daily Buzz made him happy. "And good morning to you."

"Why are you wearing makeup to build? Makeup is for your mother's activities."

She sipped her half-caff soy latte. "There's no reason why I can't wear makeup to this, too."

Her father grunted, stroking his salt-and-pepper beard thoughtfully. "Something's going on."

"Nothing's going on." Geez, he was nosy. She was, too, but it was only in the other person's best interest. She was like one of those diabetes support dogs she wanted her dad to get. She sniffed at people's problems because she cared. Whereas he just . . . sniffed.

"Uh-huh." He did not seem convinced. *Not in the slightest.*

It was only seven thirty, but there were a few volunteers already around. Ainsley wandered toward the trailer, yawning, casually avoiding the additional questions she could feel circling her like sharks. She unlocked the trailer and rummaged around until she found the sign-in clipboard and attached this week's roster, which she'd tucked under her arm. She yawned again. She'd gotten up at five to shower and wear real clothes and fix her face . . . she usually slept until six, then left at 6:10. But Kyle was coming today . . . She shook her head, chuckling at herself. *I'm an idiot. He's not here to see me.*

"Something funny?"

Speak of the devil.

She turned to see him, arms crossed, in the open door. He was wearing stone-washed jeans and a black fleece jacket with some kind of green thermal top under it that somehow made his eyes look browner, warmer. "Nope." She pushed the clipboard at him. "Here's the sign-in. Put it next to the coffee when you're done." *Put some distance between you,* she thought. *That's it.*

Ainsley could hear him following her as she descended the stairs, but ignored him.

"Pop."

"Yo." Her father was on the other side of the trailer, chatting with some of the other regular builders.

"Got a build virgin for you," she said, throwing her thumb over her shoulder, and she heard Kyle chuckle.

"Well, if it isn't Dr. Durand 2.0. How are you, son?"

"Good, thank you, sir." The two men shook hands, and her father gave her a pointed look. "How are you, Mr. Buchanan?"

"Fine, just fine."

"How's retirement?"

"Oh, as long as I stay out of my wife's hair, it goes just fine."

"Don't be like that. Mom loves having you around more," Ainsley said, sipping her coffee.

They ignored her. "How's your brother? Heard he had another kid."

Kyle nodded. "Philip's good, still doing the physical therapy thing. Daniel's still in residency, but it seems to be going fine."

"You've got a sister, too, don't you?"

His eyes dropped to the muddy ground. "Yup. Maggie's still in high school."

She shared a glance with her father that said "Something's happening there." His answering look said "I agree."

"Well, it's good to have you here," her father continued. "Help yourself to some coffee, and Ainsley will get you started after she does the orientation spiel."

"Oh no," she said quickly, "I really wanted to get the flooring in the kitchen done today, that'll take me a while. I was hoping you could do his orientation."

Her father smiled and slung an arm around her neck like she was twelve. "But sweetheart, you know I could never orientate him as well as you can."

"Pop, for the ten thousandth time, *orientate* is not a word. You can orient something, you can do orientation, but you cannot 'orientate' anything."

"Oh gosh, I was hopin' you'd say that," he said, as he whipped a folded piece of paper out of his pocket and handed it to her.

She opened it cautiously, then read aloud, "'*Orientate.* Intransitive verb. To turn or face to the east.'" Ainsley looked up and popped her lips loudly. "Fine. I promise to point Dr. Durand east before I get started on the kitchen."

Gary pointed to the bottom of the page. "Keep reading, pumpkin."

"'Transitive verb. *Orient.*'"

"HA!" her father cried. "HA! Suck it, daughter."

"First of all? Rude. Second of all, where's Mr. Trask, I know he's the one who told you it was really a word, and thirdly, if you'd kept reading, it says 'chiefly British.' Is that the kind of American you want to be? One who uses *British* words? What's next, tea and crumpets for breakfast?"

"I'm just gettin' in touch with my roots," he said, kissing her temple before he walked away, chuckling.

"We're not using that word! And you're half-Scottish, half-German!" Ainsley called after him, fuming. Crumpling the paper, she turned to go back to the trailer and startled. Kyle was still standing right behind her; in her word fury, she'd completely forgotten about him. "Sorry," she muttered, even though she hadn't run into him.

"For what?"

"I almost ran into you." *And I forgot you were there.*

"But you didn't."

"No, I . . . guess not." Ainsley sipped her coffee. She really wished her brain would hurry up and *orientate* itself to Kyle's presence.

"I already know which way is east, but I don't know anything about building houses." His face didn't indicate that he was joking, but his dark eyes had a twinkle in them. She would have found him unnervingly good-looking, but he was just Kyle. She wouldn't worship him like the other women in town, no matter how funny and smart and thoughtful he was. *It's not like he's perfect. I'm sure he has flaws.*

She started toward the trailer again, carefully walking around him this time, and once again, he followed her. *I guess it can't hurt to humor the old man.* "Well, maybe you'd like to help me with the flooring." It was the only logical thing to do with a newbie on-site, she told herself. Left to their own devices, they could really screw things up, and that wouldn't be fair to the Sadiq family. Life was hard enough as a Somali refugee, from what little she knew of it; they didn't need poor tile installation in their bathrooms to add to their troubles.

"What does that entail?"

"Are you good at puzzles?"

"Word puzzles or cardboard puzzles?"

She suppressed a small smile. She'd forgotten he was like this. He always wanted more information, was always cautious.

"Cardboard puzzles. You know, five hundred pieces all look the same, and then you get a picture of a field of sunflowers when you're done?"

"Mine are always famous historical sites, but sure. I guess I'm okay at them."

"Well, this is a lot like that. We have to piece together the laminate flooring without the seams showing. Do you know how to use a circular saw?"

"I thought saws were long and flat, so apparently not."

Ainsley laughed as she walked up to the driveway, where the regular coffee she'd brought from home was sitting on a folding table beside a small crowd of volunteers. "All right, listen up, please." She used her classroom voice, and as they always did, people quieted down to listen to her. "Today, you're here to help build a house for Abshir and Bilqiis Sadiq and their daughter, Fawzia. In case you don't know where you are, Habitat for Humanity builds houses for people who can't afford them, but every homeowner puts sweat equity into the house.

We do more than just build; we also advocate for safer housing policies, less discrimination in housing practices, and training to help families improve their situations. If you decide building the houses isn't for you," she said, eyeing two high school girls in skinny jeans and tight T-shirts, "you could always volunteer at the ReStore in Salem. They sell salvaged and donated items to benefit the organization."

One of the girls raised her hand. "Do they have vintage stuff?"

"You could call it that." Truthfully, most of it was more thrift store than vintage, but she'd gotten a nice end table there last year that fit perfectly in her living room. "If you are doing this for community service hours of any kind, you must sign in *and* sign out. If you just sign in, we won't know how long you were here and my dad will not vouch for you, because he's a grouchy old man." Light laughter came from the group of ten. "If you don't know what to do, don't guess. Ask the mean old man, because he'll make me fix it if you screw up. His name's Gary." She pivoted. "All you, old man."

"That's the third time you've called me old today," he grumbled, then grinned. Gary took off his John Deere hat, and said, "Let's pray. God, thanks for today, thanks for a good crew. Keep us safe as we work, may this home be a blessing to the Sadiqs. Amen." Ainsley wasn't surprised Dad kept his prayers short. It had been a site tradition before they'd taken over to pray at the beginning, and he didn't want to break it, but he was also not the public-speaking type.

Ainsley felt the women gravitating toward her, so she set them up with a simple caulking project in the upstairs bathroom, then went back down to the trailer to grab her tool belt.

Kyle was waiting for her in the kitchen, looking around, poking into the cabinets.

"You looking for a snack or something?"

"Just killing time until my instructor gets here."

She grinned. "That's my day job. Today I'm just another lady with a tool belt."

"How long have you been teaching now?"

"Five years." She shook her head as she opened the box of premade planks. She handed Kyle the instructions. "Seems like less than that."

"Why?"

She shrugged. "I've got different kids every year, curriculum's always changing, the state standards are always shifting. I think I thought it would be easier after I'd been doing it a few years." *Why am I telling Kyle Impressive Durand about my professional misgivings?* "That's not to say that I don't like it—I do like it. It's been fun having Cooper in my class this year."

Kyle snorted. "Fun, huh? Is that code for something else?"

"No." She smiled. "I love Cooper. He's a problem-solver."

"He is that," Kyle said, but his voice lacked feeling as his eyes scanned the page. "Did you acclimate the planks?"

"Yup, I put them here last weekend, so we're good. And I already installed the moisture barrier underneath."

He got to his knees next to her. "Okay. Show me how to put it together."

"Hold your horses, cowboy. We've gotta get the shop vac and clean the floor first."

"Can I see all the directions before we begin? I like to have a complete picture of the scope of the project."

Ainsley smiled and handed him the directions. She watched as he read them carefully, his dark eyes scanning the page. It was impossible not to appreciate the way he gave something his whole focus; she thought she could probably dance a jig right now, and he wouldn't notice. In her case, it was impossible not to find that adorable.

He nodded after a moment. "Okay, I think I've got a handle on it. Where's the vacuum?" She walked him to the garage, and he got to work while she went upstairs to check on the caulking women, who had abandoned their project in lieu of painting cabinet doors in the garage.

She took the lid off and downed her latte before it got any colder. Kyle was almost done vacuuming when Mrs. Sadiq came in.

"Bilqiis, you made it! I thought you were working today."

She gave Ainsley a hug, as she always did, and then linked arms with her. "No, I'm off today. Fawzia and I thought we would come down." The young girl bounded into the house, a blur in leggings, a colorful long-sleeved dress, and a neon-pink head covering, then tore up the stairs. Bilqiis chuckled. "They're doing something with the machinery in the backyard, and she wanted to watch from *her* room." Ainsley smiled, too.

"Hello, I'm Kyle Durand," he said, sticking out his hand.

Bilqiis looked up at him for a brief moment, then lowered her gaze. "It's nice to meet you, Kyle; I am Mrs. Sadiq. Thank you for coming to help with my house." Kyle let his hand fall.

"Most of the women are out in the garage," Ainsley said, untangling them, and Bilqiis nodded, then disappeared down the hall.

"Did I say something wrong?"

"No, she just doesn't shake hands with men. She doesn't with Dad, either. But she's not offended. She really is glad you're here. She just doesn't want to appear flirty with you."

"Right." He eyed her. "Ready to plank now?"

"I am." She got to work, laying out planks so that the grain wouldn't look too manufactured despite the fact that it repeated often. Kyle was a quick study; he worked in front of her, snapping together the pieces she placed. It gave her a nice view of his backside, which she decided pointedly to not appreciate. *No point in that.*

She took the too-wide, too-long pieces out to cut with the circular saw, but her father's friend Perry Helsing was already using it.

"I'll cut it for you, gorgeous."

She stacked the planks next to him and straightened, rolling her eyes. "Shameless."

"Why? Because I'm seventy-two? I'm not dead, you know." He cackled.

"Neither is your wife, Perry!" she called over her shoulder. Her father's friends were always giving her a hard time; they seemed to feel personally responsible for her single state. She went in through the garage, stopping to remind the ladies to wipe the drips off the floor. Kyle was done placing the planks she'd laid out for him.

"Nice job, Doctor. I should've figured you'd be good with your hands."

He turned to look at her, eyebrows raised, and she played back the tape in her head to figure out what she'd said wrong.

"Oh"—she felt her face flush—"I didn't mean . . ."

"That's okay," he said, brushing off his hands as he got to his feet, "I am good with my hands. In more than one sense." He was staring at her. No, *gazing* at her, letting his hip rest on the kitchen island.

I should look away. I don't want to give him the wrong impression. But she didn't. Ainsley stood with him in the kitchen, looking deep into his brown eyes, until someone behind her cleared his throat.

"Can you help me bring up some boxes of flooring to the master bath?" she asked Kyle, pointing over her shoulder.

"Sure," he said, but he was looking over her shoulder now, and she turned.

"Hi, Pop. Need something?"

Her father was glaring at Kyle. "Nope."

She looked between the two men, unsure how to break the weird, silent conversation they were apparently having. "Well, then." She turned and went out to the trailer, climbing over all the stuff people had stacked in the middle to get to the flooring boxes. She passed them out to Kyle, who, predictably, had followed her out. *Possibly, there's a good reason I'm still single. And that reason is an overprotective ex-cop dad named Gary Buchanan.*

Her planks had been cut when they came back down; the two of them placed the last pieces, then added the molding.

"You finally got to use a hammer!" Ainsley teased Kyle, and he scowled.

"I was trying to be nice, offering to bring a hammer. Won't make that mistake again," he said haughtily, carefully keeping his eyes on his fingers as he tapped in the finishing nails.

"I'm sure you won't," she said, using her soothing teacher voice.

"What are you doing after this?" he asked.

Ainsley's nerves were starting to get raw. It was just too weird, having him here in her domain. "My dad usually takes me out for Mexican."

"Ixtapa?"

"No, Muchas Gracias."

"Ever been to Rico's?"

Ainsley forgot she was nervous. Thinking with her stomach did that to her. "No, where's that?"

"Sublimity. It's a little farther, but it's worth it."

"Good nachos?"

"Yeah, they're good," he said, standing up. "But the breakfast burritos are my favorite. I like to grab one after I work a night shift."

"Do you have to do that a lot?"

He nodded, placing the hammer gently on the island. They were gazing again.

"Well," she said cheerfully, "thanks for coming today, it was great to have your help." Ainsley stuck out her hand, and he shook it, half a smile on his face.

"You're welcome. I'll see you for Cooper pickup on Monday."

"I'll be there."

He moved past her toward the front hall.

"Don't forget to sign out," she called.

"I never signed in," he called back.

"Why not?"

Kyle smiled, then disappeared out the door.

CHAPTER SEVEN

KYLE DROVE TO HIS HOUSE and sat in his car in the driveway. He was tired. Yawning, he scrubbed a hand over his face and heaved himself out of the car to go inside. He'd just take a quick shower—building was surprisingly dirty work—and then head over to his parents' house for dinner—

Ugh. Again? Daniel and Winnie were on the couch, trying to act innocent, but he could see the color on both their cheeks was higher than normal. And it wasn't because Daniel had turned up the thermostat again. Their presence here was becoming a problem. Why weren't they at Winnie's apartment? Ainsley would be out most of the day, if he'd overheard her correctly. People made no sense sometimes. They just didn't think things through.

From his bag, he pulled out the list he'd printed last night. "Here."

"What's this?" Daniel asked, taking the paper. "Grievances?"

"I considered nailing them to the front door, but you don't usually come in that way."

"Lack of dish-doing, that's fair. Failure to contribute to the cleanliness of shared spaces . . . I know I was supposed to vacuum, but I got called into work. I'll do it tomorrow, I swear. Poor hygiene? What?"

"You left dirty clothes on the bathroom floor. It's unacceptable." Kyle crossed his arms over his chest as Winnie gave them a bemused glance. "Look, I know you're moving out soon, but in the meantime, you need to change your ways. Consider it practice so that Winnie doesn't throttle you."

"Kyle . . ."

"No." He held up a hand. "This is my house. These stipulations were in the contract you signed. You either start upholding your part of the deal, or I'll double your rent." Kyle started up the stairs.

"You can't do that!"

"Yes, I can," he called back. "And read the fine print before you sign anything for your next place." He shut the door behind him and breathed a sigh of relief. At least Daniel never came into his bedroom; he was safe from his brother's slovenly chaos in here. He touched his bookshelf protectively; his football trading cards were still laid out in order. It made him breathe easier to look at them; a little visual stimulation when he was tired or stressed. When he'd lived with his parents, his siblings had found it amusing to move them while he was out, and it still annoyed him to think about it. They'd even timed how long it would take him to notice, like it was hard. Like anyone wouldn't notice that immediately. He just didn't get them sometimes. Neurotypicals were so weird.

Kyle took his shower and changed into basically the same clothes he'd just been wearing before he lay down on his bed and retreated into Twitter. Unlike other social media platforms, there were no real friendships here; he could lurk anonymously and leave without anyone knowing he'd been there. If people tried to DM him, he just ignored them. It was just the right amount of stimulation, little bites of all the stuff that interested him: sports, video games, politics. The politics was too much and got him fired up sometimes, but he seldom responded to the provocation. He did, however, answer a lot of questions for people stuck on a game level or unable to find the stat they were looking for, and it had garnered him a few thousand followers.

His favorite account had been active. Brad was a gamer in Massachusetts, autistic like him. SaveTheNeurotypicals was a close second; she helped him put his family and friends into context sometimes. Helped him see his own condition more objectively.

BrokenBrad: Anyone up to Minecraft this afternoon?

Yeah, he had time for that. He found Brad's Minecraft server and began to build a library, losing himself in the creation. Kyle preferred games that were a little more low-key after the intensity of the emergency room. Stardew Valley with its little farm, Kerbal Space Program with its cute green alien astronauts, Minecraft with its infinite sandbox feel . . . He wanted to try Animal Crossing, but he didn't want anyone to find out and ridicule him. He broadcasted his games on Twitch occasionally, but he didn't have many followers. He didn't like the constant stream of chatter from the players and couldn't emulate it, and his schedule was variable and strange enough that he couldn't always log on at the same time.

His phone rang, and he answered it on speaker to keep his hands free.

"Hello?"

"Hey, Grumpy." Maggie had dubbed her brothers Happy, Grumpy, and Bashful at a young age, and apparently, she felt the nicknames still applied.

"What do you want? I'm coming over soon and I'm busy."

"Just wanted to give you a heads up about something."

He paused the game. "What?"

"I want to have a Sibling Night monthly. I don't get to see you guys much anymore, especially not together. Will you do that for me?"

"Sure." He assumed the conversation was over and moved to hit the red hang-up button on his phone, but she kept talking.

"I know it'll be a challenge with schedules and stuff, but it's just once a month. And with Daniel moving out, I know you'll be lonely by yourself."

"No, I won't," he said gruffly. "You don't need to worry about me."

"Whatever, Grump. I know you better than that."

He resumed his game, muting it so she wouldn't know. "You're mistaken."

"Do you think we should let Daniel bring Winnie? She's kind of a sibling."

He thought about it for a moment. It was setting a precedent if this kind of event was going to become a Durand family tradition. And if it was precedent, then he could bring Ainsley someday . . . if he ever managed to actually ask her out. He liked that idea.

"Yes. Definitely. Winnie is welcome."

"Okay. See you later?"

"I already said you would," he said, disconnecting the call before she could start laughing.

He played for a few more minutes, then decided to take a nap. He'd only been at the build site for four hours, but between the learning curve, the physical work, and the drive there and back, he was almost as tired as if he'd worked a full shift at the hospital. Not knowing what was going on or what he was supposed to do was hard, but putting himself in Ainsley's hands? That was easy. He'd lucked out that her dad had made her train him. Was it luck? He didn't know; Gary hadn't seemed too thrilled about their moment in the kitchen, but the man was hard to read. But he did know one thing . . . tabbing over to an internet browser, he logged onto the Habitat site and signed up for another half day the next weekend.

CHAPTER EIGHT

AINSLEY HAD JUST WALKED into Muchas Gracias when her phone pinged with an email. She scanned it as they walked to their usual table. *He signed up for next weekend.* Her heart felt bubbly, but she quickly popped the happy feelings. *It's got nothing to do with me. Maybe he wants to work on his house and he's using Habitat to learn how. Maybe he has a guilty conscience about something and he's compensating. Maybe he just likes to work with his hands . . . Nope, nothing to do with me.*

"What's got nothing to do with you?"

She looked up at her dad. "What?"

"Ainsley, if you're going to talk to yourself, do it inside your head."

"Sorry." She put the phone away and grinned at her dad. "What's new, Pop?"

"Nothing. That's what it means to be retired. Nothing's new. It's nice." He sipped the water the waitress had brought them. "What's new with you?"

"Starla conned me into doing the bake sale again." Two dozen snickerdoodle cupcakes with browned buttercream frosting . . . She'd probably be up until midnight again, waiting for them to cool, because she had a PTA meeting that night, so she wouldn't be able to start until late. She blew her bangs out of her eyes in annoyance. Why did everyone act like they could prevail upon her time? Just the idea of saying no made her chest feel tight. She wouldn't think about why that was.

He rubbed his protruding belly. "Good news for me."

"No, it's not, Mr. Diabetic. You need to steer clear of that stuff."

Gary ignored her, and she frowned at him before changing the subject. "Did you go golfing with Randy?"

He nodded. "Did a round at Elkhorn."

"Who won?"

"I think you already know the answer to that."

"Why do you even play with him if he's so terrible?"

"Darlin', I've known Randy since before you were born, going on thirty years. His ability or inability to play golf is immaterial to me at this point. We like taking a walk on green, level grass and we can afford to pay fifty dollars to do so at Elkhorn."

She gave him half a smile.

"Speaking of old friends," he said, and she knew what was coming next, "did you enjoy catching up with Dr. Durand?" He said his name with too much emphasis.

"We weren't really friends as kids, Dad."

"See, that's funny, because I remember you coming home with stories about him all the time."

"Daniel was in the after-school orchestra with me in middle school, as you already know. The only time I saw Kyle was when he picked us up, and he was always in a hurry to go, let me tell you. No time to stand around and chat, that one."

"He broke my mailbox, you know."

She rolled her eyes. "Is that why you were glaring at him?"

"It was a brand-new mailbox. Custom made, Ainsley. But no, I was glaring at him because he was lusting after my beautiful daughter. Never would've had you orientate him if I'd known he was gonna be like that."

She ignored his attempts to bait her with bad grammar. "Dad, Kyle Durand did not break your custom-made mailbox in the shape of a rainbow trout's head. And if he did, he did us all a service, that thing was ugly as heck. And he was certainly not *lusting*."

Ainsley was saved from having to endure more mailbox complaints when the waitress came to take their order . . . but her reprieve from the questions was short-lived. With nachos and enchiladas on their way, her father returned to his previous line of questioning.

"Sure seemed like he was willing to chat with you today."

"He just needed instructions. He doesn't know anything about building."

"Darlin', he stuck to you like fly paper. Followed you around like a puppy. Not me, not Perry Helsing, *you*."

"Just wait until he gets his confidence up. You'll see."

Her father's eyebrows disappeared from view under the brim of his hat. "He's coming back?"

She wiggled her phone. "Just got the notification. Surprised me, too."

"Well, he wouldn't be the first man to admire your confidence around a construction site. And you're welcome for that."

Ainsley laughed. "Yes, but the rest of them qualify for AARP."

He snorted. "You gonna sleep over tonight? Eat my pancakes in the morning?"

Her heart warmed at the idea of sleeping at her parents' house. She liked her apartment, but it lacked a certain hominess that they provided. She missed her family.

"Is maple syrup the best?"

Her dad shook his head, smiling, and lapsed into silence, watching the basketball game on the TV behind her. Ainsley looked around the small restaurant. A child was waving at her; it was Emily Miller. With a smile, she slid out of the booth and crossed the seating area to give Starla a side hug and greet her family—even Señor Douchebag, who was currently eating a *dos manos* burrito, living proof that being handsome wasn't everything.

"Hi, Ms. B!" Emily chirped.

Ainsley plucked a chip from the girl's basket and enjoyed her fake outrage. "Then eat, girl!" she chided; Em was always too busy talking to eat. "What're you guys doing here?"

"We came to meet Daddy for lunch!" That made sense; the dealership was just down the road.

"Oh, is he working today?" Ainsley asked innocently. She gave him about a 25 percent chance of actually working versus meeting one of his girlfriends.

"Unfortunately," Charlie said, but his fakety-fake-fake grimace gave way quickly to a smile. "Haven't seen you in a while, Ainsley. How've you been?"

"Oh, I'm fine. Busy, but fine. How's business?"

Charlie's face brightened. "Oh, it's been great. We're selling lots of four-wheel-drive vehicles, people getting ready for winter. Jason's been busy in the shop. We're running some great deals; you ought to come in and replace that junker you're driving."

"No, I'm good, thanks." She loved her funky old truck. Truth be told, it was her favorite accessory. The bright salmon paint job made her smile; you'd never lose it in a parking lot.

"How about you, Aiden? Still playing chess?"

He mumbled an answer, but didn't look up from his food. He'd loved chess when he was in her class, but he'd been extra surly lately. She'd thought it was just boy hormones, but her teacher sense told her there might be something else going on.

"He's doing great, aren't you, Aid?" said Charlie, slapping him lightly on the knee, and Ainsley bit her tongue to keep from snarling that she hadn't asked him.

"Maybe we could set up a game this week at the library after school?" That earned her a small smile and some fleeting eye contact, at least. Maybe that's the best you could expect from a nine-year-old whose home life was a bit tense.

She glanced at Star, and she didn't need to ask how she was doing; her annoyance was in the tightness around her eyes, the dip of her eyebrows, but she was forcing a smile. Ainsley was tired of seeing that look on her beautiful friend's face. She put a gentle hand on her shoulder. "I'll give you a call later tonight so we can catch up, okay?"

Starla nodded, giving her a little wave as she left. Ainsley made herself walk back to her own table; she knew it would still be hard to get the details out of her friend when she called later. Starla didn't like being a martyr; she just hid from the world, playing possum, until people left her alone. Fortunately for her, Ainsley loved her far too much to do so. Her phone vibrated with a text.

Starla: Found an earring in my bed this morning when I was changing the sheets.

She shot her a look across the restaurant, and the defeated look on her friend's face almost made her cry.

Ainsley: Not yours?
Starla: Not mine.

"Everything okay?" her dad asked, eyeing her. Her heart must have looked as bruised as it felt on behalf of her friend.

"Just more Charlie stupidity," she said, tucking her phone away to focus on her dad. But he was staring over at the Millers' table, and she knew the cop in him was pissed.

"She and her kids are welcome at our house, too," he said gruffly. "Anytime. And I can make a phone call to one of my buddies at the sheriff's office if—"

"It's not that kind of mistreatment," she said with a long sigh. "It's just her heart that's getting kicked around."

CHAPTER NINE

THE NEXT FEW DAYS WENT by quickly for Ainsley. Sunday, she worked on her presentation for the playground improvement committee. Monday, they did a fire drill, which riled the kids up enough to spoil most of the afternoon for real work. Tuesday, Posey threw up during circle time, and they had to send her home and have the janitor come and clean the carpet. Wednesday, her kids had two specials, so she had extra prep time, which she spent cutting out thirty paper pumpkins. That extra time midweek was golden, because it meant she didn't have to walk Aiden and Emily to the library and then go back to work. Today, that meant a quick grocery run . . . She was down to half a box of Frosted Mini-Wheats. Not enough to get through the next week.

She'd have to go into town; the little grocery store in Timber Falls wouldn't have what she needed. No matter; it wouldn't take long. Twenty minutes later, she was grabbing a big cart at the Safeway in Stayton. Kyle Durand was in the produce section, and he nodded to her as she came in. Her stomach dropped a little to see him unexpectedly, but she disregarded the feeling as fatigue after a long week, nothing more. Just to prove to herself that it was nothing, she'd go talk to him.

"Following me again?" she called, shaking her head. "What would my cop father say?"

"I'm afraid to find out," he said, bringing his cart up next to hers. "How was your week? No more tree-peeing, right?"

"No, we got that sorted out," she said, shaking open a plastic bag and filling it with Fuji apples. "No worries. How was your week?"

"Fine," he said, claiming a large bunch of bananas. "I treated a head injury for a man who tried to hang drywall while drunk."

"Really?" Ainsley laughed. "People are so ridiculous." Her laughter seemed to encourage him, and he followed her along the side of the store.

"I also saw more children than usual, which is unfortunate. Did you know that patients eighteen and under make up at least a quarter of all visits to the emergency room? I'm actually thinking of taking a safety curriculum around to the schools to see if I can do some presentations. I think it would cut down a lot on accidents. Their parents are clearly not informing them about the kind of hazards they need to be aware of."

"And what kind of hazards are those?"

"Snakes, poison ivy, electrical cords, burns—saw lots of burns last week for some reason."

"Well, people lit their woodstoves for the first time in a while, probably." She paused. "Kids do that, you know. They just get curious and they hurt themselves. I don't think taking a curriculum around will do any good." But that was Kyle Durand's brand of caring: just drown people in safety information, and they'll feel your love.

"If you say so. But I'm not good with kids like you." He stared at her, and Ainsley had no idea what he was thinking. I mean, she didn't usually, so it wasn't really any different, but now, for the first time in a while, she wished she did.

"And at the end of the night, a woman having a bad reaction to Ambien came in. She kept saying that her thumbs were controlling her. Then she took off her shirt and asked me to rate her breasts on the scale of one to sixteen. That was awkward."

"No!" She cackled. "What score did you give them?"

"Her husband was standing right there!" he protested, scowling. Delight at being able to tease him a little suffused her chest.

"Come on," she laughed, nudging him with her elbow. "Just between us. What score?" She held up two grapefruits in front of her chest, and he chuckled, pushing on her shoulder gently.

"Quit it. That's unprofessional."

She put the citrus back and pushed her cart forward, but couldn't resist pressing him a little more. "They were an eight, right? And you didn't want to hurt her feelings?"

He laughed as he grabbed some whole wheat hamburger buns, pointedly ignoring her continued needling. "Her husband said she also ordered a case of industrial-strength hydrogen peroxide online."

"Well, she'll be able to get that bottle blonde look for quite a while on that," Ainsley said, turning down the booze and cheese aisle. The Chateau St. Michelle wine she wanted was on the top shelf. Ainsley sighed.

"Problem, short stuff?" Kyle smirked.

"No." She pushed back her shoulders. "It's no problem." Putting one foot on the lowest shelf, Ainsley proceeded to climb high enough to grab the bottle she wanted, as Kyle looked on, his face painted with shock.

"I would've gotten it for you!"

"I didn't need you to," she informed him, flipping her hair. Short girls knew how to get things done. There wouldn't always be a tall friend around.

Kyle was quiet for a moment as they pushed their carts farther on. "I should see if he wants to sell some of that hydrogen peroxide to my mom," he mused, "if he can't cancel it."

"That's a good idea," she agreed, grinning. "How is your mom, by the way?"

"She's good. You want to come to dinner on Sunday?"

Ainsley froze, her hand almost to the baby brick of pepper jack she'd been reaching for. "Oh. Um, I'm not sure if I should."

"You used to come when we were younger."

She waggled her head a little, considering. "That's true . . ." *But we were kids. And Daniel invited me, not you. It didn't mean anything then.* And yet, she'd love to hang out with his family; they were the best. Daniel had asked her once if she had a favorite (besides him), and she honestly couldn't choose. They were all so great in their own way. She loved Philip's warm big-brother thing and Kyle's quiet, dependable way and Maggie's salty snark. And the parents: she loved how Farrah could turn anything into a celebration and how Evan always had a new dad joke to tell.

"Are you concerned that the host didn't invite you? I can text her right now." He was whipping out his phone, and she panicked.

"No, Kyle, don't. I think I'm already busy, don't bother her. Maybe another time."

That seemed to assuage him, but he was quiet as they neared the end of the cereal aisle, and she glanced at him, worried that she'd hurt his feelings. That was the last thing she wanted to do.

"Why don't you just go back where you came from?" A man's voice punched through the elevator music playing in the store. She peered around the end of aisle, and her stomach dropped when she saw Bilqiis facing down Ranger Zane alone; she'd know his shaved head and red face anywhere. As she approached, Ainsley tried desperately to remember the active bystander article she'd read a few months ago.

"Bilqiis?"

"Ainsley?" The young woman's eyes locked onto hers and she read the terror there. Giving her a nod, Ainsley placed herself between the angry man and her friend, but gave Ranger her back.

"Hey! Are you listening to me? I said you should get the hell out. We don't need you here, don't want your kind." Ainsley felt herself trembling, not with fear, but with anger. She wanted nothing more than to whirl around and scream at him that Mrs. Sadiq would probably love to go back to where she came from. That her home had been taken from her, her childhood destroyed. Instead, she focused on her friend.

"Bilqiis," she said, smiling at her, "I'm glad I ran into you. I've been meaning to talk to you about going shopping for some furniture for the house." She put her arm around the woman's shoulders, turning her away from her cart and her attacker. "When would be a good time for you to do that?" Bilqiis's eyes were wide, and her shoulders were taut under Ainsley's touch.

"Hey. Zane. What are you doing?" Kyle's voice was calm, but firm.

"I'm just having a conversation. Not that she can understand me."

"She can, actually," he said. "But she doesn't want to talk to you right now."

"You don't belong here!" he shouted past Kyle.

"That's enough, Ranger. Just walk away."

As Ainsley and Bilqiis turned the corner at the end of the aisle, Ainsley could see out of the corner of her eye that the store manager had come over to stand behind Kyle.

"Let's go to my car, okay? I'll come back and get your groceries. Were you almost done?"

"Yes, I was almost . . ." Mrs. Sadiq choked out a sob. "I'm sorry."

"Don't apologize. It's not your fault he's an idiot." She paused their conversation as they passed through the sliding doors into the parking lot. "Do you want to call Abshir?"

"Yes. I will call him in the car."

"Do you want to go home?"

"I don't know, I don't . . ."

"That's okay," Ainsley soothed, rubbing her back. "Let's just get to the car, and then we can figure out what to do next." She opened the door for Bilqiis, then her phone plinked.

Kyle: Don't leave. I'm paying for the groceries now.
Kyle: Is she okay?
Ainsley: Okay, we'll wait. I think so. She's in my car.
Kyle: Let's follow her home and make sure.

Ainsley: No argument here.

Kyle: That's a first.

Ainsley was texting him back a face with a tongue sticking out when a shadow fell over her phone, and she looked up to see Ranger.

"What's your problem, Buchanan? I was just talking to her."

"No, you were just belittling, insulting, and harassing her, Ranger. She doesn't deserve that. No one does."

"It's a free country."

"That's right, it is. And she's as free to be here as you are. You're entitled to your opinion, but you're not entitled to share it so viciously. It was disrespectful and rude, and she's not obligated to just stand there and take it." Out of the corner of her eye, she saw Kyle coming out of the store.

Ranger stepped into her personal space. "She doesn't belong here. Nobody's going to censor me." Kyle now appeared to be hurrying.

"I'm sorry you see it that way. Her presence here is perfectly legal, so I disagree. And as for censorship, it's not that we're saying you can't say it; we're just saying that we're not going to listen."

Kyle arrived at the car and began loading the groceries into the bed of the truck.

"Zane," he said without looking at him, "the next time I see you, you better not be sick with anything I can cure."

"What's that mean, Durand?"

"It means if you don't step away from this car, the next time you need my help, you might not get it."

His eyes narrowed. "You wouldn't."

"According to the AMA, 'a physician shall, in the provision of appropriate patient care, except in emergencies, be free to choose whom to serve, with whom to associate, and the environment in which to provide medical care.' Salem's not that far. I'm sure you'd be fine." He looked him up and down. "If you lay off the six-packs." He slammed the trunk and touched the small of Ainsley's back to move her toward the driver's seat. Ranger stepped back to make way for her, but she didn't miss the way his hands flexed into fists.

Kyle opened the driver's side door for her, and she slid in. She took a breath to say something to Kyle, but he'd already shut the door. The two men were still talking, but she couldn't hear what they were saying. She turned to Bilqiis. "Are you all right?"

She nodded, but the tension around her mouth and her eyes told another story. Ainsley noticed her jersey head covering had slipped back a little in their rush to the car.

"Can I help you adjust your hijab?"

Bilqiis raised shaking hands to touch the fabric. "He doesn't understand."

"No," Ainsley agreed quietly, letting her hands fall to cover Bilqiis's cold hands as they fell back into her lap.

"Coming here, it was so much work. So many tests, so many interviews, so many things we must do. Money and more money. And now, the people hate us."

"I don't hate you." She squeezed her hands tight, so tight her knuckles turned white. It wasn't tight enough, not by half, to express the deep sorrow she carried for her friend. "I don't hate you at all. Neither does Kyle or my dad or any of the guys building your house. I promise you, we don't. Don't let one a—" She caught herself just in time; she didn't know how her friend would receive that kind of cursing, even if it was meant in solidarity. "Don't let one jerk get in your head. Do you understand me?"

"It is difficult. He is not the only one. Things people say, the way they stare. It is difficult."

"I'm sorry, Bilqiis." What more could she say? A helpless rage welled up inside her, and she felt tears threatening to fall. There was a knock at her window, and she turned and rolled it down. Kyle looked chagrined.

"Are you okay, Mrs. Sadiq?"

"Yes, I am all right. Thank you, Dr. Durand." At the sight of him, she touched her hijab, then pulled down the vanity mirror to adjust it more fully.

"Would you like me to drive your car home for you?"

"No, I will ask Abshir to bring me back later. Thank you for the offer."

"What about you?" His voice was softer as he turned to Ainsley. "You okay?"

She nodded, but tucked her hands under her legs so he couldn't see them shake. His eyes narrowed. *So, it seems like maybe he knew anyway.*

"I'm going to follow you to Mrs. Sadiq's apartment . . ."

"There's no need."

He cut her off with a "stop" gesture. "I want to. It wouldn't be right not to. Please."

Ainsley sighed, then nodded.

"Don't drive like a maniac, I won't be able to keep up." His gaze was still searching, and she knew this subtle attempt to get under her skin was his way of probing for a real answer as to whether she was okay.

She lifted her chin. "I never drive like a maniac."

Kyle snorted. "That's a matter of opinion."

She didn't know what to say, keeping her gaze steadily trained on his sober brown eyes. *I am okay, Kyle. Really. We are okay.* Kyle swayed forward, and she tensed. She could've sworn . . . No, that couldn't be. She could've sworn he was about to kiss her. His gaze dropping, he shuffled backward, rapping out a staccato rhythm on the door of her truck with his knuckles in a poor attempt to seem casual.

"See you there."

"Okay."

She rolled her window back up as she started the car, taking care not to run over him as she backed out.

"Dr. Durand, you are dating him?"

Ainsley tightened her grip on the steering wheel. "What? No. We're just friends."

"You don't need to hide this thing from me. I know how it is for you, how Americans choose their husbands. I've seen *Friends.*"

"Oh, Lord, Bilqiis. Seriously, Kyle and I are just friends."

"*He* is not just friends."

"Didn't you have an arranged marriage? What do you know about dating?"

"No. And you should not assume. Abshir and I met in our university classes. He liked me, we would meet to study together, and then he went to my father." She paused. "Has he spoken to your father?"

"Not that I know of, but that's not really a thing here anymore . . ."

"He will." A secret smile. "Before long, he will."

"Well, my dad's mad at him for destroying his ugly mailbox back in 2013, so good luck to him."

"I like him for you. He is . . ."

"Opinionated? Overconfident? Bossy?" *Funny? Hot? Thoughtful?*

"I would say 'handsome.' But he is those other things, too, at times. Perhaps he sees you hurt yourself on the site. You are not careful."

Ainsley rolled her eyes. "Not you, too. Listen, I'm doing just fine over here. I don't need any of you clucking around me like mother hens. My own mother doesn't even do that."

Bilqiis held up her hands in surrender, but Ainsley saw her smile as she turned to look out the window. Before long, Ainsley pulled into the apartment complex where the Sadiqs lived; Kyle parked next to her.

She nodded to a few residents coming out of another building as they pulled out the groceries, but Kyle didn't bother acknowledging them.

"Which one's hers?"

"12B, I think."

"Okay, let's get this stuff inside. Don't dawdle."

Ainsley groaned, exasperated. "Why are you so grumpy all the time?"

"I'm not grumpy, I'm just focused. Unlike you, trying to socialize with every stranger who walks by. So unnecessary."

She smiled. "Why is it unnecessary?"

"Because we're just here to drop off Mrs. Sadiq and her groceries. That's it. I see no need to make new friends just because I'm here for the first time."

"I'm not trying to make friends, I'm just being friendly. Try it sometime. It's fun."

He snorted as he started up the sidewalk. "I don't think so."

"You might like it. You might be surprised." Kyle was silent as they walked up the steps, Bilqiis leading the way.

"You know what we should do?" Ainsley said, taking the bags into the kitchen, putting the milk into the fridge. "We should go somewhere fun on Saturday. Get out of town. Where have you wanted to go?" She could hear Kyle trotting back down the stairs to get more bags.

Bilqiis got a heartbreakingly wistful look. "The ocean. In Mogadishu, we could see the ocean often. We still haven't been since we arrived in Oregon."

"Two women and a child? No. You cannot go alone, it's not safe." Abshir was understandably nervous.

"Mr. Sadiq, I've been to the beach many times, I assure you. I know the way. It's a very safe place."

"I'm sorry, Ms. Buchanan. My wife and child cannot go with only you, and I must work. There is an American proverb: there's safety in numbers. We can't be too careful after...what happened. People who agree with Mr. Zane, they are everywhere."

"What if someone else came? My . . . Dr. Durand, he might be willing to go with us."

Abshir stared at the carpet, then he nodded slowly. "Dr. Durand is a good man, and I think other men would not confront my wife if she were with him. Yes, you may go if he will accompany you." Ainsley privately agreed; Kyle was no body-builder, but she wouldn't mess with him, either.

Fawzia started jumping up and down, her small feet producing more noise than one would think possible, but Ainsley could see that Bilqiis wasn't letting herself be excited yet.

After several trips, they ended up back in front of their cars. He still looked stressed; Ainsley wanted to hug him, but they weren't that kind of friends, and she knew he had touch issues occasionally. She settled for a gentle punch on the arm, but as she went to do it, he misinterpreted her movement. Kyle lifted his arm, as if to hug her, and her fist, having nowhere to land, found open air. The motion propelled her forward, and they were suddenly getting that hug after all; it was one-armed and cringe-worthy, but it was warm. Ainsley found herself hesitant to pull away: she hadn't meant to hug him, didn't want to weird him out . . . but also wasn't ready to leave this somewhat tender if unexpected moment and go back to their usual brand of awkward.

Nestled under his arm, she murmured, "Thanks for your help today."

"You're welcome. And I'm not grumpy all the time."

She rolled her eyes, but smiled. "Fine, I take it back. You're a ray of pleasant sunshine." She gave him a quick squeeze as they released each other.

"Thank you." He caught her gaze and held it as he backed toward his car. "See you."

"Yup. See you." She only realized later that she'd forgotten to ask him about the beach trip.

CHAPTER TEN

THURSDAY AFTER SCHOOL, Kyle was there as usual to pick up Cooper. Ainsley felt pressure to talk to him about the beach. Their families had happened to meet in Pacific City a few years ago on a rare sunny spring day, and he'd looked miserable. She didn't know if it was a sand thing or a sun thing or a not-being-at-home-playing-video-games thing, but she didn't anticipate that he'd actually want to join them. Maybe she could bribe him with brownies . . . She really wanted to make this happen for Bilqiis.

Just as she was about to hand Cooper off, the boy slapped his own forehead comically.

"I forgot my lunch box!"

"Where'd you forget it?"

"I'm not sure . . . in my cubby, maybe?"

"Okay, hang on. I have to walk you back inside. Go tell Uncle Kyle." Cooper dashed across the concrete to talk to him, and Ainsley delivered the rest of the class to their buses. Kyle and Cooper were waiting for her by the front doors, and they followed her inside.

"Hello, Ainsley."

"Hey, Kyle." He was dressed for work, and she gave herself a moment to admire his suit. Or rather, to admire him in a suit.

"Just as a heads up, I was thinking I might not build on Saturday."

He looked up, scowling. "Why? You always build on Saturday."

"I know, but Bilqiis really misses the ocean, and she doesn't get a lot of time off. I thought maybe I would take her, make a day of it." She swallowed. "I thought maybe you'd come with us."

"Why?" He sounded as surprised as he looked, and both were considerable.

"Abshir doesn't want us to go unless we have another dude with us. He thinks racist guys will be more likely to leave us alone."

"He's not wrong. Cowards hate an audience. And he approved of me?"

"After a little cajoling, yes."

He was biting the inside of his lower lip, and Ainsley held her breath. She was tempted to do some cajoling of her own, but she thought she'd wait for him to say no first.

"Okay." She wanted to stick a finger in her ear and clean it out to make sure she was hearing him right.

She blinked at Kyle as Cooper ran back into the classroom, only to run right back out.

"Not in there, gonna check the lunch room!"

"Okay, Coop." She turned back to Kyle. "Did you just say 'okay'?"

He nodded. "Yes. But I have some conditions . . ."

She threw her arms around his shoulders, squeezing him tight. "Thank you, thank you, thank you, Kyle! Oh, thank you so much!" When he stiffened, she pulled back quickly. *That was too much.* She turned away under the guise of putting her hair back up, letting her face go hot while he couldn't see.

"Ains . . ."

She trampled his attempt to talk about it like she was a bull at Pamplona. "So I was thinking we could leave early; that's your preference, right? I think they get up early, too, so it shouldn't be a big deal. I was thinking of Lincoln City, but I could probably be persuaded to go to Pacific City if you like it better. They're both kind of tourist traps, but they might like that better, I don't know. I like the beach better at Lincoln. And of course, a stop at Tillamook for ice cream is essential, even if it does add a lot of extra—"

"Hey." He grabbed her arm and spun her around. Kyle engulfed her in an ardent hug. She felt her face pressed into his clean-smelling chest, and she completely forgot what she was going to say next. Her hands lifted on their own and returned his embrace, pressing her palms into his back, worried she was somehow doing it wrong. *A hug? You're worried that you're doing a hug wrong? He's autistic, but he's not going to disown you if you don't touch him exactly the way he wants. You are officially too wrapped up in this . . . whatever this is.*

"I'll leave whenever you want to leave," he said, his lips brushing the top of her head, making her heart beat faster. "And we can go wherever you think is best. But I'm not driving all the way to Tillamook for ice cream we can get at the grocery store in Salem." He left his arms loosely around her; she could've easily pulled away, if she wanted to. But she didn't. Ainsley tipped her head back to stare up into his solemn face, but she could see a spark of pleasure in his eyes, and his hands were warm as he touched her gently.

She couldn't bring herself to leave that touch, but she wanted to put them back on solid ground, and that meant arguing. "But everyone knows ice cream is better when you eat it next to a giant black-and-white cow statue. And they won't get to take the tour that way! Also, there's an aviation museum nearby, so we could—"

He put a finger over her lips. "Fine. A quick stop at Tillamook, but no one is eating in my car." *He's touching my face. Kyle Freaking Durand is touching my lips.* This was even better than the wedding cake moment.

"Deal."

"Do you have an umbrella?" She gave him a perplexed look, and he shook his head. "Never mind, I'll grab the one at my mom's."

"Like a rain umbrella or a sun umbrella?"

He flexed his arms inward a little bit and then let her go. "First of all, rain umbrellas are for Californians."

"Well, that's what I would've thought, but . . ."

"No, you're right. They are. But I hate sitting in the sun, so I have a big beach umbrella. It's very helpful. We should also plan to get some buckets and shovels before we go, because they always mark that stuff up at the grocery stores near the beach . . ."

"You're right, that's a good idea. See? You're not so bad with kids."

That earned her a bright smile from him, and she gave him one back.

"Found it!" Cooper crowed, and Kyle and Ainsley both stepped away from each other as he blasted back into the room. "But now I lost my backpack."

Kyle picked it up where the boy had dropped it and held it out to him.

"You can carry it," Cooper said, turning for the door.

"It's not my backpack. Come get it, Coop." Dragging his feet, Cooper came back and claimed his possession.

"So Saturday? Seven?"

"Saturday," she confirmed, watching as they started back down the hall, still not sure how she'd just gotten Kyle to agree to go somewhere he hated.

CHAPTER
ELEVEN

ON FRIDAY NIGHT, AINSLEY drove to the town meeting like usual. But unlike usual, Kyle was standing outside by the doors. And he was talking to people; in fact, he spoke to everyone who approached the doors. It seemed to be voluntary; she didn't see a gun to his head or anything, and yet . . . this was very un-Kyle-like behavior.

"What are you doing out here?" Ainsley crossed her arms over her chest against the autumn chill. She was so glad Bilqiis wasn't here to witness this; it would cement her opinion about Kyle's interest in her even more.

"I'm greeting people."

"Greeting them?"

"Yeah. You know. Being *friendly*."

Ainsley sighed. "This is because of that thing I said, isn't it?"

"Yes." Kyle faced the Turners. "Hey. Welcome to the town meeting. Someone is glad you're here."

"Thank you," Mr. Turner replied, nevertheless taking his wife by the arm and guiding her inside, as if Kyle and Ainsley had some malicious intent that he hadn't yet ferreted out.

"I'm sorry I said anything. I didn't mean for you to go all Walmart on the good people of Timber Falls, Kyle."

"It can't hurt to practice, can it?"

"It might," she muttered. Ainsley sat down on the bench outside the town hall in order to think. Starla was right across the street in the library; she could see her packing up to go home, most of the lights off already. Pulling out her phone, she texted her.

Ainsley: Packing up?

Starla: Don't do that.

Ainsley: Don't do what?

Starla: Don't be a creeper through the windows. I'm fine. Everything's fine.

It didn't seem fine to Ainsley. If anyone she cared about had left someone else's earring in her bedroom, she'd have feelings about it. Big ones. Loud ones. Angry ones.

Ainsley: Okay, well, have a good night.

Ainsley turned to Kyle. "How long are you going to do this? I'm cold, and you're freaking people out."

"How am I freaking people out?" He turned back to the couple approaching. "Hey. Welcome to the town meeting. Sit anywhere you like." Mrs. Kirschbaum smiled at him, amused.

"That. That's freaking people out, because they already know they can sit wherever they like, it's not a wedding, for goodness' sake."

At the word *wedding*, he went eerily still. "Why would you mention weddings?"

"It seemed to fit the scenario," she said, confused. "Just come inside."

"Daniel isn't here yet. I'll come inside when he gets here."

"Why would Daniel come to the town meeting, anyway? Why are *you* at the town meeting for that matter?"

"I learn a lot of useful things at the town meeting. Like where we're building houses in the community."

He still hadn't signed in at the build. He was getting no credit for it from anyone. She didn't want to stand out here in the cold and argue with him. She wanted to shake him until he started being candid, which was funny, because Kyle was always candid. But she wanted answers to questions she was too afraid to ask.

"I see. And this has nothing to do with Jennie Wallace's presence?" It was a petty thing to say. He hadn't seemed all that interested in her, really, the last time she'd seen them together.

His scowl was deep and instantaneous. "No. Why would it? What would—" Kyle interrupted himself. "Why, it's the Danniver family," he announced loudly. "Come on in out of the cold and find a seat, the meeting's about to begin!" His smile was big and cheesy, and Carmen Danniver literally cowered next to her mother at the sight of him.

"Hey, it's my best friend and my brother! What's up, guys?" Daniel gave Ainsley an affection head ruffle, and she hugged him in response. Good old Daniel. Predictable, amiable Daniel; she was so relieved to see him. He moved to tousle Kyle's hair in the same manner, but he stepped back before Daniel could touch him. Ainsley saw Daniel's sly smile appear, and she knew that brotherly shenanigans were about to occur.

"I'm going to go make sure no one took my normal seat," she said, "since someone's been telling them they can sit *anywhere*."

Ainsley meandered into the building, giving Mrs. Durand a friendly smile on the way. Her mother was sitting up front; Ainsley's normal seat was toward the middle, near his mom's seat. Their mothers often sat together; Ainsley's friendship with Daniel meant that they'd gotten to know each other over the years. They were quite different: Farrah was always put together, while Ainsley sometimes suspected her mother just reached into her closet and pulled out whatever she came up with. It usually coordinated, more or less, but she hadn't been shopping for new clothes in years. It might bother another boss, but Mr. Carpenter had been smart enough to realize that her mother was organized and diplomatic, and had an uncanny way of knowing what was going to happen before it happened. Ainsley had thankfully inherited this trait as well, and it served her well in working with children. By October, she'd have them all pretty much nailed.

Her mother was presenting today, which was why she was sitting up front. It wasn't too early to start thinking about Christmas, and they were trying to convince the town to participate in a giving tree program this year. Families who couldn't afford presents for the holidays could anonymously sign up for a wish list with their children's ages and two or three items. Ainsley had snorted through the list: yes, I'm sure your four-year-old would like an eighty-inch flat-screen, but there was probably some prompting on the part of the parents for that one.

"All right, Timberites," Councilman Park said, coming to the front, and everyone quieted, trying to find their seats. Kyle and Daniel filed in, both looking a bit more wrinkled than they had a moment ago. Were they going to wrestle like that into their thirties? She'd have thought they would've grown out of it by now. She was never sure if Kyle was actually a willing participant in these things or if he was just defending himself against Daniel's fun-loving, touchy nature. Ainsley sat in the third seat in her row. Daniel went to file in, but Kyle reached out a hand and grabbed him by the hood of his jacket, towing him backwards. He claimed the seat in the middle, right next to her. She stared at him.

"I thought you liked the end because of your super long legs?" she whispered.

He shrugged, turning his attention to Councilman Park. She elbowed him.

"Well?" she whispered again, but he didn't turn his head, pressing his index finger to his lips in a "quiet" gesture. Shushing her? He was SHUSHING her? Well, fine. Since when had he become such a model citizen? At the last meeting, she'd almost thrown a pencil at him, he was making so much noise with Maggie. She turned back toward the front.

"Today, we'll hear from Mrs. Buchanan about an exciting new program . . ." Ainsley zoned out. Her part of the meeting wasn't for a good ten more minutes at least, and she was still trying to figure out how to help her kids understand algebra better. True, they wouldn't start learning it in earnest for several years, but their spiraling curriculum mandated that she introduce the concept now. Maybe if she tried another symbol? A question mark? Maybe even a little box—sort of a Schrödinger's box situation? If she wrote a little story about a situation with an unknown quantity, maybe it would . . . Oops, her mom was done. She clapped extra loud for her, knowing she preferred to be behind the scenes and not up front. She was rewarded with a shy, glowing grin as Nancy went back to her seat.

Kyle widened his stance in his seat, slumping down, his arms crossed over his chest. But his knee was bumping hers as it bounced. He was usually moving—that wasn't unusual—but they usually had Daniel between them. He clearly hadn't wanted that today. It made no sense: Kyle preferred the aisle, didn't he? She turned back to Councilman Park, who was still talking.

"The Turkey Trot is coming up fast," he said. "We're still looking for volunteers to help with the medical tent. Dr. Kyle Durand has volunteered to man it, but if last year's black ice pile-up on Main Street is any indication, one person won't be enough." He looked out hopefully over the sea of faces, and Ainsley felt her hand twitching. She really wanted to run this year; she'd actually been training. But as usual, it was more important that the town have what they needed. With a flat smile, she raised her hand.

"Thank you, Ainsley. We sure appreciate that."

She nodded, then sat back hard in her chair. It shouldn't feel like a punishment, helping your community. Why couldn't someone else step up for once? It was hard not to feel resentful. Someone poked her: Daniel was leaning around his brother. He cupped his mouth so no one else could read his lips. "Thought you were going to run this year."

"I was."

Kyle glared at her. "So why don't you?"

"Because you need help."

He snorted, and several people around them gave them subtle "shut up" looks. They let it go, and with relief, she sat back in her chair. She wasn't about to let either of them push her around.

CHAPTER
TWELVE

"WE'LL NOW BREAK FOR a few minutes to give people a chance to . . ." Ainsley did not get to hear the rest of Councilman Park's announcement, because she found herself being dragged outside by two annoyed Durand brothers. Coatless, she wrapped her arms around her middle. Kyle took off his coat and draped it around her shoulders.

"Why did you sign up for the medical tent? You said you were going to run," Kyle said, hands on his narrow hips.

"I *was* going to run. Now I'm not. No big deal."

"You've been training, right? She's been training," Daniel added.

"She didn't run last year, either. She said 'something came up.'" Kyle said, pointing at her.

She narrowed her gaze. Kyle was shivering, but he still looked so stinking solid; how did he manage that?

"I don't want your help," Kyle announced. "I want you to run. I'm firing you."

Ainsley saw Daniel sliding away, back inside, but he gave her a wink as he opened the door. What was he winking about? *The sleep deprivation is getting to that boy . . .*

She laughed. "You don't control the sign-up, the council does, so . . ."

"Well, wear your running shoes, because I'm not letting you help me. I'll draft Maggie or something. Let me worry about it. You do too much; you're already running the fall festival." *And the PTA, and the playground improvement committee, and I'm doing the bake sale . . .*

"Why aren't *you* running?"

"I ran last year."

"No, you didn't. You were out of town for your grandma's funeral."

He waved a hand. "Then I ran the year before. I hardly do any community service. This is my chance to make up for my laziness the last few years."

"I highly doubt you're lazy . . ."

"I am where the town's concerned. I haven't been very involved."

She blinked. "Did you want to be? You always struck me as kind of a lone wolf."

"I don't mind that description. But most wolves need a pack. I haven't had one for a long time, besides my family."

"Why's that?"

He shrugged, looking toward the door. "Spent a lot of time studying, preparing to be a doctor."

"That's important, too."

"It is," he agreed. "But there's a lot of things, a lot of relationships that have been neglected because of that . . ." He wasn't just looking into her eyes, he was pouring himself into her. The mild frustration he usually carried when he talked to her wasn't there. He wasn't somber, but there was a stillness to him, a peace, almost. Ainsley felt as though she were looking into a glassy lake hidden up in the mountains . . . There was a secretive streak to the man, but she felt like he'd just opened the door a crack for her, let the light stream out.

"What kind of relationships?" She played dumb. She had to. Because if she considered what it meant that he'd been steadily moving closer to her, that his breath was warming her face, that he was touching her elbow . . . she couldn't. He was Kyle Unattainable Durand—there wasn't a single woman in this town who wouldn't give her right ear to have his attentions on her. Everyone knew he was a shoo-in for his father's seat on the hospital board in a few years. He was as much a pillar of Timber Falls as she was . . . but she couldn't let herself imagine what he wanted from her. Not after what had happened with Shane, her first boyfriend. Or rather, the boy she'd thought was her first boyfriend. Just thinking about that incident was still enough to put her on edge.

"Ains, I—"

"Meeting's starting again!" Daniel sang out as the front doors popped open. Kyle shuffled back quickly, rubbing his arms.

Ainsley shrugged out of his coat and handed it back to him, murmuring her thanks. He opened the door for her, tipping his head toward the warm interior of the building. There was no time to grab a cookie; they'd spent the whole break talking. No, not talking—bantering. Time was when she could hardly get Kyle to talk to her . . . until that wedding picnic. Ever since she'd mentioned weddings, that day kept floating back to her. She'd seen that moment in her mind a million times since then. It was definitely on her brain's "greatest hits" list when she was bored or tired.

When the meeting was over, everyone flowed out of the hall to their cars. Kyle and Daniel had walked; their house wasn't far from the middle of town. So it surprised her when Kyle started into the darkened parking lot.

"Where are you going?"

"Just making sure you get to your car okay." He spun his keys on his index finger.

"Why?"

He scowled at her. "Because it's dark? And you're a woman alone? And we're friends? Do I need another reason?"

"I guess not . . ." It was hard not to be skeptical. He was just acting . . . *weird*. But she was too tired to fight with him anymore. He shadowed her to the back of the large gravel lot, where her truck was waiting. She put her keys in the lock, but he stopped her with a hand to her arm.

"Your car door isn't closed all the way. Check inside, make sure there's nobody in there."

Ainsley chuckled. "It just doesn't work right. I think I slammed my seat belt in it one too many times."

"You should get it fixed."

She peered at him. "Why?"

"Because it doesn't work right?"

"Don't have the money for aesthetic fixes right now. The 'check engine' light keeps me plenty busy." She climbed up into the driver's seat, tossing her bag onto the other seat, slamming the door behind her. Kyle knocked at the window. Was their conversation not over?

Amused, she rolled down the window. "Yes?"

"It's more than just aesthetic, it's dangerous. If I had a screwdriver, I could pry that thing open in two seconds flat." His high cheekbones and broody eyes were doing things to her in the dark. Ainsley had the sudden desire to kiss him—just to shut him up, of course.

"And someone in town would see wherever you parked it and call me to come get it. Next objection?"

"What if it comes flying open on the highway?"

"I always wear my seat belt, Dr. Durand."

"That's not the point, Ms. Buchanan."

She leaned forward, dangerously close to him now. "And what is the point?"

Oblivious to her interest in his lips, he turned and bumped the door with his hip, then pushed on it. Kyle lowered his shoulder and slammed himself against the door, which finally clicked shut completely. Then he opened it and began to examine the hinges. She pretended that his show of strength hadn't impressed her.

"Hey. Nosy McGee. Please close my door, I'm tired. I want to go home."

"Are you getting married?" He held her door open, his arms bracing his large body between it and the rest of the car, his gaze still focused on the machinery.

Ainsley felt her eyelids fluttering rapidly as she tried to process his nonsensical question. "I beg your pardon?"

"I was curious if you were getting married. Cooper mentioned something about it a while back . . ."

She was still shocked speechless. *Why would Kyle Awesome Durand care if I'm getting married?* Her heart rate sped up as she considered the possible answers to that question, none of them simple.

"No," she finally choked out. "I'm not. I'm not even dating anyone."

Kyle straightened, nodding, rubbing his hands together, which did nothing to remove the grease that was now on his fingertips from poking around in her car.

"Okay." He closed her door hard, then bumped it closed with his shoulder.

"Okay," Ainsley echoed vacantly, starting her car. *What is happening?*

"So I'll see you tomorrow? Seven?"

"Okay." It seemed to be the word of the day. She felt like an idiot just nodding, staring at his handsome face. *Drive away, Ainsley. Put the car in drive.* She fumbled for the gear shift.

"Drive safe," he called, giving her a little wave.

"Yes, you too. Walk . . . safe."

This man is going to be the death of me, she thought as she pulled away.

CHAPTER THIRTEEN

KYLE PULLED UP IN FRONT of Ainsley's apartment building at precisely 6:50. He figured ten minutes was more than enough time to get three people loaded into the car. What he'd forgotten was that when Ainsley was one of those people, ten minutes was not nearly sufficient.

To her credit, she was dressed when she answered the door, and Bilqiis and Fawzia had already arrived.

"Coffee," she blurted, rubbing her eyes. Her blonde locks were still very askew, and he thought to himself that if this was how she looked when she first woke up in the morning, he wouldn't mind waking up next to her from now on.

"We'll drive through. Come on."

"Got stuff," she said, pointing to a large pile of striped beach towels, plastic buckets and shovels, a kite, and what appeared to be some kind of tent.

"Oh good. Let's get this stuff to the car; has everyone used the bathroom? I'd prefer not to stop until we get to Lincoln City." He pivoted to see Ainsley's face. "That's where we're going, correct?"

She nodded, then stood there, still nodding, looking around like she wasn't sure where she was.

"Did you run out of coffee?"

She nodded again, then whimpered so pitifully, Kyle just wanted to hold her.

"Okay. Go get in the car, Ains. We can get this stuff. Then we'll get you your coffee. Cuppa Joe."

She smiled, and he remembered why he was doing this. *Phase Three: Win Ainsley's Heart.* Now that he knew she was single, he anticipated he would be in this phase a long time. He hoped so, anyway. Kyle gathered up all the stuff he could, and Bilqiis and Fawzia got the rest. It appeared Ainsley had packed lunches for all of them, and he hoped it wasn't something he hated. She was a pretty good cook; her brownies were his favorite.

"You can sit in the front, Bilqiis," he offered as he popped the trunk of his minivan. He really wanted to sit next to Ainsley, but he figured the most senior adult in the car should be offered the best seat first.

"Oh, no, thank you. I will sit with Fawzia. I want to see her face when she sees the ocean. I don't think she remembers." Ainsley was giving the other woman a funny look, and he wondered briefly if he was missing something. *Whatever.*

"Seat belts, everybody."

Once they got Ainsley her coffee, she perked right up. He'd brought an audiobook, fearing awkward silence in the car for two hours. What he'd forgotten was that Ainsley could entertain a slug, just by virtue of being herself.

"Let's see, I've got G. Hi, my name is Gertrude, my husband's name is Grant. We come from Georgetown, and we sell grapefruit."

"Grapefruit don't grow in Georgetown," replied Kyle.

"I didn't say they did." She grinned. "I said we sold them in Georgetown. We import."

"This is a weird game."

"Hush, driver. Your turn, Bilqiis."

She cleared her throat. "Hi, my name is Habeekah, my husband's name is Haamid. We come from Hargeysa, and we sell horses."

"Ooh, good one, Hooyo!" Fawzia exclaimed, and she and Ainsley both applauded.

"Kyle's turn," Ainsley sang, "and you've got *I*."

He groaned. "The only letters harder than *I* are *Q* and *Z*."

"Not true," said Bilqiis. "Just sell qatayef and zaatar spice."

Kyle smiled at her in the rearview mirror. "Maybe I will. Okay, *I*? Hi, my name is Ivan, my wife's name is Irene. We come from Iceland, and we sell ice."

"Iceland is very green, you know," Ainsley teased, sipping her coffee.

"Yes, I know. But you threw logic out the window when you told me you sold grapefruit in Georgetown. Next."

Ainsley threw back her head and laughed, and he had to make himself watch the road instead of her. He treasured the sound of it: he was going to play it over and over tonight in his mind. It was very good at collecting facts and memories regarding her, and this one was definitely getting saved.

As they started cresting the coastal range, the beach looked like it was completely fogged in.

"No problem," Ainsley declared. "We could hit the aquarium. Or just find a bakery and gorge ourselves on treats. Or . . ."

Kyle put a hand on her leg. "Or we could see what it looks like when we get there. They came to see the ocean, Ains."

"Yes. You're right," she said, but she'd gone sort of quiet. Was she that disappointed? Had he said the wrong thing? He glanced at her, and she was staring at his hand. *Oh, right.* He'd just wanted her attention; it wasn't easy to get when she was all bubbly and excited like this. Kyle quickly pulled back and put both hands on the wheel.

When they arrived at the parking area, there were few other cars, but amazingly, there was some blue sky. He even needed his sunglasses; darn. He'd hoped it would stay overcast, as he hadn't had time to get the umbrella from his mom. Sand was terrible as it was, but now the sun would be glinting off the waves and beating down on his head. At least it wasn't hot. By the time he got down to the sand, Ainsley had set up her tent.

"Ta-da!" she exclaimed. "I brought this for you. My mom keeps it for Travis's kids to nap in. It'll give you a place out of the wind and the sun."

He peered inside; it was large enough that he could sit up inside it, but the door was wide enough that he could see what was happening outside. It was kind of . . . perfect.

"I can see that you're speechless with gratitude. I'm gonna go fly this kite with Fawzia. I'll be back."

He opened his mouth to thank her, but she was already gone, barefoot with her blonde hair whipping behind her like the wind wanted to fly her, too. Kyle retreated to his tent, spreading a towel so he wouldn't have to sit on the cold sand itself. Bilqiis was right behind him.

"Your ocean is *very* cold. Beautiful, but very cold."

"That's true."

They sat in silence, just watching the waves roll in and out, the occasional brave walker go by. After half an hour, Ainsley came back, her chest heaving.

"Your turn, Bilqiis," she gasped out. "She's ... I ..."

"She exhausted you?" Bilqiis chuckled.

"Yes!"

Bilqiis smiled as she exited the shelter. "I will take my turn, then, but I will not run races."

"You're smarter than me," Ainsley said, collapsing onto her vacated towel, rolling onto her back, but she was still smiling. He hadn't seen her smile this much in a while.

"You're having fun."

"Yes. Are you?"

He shrugged. "I'm enjoying watching you have fun."

"You're too nice," she said, propping herself up on her elbows. She was winded, tousled, still talking a mile a minute . . . the thought had barely crystalized before it was out of his mouth.

"This is how I remember you," Kyle said.

Ainsley ran a hand through her long hair. "What do you mean?"

He shrugged again, trying to figure out how to express what he wanted to say. "Lately, you're so stressed and responsible and in charge. But not today. Today, you're free."

She looked out at the water. "Everyone's different on vacation."

"Just haven't seen you this happy for a while."

"I haven't been."

"Why?" *What are you trying to prove? Why do you pile on responsibility like that?*

"I don't know," she mumbled, still watching the waves.

"Well, I hope it lasts. For your sake."

She looked at him then, and the emotions in her eyes were as choppy as the sea. Ainsley cleared her throat, then suddenly changed the subject.

"Okay, so ice cream is out, I think, because we're all going to be frozen. And pepperoni pizza, because, you know, *pork*. But I'm sure we can find something . . . Ooh, sushi! Kyle, do you like sushi?"

"You want to feed them uncooked fish, then put them in a car for two hours? I don't think so."

"Spoilsport."

"You gonna clean out my car if someone throws up? Or worse?"

She grinned, lying back down. "Nope."

"Then that's settled. No sushi. What'd you bring for lunch?"

"Tuna sandwiches." When he wrinkled his nose, she laughed. "I had to, Durand! It's the beach, seafood is a requirement!"

Kyle rolled his eyes, then got to his feet, brushing off his hands and clothes. "Ugh. Sand."

"Why'd you come with us?" That breakwater look in her eyes was back, and now he was the one groping for answers.

"Sounded like fun."

"No, it didn't. You hate the beach."

"I don't *hate* the . . ." She lifted an eyebrow at him skeptically, and he paused. "Yes, I hate the beach. But you asked me to come." Ainsley was staring at him, and he didn't know what she was thinking, but based on the softness of her face, it was complimentary. He reached out to help her up, and she took his hand.

"Bilqiis! Fawzia!" she called. "Let's eat!"

CHAPTER FOURTEEN

A WEEK LATER, KYLE had pink fluff in his hair. He'd been up in the attic all afternoon, installing insulation with Abshir, and it seemed like they'd had a pretty good time based on the way they were shaking hands. He went to brush off his clothes, but Ainsley stopped him.

"Let's go outside to do that, eh?" She led him into the back-yard. This was the first day he'd worked apart from her, and she'd had to tell herself not to feel sad about it. It was good for him to branch out, learn more skills. But he'd been quiet when he'd picked her up this morning, and she didn't know how to interpret that. "Did you have fun working with Abshir?"

He nodded. "Yes, but I turned on my phone's flashlight to help us see better, and now it won't go off. But I like Abshir; he's led a fascinating life. They seem like a nice family."

"Yeah, they are." She pulled her heavy gloves from her tool belt and put them on. "You have to be careful with insulation; it'll sting like crazy if it gets on your skin." She started brushing off his chest, his arms, his neck, his hair. Kyle just stood still, watching her with an unreadable expression. "Didn't you wear gloves?"

He lifted his hands, which were already red, and inspected them. "No, I didn't know."

"Go wash them off and I'll give you some lotion from my purse."

"I don't do lotion."

"You do today," she said, pushing him back toward the house and into the bathroom. "Don't fuss at me. You'll need those hands later today. Can't hold an Xbox controller with your teeth. And take off your clothes and shake them out in the shower."

"Take off my . . ." Kyle looked pale, like he might pass out, and Ainsley laughed.

"You can close the door first."

He was still giving her a wide-eyed look as she shut the bathroom door on him, trusting that he'd obey her. Ainsley smirked as she heard the water run, then the rustle of fabric as he stripped down.

"Are you sure this is necessary?" he griped through the door.

"Yes," she replied, ignoring the strange look Abshir was giving her. "Just do it."

A moment later, he stepped out, his face and hair damp. "Fine, but I'm not doing the lotion."

"It doesn't have a scent. It won't make you smell flowery."

"It's not that." He looked around, but no one else was listening. "It's kind of a trigger for me, autism-wise."

"Oh. Of course." She felt stupid for not having realized that earlier. She lowered her voice, mindful that he'd tried to ensure privacy in the moment. "What if I did it for you?" She was used to doing things for small people: tying their shoes, wiping their noses, cleaning up their scraped knees, drying their tears. Helping a sensory-sensitive adult friend protect his skin just felt . . . natural. "Then you only have to feel it a little bit."

"Okay." His voice was soft, but not sullen. If anything, she noted a spark of curiosity in his gaze. That little zing, that little interest, had her hypersensitive, and she wondered if she'd made the wrong decision in offering to help. Because she wasn't supposed to let herself fall for Kyle; their closeness was proving dangerous already. That's how she'd gotten her heart broken before. She found her purse in the kitchen. "That reminds me, my phone's dying, too."

"You should charge it."

"Thanks, Captain Obvious."

Kyle scowled at her. *That was too harsh. He's just trying to help.* Her heart felt like a mud puddle—undiscernible, murky—and each interaction just added more ripples to the mess. At least the day was almost over. The phone situation happened to her fairly often, so she had a charger in her purse. She pulled out her lotion at the same time.

"What are you up to tonight?" she asked as she took his right hand, holding his gaze, and rubbed the lotion into his skin gently but thoroughly. Her intent was to distract, but she found herself struggling to stay focused on both tasks at once.

"Not much. I have some medical journals to read."

"No video games?" she teased, gasping in mock shock.

"There might be video games," he admitted. "But I also need to clean my house. My brother's a slob."

She laughed and picked up his other hand while he was distracted. "That he is. But won't you miss him? I can't imagine living in that big, drafty farmhouse by myself. I like having people around."

"You don't like my house?" he asked, suddenly intent on her. It was not lost on her that he hadn't answered the question about Daniel . . . she had a suspicion that he felt more emotional about it then he was letting on.

"No, I like it."

"But you wouldn't want to live there?"

"No, I would, just not by myself. If there were more people, it'd be fine."

"It *is* a little drafty," he said, sounding troubled. "Maybe I should work on that. I could replace the windows."

"Just throw on a sweater. That's the Gary Buchanan school of thought when it comes to heating, anyway." Looking down, Ainsley realized that she wasn't just rubbing the lotion onto his hand, she was massaging it . . . letting the warmth from his comparatively giant hand seep into her own, pressing her thumbs deeper into the tendons, letting her fingers explore all the delicate skin between his fingers. She drew back suddenly, wiping her hands on her jeans.

"There you go!" she said, her voice sounding too chipper to her own ears. "All done!" *Tone it down, Ainsley,* she chided herself, then, needing a distraction, she turned and began to gather things up for the end of the day. In no time, she was juggling a can of blue paint, two hammers, a caulk gun, an extension cord, and a painting drop cloth. The brushes were still soaking in the house . . . someone had left them before lunch without cleaning them. She'd gotten to them just in time.

"You've got that stuff, honey?" her dad called across the yard, his breath clouding in front of him. The sun was starting to tint the horizon orange, and the chill in the air was getting stronger.

Ainsley nodded to her father. "Yup, I'll finish up with the tools. You can head on home."

"Thanks, sweetheart." He gave her a prickly peck on her cheek as she passed by, then turned back to his conversation with the regulars. She shifted the tools in her arms as they started to slide.

"I got it." Kyle caught the extension cord as it started to fall, looping it around his forearm.

"Look at you, coiling cord like a pro. You'd never know you were just a dumb doctor."

He scowled at her. "Do you want help or not?"

"Your help? Always." The scowl softened then, and the heat in his gaze made her stomach flip-flop. So apparently, that made up for her snarkiness earlier. He'd been doing that at pickup with Cooper, on their ride over today, on the way to the beach, basically ever since they'd talked after the town meeting. Ever since he'd asked if she was getting married. Kyle wasn't being forward exactly, just . . . intense. Even more intense than usual. She toed the trailer door open just enough for them to slip inside, leaving it mostly darkened.

"Where do you want this?" he asked.

She sighed. "I don't know. Just dump it on the floor. I'll have to put it in order next weekend, I guess."

"You don't have to do everything yourself, you know . . ."

"It's just easier." She turned to find him very close, closer than she'd realized. *It's just a small space.* He didn't move out of her way. It was the same kind of concern he'd shared in the tent at the beach when he'd rendered her speechless with his blatant honesty. Truth be told, she had lost some of her sparkle in the last few years, and she wasn't really sure why that was.

"Ainsley . . ."

"Yes?"

"When was the last time you were kissed?"

"Kissed?" She wiped her dirty hands nervously on her jeans. "In college, I guess. My last real boyfriend, senior year."

"That's five years ago. How is that possible?"

She blinked, trying to understand his words. "What?"

"I asked," he said, putting his hands on her upper arms, rubbing lightly, "how it's possible that in five years, no one has asked to kiss a woman so gorgeous, capable, and effervescent?"

"Effervescent?" She wrinkled her nose. "I'm not an antacid."

"I beg to differ. You always make me feel better. You make me feel . . . lighter."

"That's weird," she said, looking into his eyes.

"Yeah," he said. "You know what else is weird?"

"What?"

"You've stopped trying to impress me. You stopped wearing makeup to the site. You're wearing pants with holes at the knees and faded flannels. But instead of repelling me, it has me wanting to corner you in a dark trailer and kiss you until we're both gasping for air." His hands slid simultaneously up her arms and into her hair, his thumbs stroking her cheeks.

"That is weird," she said, her voice squeaky. "Are you going to kiss me now?"

"Only if you want me to."

She nodded, and their lips connected before she could even close her eyes. She slid her hands up his sides to find his arms, traced her fingers over the inside of his veined forearms where his sleeves were pushed up. The smell of pine and dust competed with the light scent of his clothes, which smelled like Costco laundry detergent. The men outside laughed, and Ainsley stiffened. Kyle must have felt it, because he pulled back, held up one finger, and took one giant step to the door to pull it shut. "There," he murmured. "That's better." They felt around for each other in the pitch dark of the trailer, Ainsley's giggles swallowed by his hungry kisses. Kyle walked her backwards slowly, pressing her against the wall of the trailer with his body. *His very tight, fit body.* Their tempo increased, two people wound together by more than the physical, soft touches and tastes creating for them their own private world. Ainsley felt her heart break open like a can of caulk left in the sun, a big gooey mess overflowing with happiness. The male conversations outside had faded away, but her mind still registered a familiar clank.

Ainsley broke the kiss abruptly. "What was that sound?" she whispered.

"What sound?" he whispered back. Kyle was breathing somewhat hard, but he cocked his head to listen. "I didn't hear anything."

"It almost sounded like . . ."

Outside, a car started. *Her father's truck.*

"Oh no. No, no, no . . ." Scrambling over the hoses, sawed-off PVC pieces, and broken caulk guns, Ainsley lunged for the door. It bounced outward, but didn't open. Ainsley cursed loudly. She turned back to Kyle, her eyes wide, both their chests still heaving. "We're locked in."

CHAPTER FIFTEEN

"LOCKED IN?" HE ECHOED, and he stumbled toward her in the dark. His eyes started to adjust, and she stepped out of the way just before he would've run right into her. Kyle tried the door himself.

"We're locked in," he said flatly.

"I heard that somewhere before," Ainsley quipped. "Oh wait, I know . . ."

"Okay, okay. Let's not panic. I've got my phone, we'll just call your dad and . . ." He went very still. *Of course it was.* This was not happening.

"What?"

"That flashlight thing—remember? I had the flashlight on, and I couldn't get it to go off . . . and it's dead." He pivoted. "Where's yours?"

"In the house," she whispered. "I was charging it."

"And it's a padlock, right? Nothing to be done from the inside?"

"Not unless you want to break it down."

He looked at the door, running his hands over the edges. "Hinges are on the outside. I don't think I could get up enough speed to break it down."

Ainsley clapped her hands. "Well, let me find a flashlight, there's gotta be one around here somewhere . . ."

"Do you have any food?"

"Why, are you hungry?" She groped along the shelves, searching for something, and he heard her fingers moving along the tools.

Don't hurt yourself, he wanted to say. *If you're hurt and we're trapped in here, I'm going to lose my mind.*

"I'm going to be. And since we're stuck here all night . . ."

She laughed. "Oh, don't be silly, Dr. Doom. We're not going to be stuck here all night. Someone's going to notice I'm missing." She found a flashlight and turned it on, setting it on its end to point the beam at the ceiling and illuminate the whole room. Kyle crossed his arms, his expression grim.

"Who?"

"Who?" she echoed, moving a box of screws.

"Yes. Who's going to notice if you're missing?"

"Winnie."

"You usually go home with your dad on Saturday nights because of your weakness for pancakes."

She tossed her head, which was unfortunate, because her hair was still French braided, so the effect was lost. *Adorable.* "First of all, it's not a *weakness*, it's a *proclivity*, and second of all—"

He snorted. "Fine, your proclivity. But wouldn't she think you were with him?"

Ainsley seemed to be considering this. "Well . . ."

"And your dad thinks you went home to your apartment. So I say again: who?"

"Well, your brother . . ."

". . . is working the night shift at the hospital and won't be home until 8 a.m., assuming he comes straight home. And frankly, he's somewhat self-absorbed and Winnie-obsessed and rarely notices whether I'm there or not."

Ainsley crossed her arms, too. "Huh."

"Yeah."

A long silence passed in the darkened trailer. His fingers were tapping furiously against his leg in an effort to stave off real panic. He couldn't spend the night here; this wasn't right. This wasn't home. There was no bed, no toothbrush, no . . .

"How are we going to get out of here?" he blurted out.

She tapped her chin. "Yell really loud?"

Kyle's chin fell to his chest. "I can't believe this."

"Wait, are you giving up?"

"Aren't you?"

Ainsley laughed. "Of course not! No, I'm just . . . I'm just brainstorming. I'm just getting warmed up." She climbed over the stuff on the floor to get closer to him, and he felt himself tense, unsure of what she'd do next. "Do you perhaps have one of those 'Oops, I slipped and fell' bracelets that we could activate?"

Kyle shook his head slowly.

"Do you have a flare that we could set off?"

What an imagination this woman has. He liked that about her in general. But not now, when they should be preparing for the inevitable night they were going to spend here. Yet Kyle decided to play along, and he felt there was no greater proof that he'd lost all good judgment when it came to her.

"How's that going to help inside a metal box? We'd just burn the place down with ourselves inside."

"Hmm, good point." She put her arms around his waist, and he stilled. He'd been so nervous to kiss her, to even ask, and now she'd just initiated contact with him, like it was normal. Like she was allowed to now, like he belonged to her. The panic over spending the night here began to ebb away as she held him. Maybe she'd be willing to sleep next to him tonight to keep warm; his body was singing like a gospel choir that *they should definitely do that, do that, best idea ever.* He lifted his hands and put them gently on her hips, trying to focus on what she was saying, but his heart was flipping around like a gymnast.

"Do you have telepathic powers? Could you perhaps signal someone with your mind?"

"My mind is powerful. But not that powerful."

"Are you secretly a superhero?"

"How could I be? I don't have glasses, and I prefer my underwear underneath my pants."

Ainsley snort-laughed into his shoulder, and he chuckled, too. Tentatively, he hugged her. She was warm, and it must be catching, because he felt like he'd never been more comfortable while touching someone; he felt his whole body sigh *finally*. Forget what he'd said about their immediate survival; it wasn't going to change anything whenever he investigated the situation further. It felt much more crucial that he kiss her again. Her lovely face was right there, tucked into his shoulder—when she abruptly went another way.

"Yeah, I've got nothing. Let's see if my dad hides any snacks in here. He's diabetic; he's gotta have sugar somewhere in this pit."

Disappointment bit him hard, but he hid the sting. They cleaned up while they searched and were rewarded with a Costco-sized box of Oreos in wrapped cellophane packages, which had been hidden behind the flooring boxes.

"Come to Papa," Kyle said, snagging two rolls for himself.

"I'd never have pegged you for a junk food enthusiast," Ainsley said, giving him the side eye.

"All things in moderation."

"Aristotle."

"Is it?"

Ainsley nodded. "I like quotes. Do another one."

Kyle tilted his head to the side, thinking, watching her eat. Her teeth were turning black from the cookies. "'I have no special talent. I am only—'"

"'Passionately curious.' Albert Einstein. A hard one, please."

He chuckled, covering his mouth so he didn't spew cookie crumbs everywhere. "Fine. 'Whatever you are, be a good one.'"

"Abraham Lincoln. I use that one in my classroom all the time."

"I'd kill for a glass of milk right now."

"I don't know that one." Ainsley smirked, and, amused, Kyle threw a cookie at her. "Food waster!" she gasped. "We need those calories right now, Durand!"

"Okay, okay." He thought for a moment. This was a chance to show her something real about himself . . . to go a little deeper. There would be no escape if he was embarrassed, but he couldn't imagine she'd laugh at him. At least, not like kids used to laugh at him, when he didn't know they were teasing him. He wolfed down another cookie for courage. "'But there was no need to be ashamed of tears, for tears bore witness that a man had the greatest of courage, the courage to suffer.'"

Ainsley squinted at him. "Shoot. C. S. Lewis?"

"Nope. Want another clue?"

She nodded.

"'What is to give light must endure burning.'"

She twisted her lips to the side, hesitating. "Buddha?"

Kyle laughed. "Nope." She wasn't going to get it. Maybe he should've picked another one. Was it important to let her win? He'd never let his brothers win at anything, but girlfriends were definitely not brothers. He didn't want her to feel dumb; she wasn't.

"Dang it!" Ainsley pounded the sack of cement she was sitting on. "Who?"

"One more, then I'll tell you. 'Everything can be taken from a man but one thing: the last of the human freedoms—to choose one's attitude in any given set of circumstances, to choose one's own way.'"

Ainsley shook her head. "I have no idea, but I love it. Especially when I'm trapped in a trailer for the night." *So not a bad choice after all.*

"His name was Viktor Frankl, he was a Holocaust survivor. Wrote a book called *Man's Search for Meaning*. It's one of my favorites."

Her expression changed, but he couldn't read it. "So when he says any given set of circumstances . . ."

"He'd been through the worst of it." Kyle swallowed. "I tell my patients that when I have to give bad news. Lots of times, an ER visit is the first sign of a bigger problem."

"Does it help?"

"Sometimes. Sometimes people just want to be angry."

"I'm sure it's a process." She dusted off her hands. "You know the upside of all this?"

"No, but I think you're going to tell me . . ."

"We're safe from the zombie apocalypse in here."

"Yes," said Kyle, his voice somber. "I think we are." *She remembered my stupid joke.* Now he *needed* to kiss her again, more than food or shelter or anything else. It had just become a matter of survival. He pitched forward a little, testing the waters of closeness, trying to see if she could read his intention . . .

"Oh! I just remembered." Ainsley scrambled up from her concrete seat and dug around in the back by the bucket of nails. Kyle held back a sigh; they were not on the same page here, but she'd piqued his curiosity now.

"What're you doing?"

"Ah-ha!" She held a deck of cards and a plastic bag full of white, red, and blue chips above her head, triumphant.

"Why is that here?"

She slid the cards out of the box. "My dad likes to play poker with the guys afterward in the house. They don't want their wives to know, so they keep their stuff in here."

Kyle shook his head, smiling. "Your dad's funny." *Too bad he doesn't like me. And this mishap is probably not going to win points in my favor.*

Ainsley shrugged. "I know, especially because my mom already knows, but she lets him think she doesn't, because it makes him happy. They're weird."

"So. Strip poker?"

Ainsley gasped. "Dr. Durand, how dare you? Besides, you see enough naked bodies as it is. It's Texas Hold 'Em, of course, the best kind of poker."

"I'd probably do better at Go Fish."

"I will abide no such foolishness," she said in her best Southern belle impression, dealing the cards. In an inexplicable string of luck, he won the first four games, and he could tell Ainsley was suspicious that he hadn't been honest with her. So he made sure he let her win the next two. She had just dealt the cards for the seventh game when the flashlight flickered. They looked at each other, wide-eyed. Ainsley twisted behind her and grabbed for something; Kyle lunged for the ten-gallon bucket he'd noticed nearby, then they were plunged into complete darkness.

"Well. I guess the game's over," she said. "What did you grab for?"

"An empty bucket."

"You gonna throw up?"

"No . . . but eventually, one of us is going to need a toilet."

"I'll hold it."

"Don't hurt yourself. I'm a doctor, I've seen worse. Also, I can't see anything right now anyway."

"I do not abide a transient toilet situation!"

"Suit yourself. What did you grab?"

"Painting drop cloth. It should do something to help me keep warm."

He moved toward her, feeling his way hesitantly over the plywood floor in the dark.

"Yeah, I wanted to say something earlier, but I wasn't sure how to bring it up . . . We should probably sleep close together for heat."

"Right," she said, and he could hear the grin in her voice. *"For heat."*

"I'm serious. This thing isn't insulated, and it's supposed to get down to forty degrees tonight. I know this looks bad," he babbled, "since I trapped you in here to kiss you, but . . ."

"Kyle, honey, it's fine. You didn't trap me; I was a very willing participant. Don't worry about it. We'll be two spoons in a drawer, two peas in a pod. I think there's more space by the door." He listened to her moving in the dark toward the entryway, trying to process the nickname bomb she'd just dropped on him. With a few muttered curses, Kyle made his way next to her and lay down behind her, pulling the drop cloth over both of them. She squirmed around on her side, probably trying to get comfortable. Her backside, which he had admired from afar many times, was pressed tight against him . . . and it was having unintended consequences. He tried to tell his hormones to take five, but they were most interested in singing about said backside and its fantastic qualities.

"Ainsley," he growled. "Stop moving around."

"I can't get comfy . . ." She wigged again, and his eyes nearly rolled back into his head.

"I'm not joking. Stop. Moving." *Please. Please, please, please.* "Please."

"Maybe if I just . . ." She tried to shift her legs farther back, but they just tangled with his and pressed her backside more firmly against him. Kyle grunted softly.

"What's wrong?"

He cleared his throat. "What?"

"You made a hmph."

He had two choices: coming clean or lying his pants off. Though not his preference, lying was probably better in this case, because the other option might lead to *taking* his pants off. And he didn't know how he felt about that just yet, as much as he liked her. It seemed like a good way to ruin things early on. So he lied.

"There's a wrench or something in my side, what do you want from me?"

"Really? I thought I cleared everything around here..."

"Well, you didn't," he growled, as she felt under them to try to remove the offending item, and he gave up his ruse lest she touch lower by accident and discover what'd happened. "Fine, there's no wrench, I just can't have you so . . . close to me." *Distract her! Quick!* "Here, lift your head."

She did, and he slid his fleece-covered arm under it. It should cushion her head and neck nicely.

"Better?" His voice had softened, like butter left out.

"Yes," she whispered. Under the drop cloth, he let his left hand rest on her hip.

"Isn't this going to hurt your arm?" Her concern was thoughtful but unnecessary. He was fairly sure he'd have it amputated if that's what she needed. Maybe that's just the way it felt.

"I'll survive."

"Are you sure we can't sleep on that roll of insulation?"

"And get cancer from breathing in fiberglass all night? No, thank you."

He could hear the smile in her voice. "Such a pessimist."

"Optimism doesn't pay the bills, Sunshine." He'd never called her that out loud, and he felt a furious blush take his cheeks. God bless the darkness. What was happening to him? How were his private thoughts and nicknames suddenly pouring out of him like this?

"I see why everyone loves your bedside manner so much."

He snorted, recovering from his embarrassment. "I may not coddle them, but I take very good care of them. I tell them exactly what they need to hear."

She rolled over to face him, and her cookie-scented breath warmed his face. He could just see the outline of her.

"I like that about you. But I wouldn't want you to tell me I had cancer."

"I don't think I could treat you anyway." He pushed a stray lock of hair behind her ear.

"No?"

"No. I'd be . . . biased. Distracted."

"You find me distracting?"

He nodded, curling her closer to him. "Very." Kyle kissed her quietly, breathing a happy sigh, finally getting what he wanted. "I find a lot of things about you distracting, though. Your body's only part of it."

"My genius with pipe cleaners is pretty impressive."

"How can you say that like it's a joke?" He knew he sounded incensed, but he kind of was.

"Isn't it? My job is definitely a joke compared to yours."

"What? That's garbage. I could never do your job. I have no idea how you handle thirty squirrely kids five days a week. Abe Lincoln would approve, especially given how you put up with my nephew."

"He's a sweet kid," she said, pushing at his chest. "I love Cooper." He loved him, too, but he had to disagree with her on the first part.

"'Sweet' is a stretch. He's just like Philip as a kid. A handful."

"I'd say he turned out okay."

Kyle nodded. He didn't want to talk about his brother; he took her chin gently in his hand and kissed her again. Their caresses were lazy, languid; she shivered, and he hoped it was because she was as affected as he was, and not because she was cold. He certainly wasn't cold; every touch of her tongue to his had him feeling like he was on fire. She was a good kisser, and he tried not to hate whoever she'd practiced with. He couldn't see her face, but he knew she was looking at him, and he wished he could see her pretty blue eyes. He couldn't believe he had Ainsley Buchanan in the dark, all to himself... and he violently wished the circumstances were different. His mind started supplying a lot of ways this could be better—a lot better.

"Kyle?"

"Ains?" There he went with nicknames again. They should kiss some more; that would keep personal things from popping out of his mouth.

"What are you thinking about?"

"When a man is holding the woman of his dreams in the dark," he said slowly, "that doesn't seem like an entirely fair question."

"Do you plead the fifth?"

He laughed softly, then kissed her. "Yes." He kissed her again, his tongue sneaking into her mouth, making her groan. "Effervescent. I stand by it."

"Tell me." That breathy voice was not helping him rein in his thoughts.

"Tell you . . . what I'm thinking about?" His voice sounded as uncertain as he felt. Kyle kept his mouth busy with more kisses while he considered her question; he was greedy for more. "That's not going to happen. I'm going to have to be content with thinking for tonight, and telling you all about it probably isn't going to . . ." He trailed off, distracted again. Those many thoughts were back again. "God, Ainsley," he whispered. "You have no idea how much I want you."

"I want you, too," she whispered. Call the coroner. He was now dead.

He groaned. "Don't. We can't." *For a lot of reasons.*

"I know," she said quickly. "I just wanted you to know."

"God, you're sweet. You put every sweet thing to shame, Ainsley Rose."

"I'm not always sweet." That teasing lilt—it was wicked. Pure naughtiness.

"I don't know what you're planning, but don't," he said with a waver in his voice. He cleared his throat, then made his voice firm. "Don't." If she made a move on him now, he didn't know if he could find the strength to make her stop.

"If you think your stern doctor voice is going to make me comply, then you're underestimating how much I love hearing it . . ." He felt a warm hand slide softly down his torso toward his beltline, but he caught her wrist just in time.

"Ainsley . . ." The tremor was back. "I'm trying to be a good guy here. We haven't even been on a date yet." Kyle kissed her hard; the heat was back. His body clearly thought his brain lacked ambition.

"Cards and cookies in a trailer don't count?"

He released her wrist and let his hand slide up her side, then he cursed as he drew back. "We're going to take this slow . . ." He was talking to himself as much as to her.

"You asked me when I'd last been kissed. You didn't ask when I'd last been—"

"Nope." He covered her mouth with one finger, his voice steely. Kyle could *not* hear that information; it would break his resolve for sure. If she hadn't had a boyfriend all this time, she probably wanted physical contact of that nature quite badly, and he already found it difficult to deny her things she wanted. He loved making her happy, but he wasn't losing his virginity in a tool trailer in the freezing cold. "Not another word. I'm serious."

"Doctor voice," she moaned.

"Fine," he kissed her sweetly, slowly. "No more talking, then. Let's just go to sleep." He pulled at her, encouraging her to roll over again. Ainsley resisted for a minute, then sighed. He listened to her breathing even out, felt her body relax into his, the heat ricocheting between them. Yeah, he couldn't imagine that sleep was in the cards for him anytime soon . . . but at least he'd avoided disaster. For the moment, anyway.

AINSLEY WAS ALREADY awake when she heard her father's truck early the next morning. She'd been watching Kyle's sleeping face, feeling his chest rise and fall beneath her cheek, enjoying the warmth of his body next to hers. Rather, she would've been enjoying it if she hadn't needed to pee like a mother of four needs coffee. She'd eyed the bucket at length, trying to decide if there was any way she could do it without Kyle waking up. But it was irrelevant now; she was getting out of here.

"Kyle," she whispered. "Wake up." He didn't even flinch. She rubbed a hand over his flat belly, and he smiled, his lids fluttering open, then frowned.

"Ainsley?" Kyle rubbed his eyes with one hand. "Oh, right. Ainsley. In the trailer. I'm trapped in the trailer with Ainsley." They could hear the lock outside being removed, and a moment later, one door opened and the trailer was flooded with light.

"What the—" her father exclaimed.

"It's just me, Dad." There was a long pause, and she used it to stand up and stretch her very sore back muscles.

"Oh, no—sweetheart, I am so sorry." He covered his face with his hands, then pulled them down his beard. "I forgot you'd come with the doc, I didn't see your car. I thought you'd forgotten to lock up the trailer when you left. Why didn't you say anything when I did the lock?"

Her face burned. "We were . . . busy. I didn't realize until it was too late. And I left my phone in the house."

"We?" Her father's chagrin changed abruptly to cold realization as her all-night snuggle buddy stepped into view. "Doc? Wait—so you two were locked in *together*?"

"It did her no good," Kyle said, squinting into the bright morning light as he tried to dust off his pants, and Ainsley winced at his matter-of-fact expression. *Read the room, honey.*

"Good morning, sir. My phone was dead, too. Flashlight problem."

Gary folded his arms across his barrel-like chest. "And just what were you doing in the trailer with my daughter, Doc?"

"Dad! He was helping me clean up." She shot Kyle a pleading look, but he clearly wasn't rushing to offer any explanations, so Ainsley stuttered, "N-nothing happened!" *Besides some very hot kissing, stroking and cuddling? Right, Ainsley.*

"I guess that's none of my business, but . . ." Gary sighed deeply. "All right. What's done is done. Come on, kids, let me buy you an apology breakfast and a hot cup of coffee. Let's go." Gary gathered Ainsley into a tight hug, but she didn't miss the way he glared at Kyle.

"First things first, Dad," she said as she hurried toward the port-a-potty. "Then we'll talk about what happened to your Oreos."

"Wait," he called after her. "What happened to my Oreos?"

CHAPTER
SIXTEEN

MONDAY NIGHT WAS AN odd time to have a social gathering in Kyle's opinion. But Monday was the only day that worked for everyone for the inaugural Sibling Night, per Maggie's suggestion. She did look very pleased with herself, munching popcorn on his suede leather couch. Kyle had opted to sit on the floor in order to not have crunching in his ear. No one gave him a hard time about it.

"So what's new?" Philip asked. Claire had made excuses, saying she'd had a tough day with Hannah . . . Kyle still wanted her to see the lactation consultant, and he decided to bring it up again the next time he saw her. Something wasn't right there, and he despised a medical mystery. Also, Hannah was his niece; he was obligated to take care of her, small and smelly though she may be. He was glad to be past that stage with Coop.

"Why don't you ask Kyle? I heard he had an interesting night on Saturday," Daniel suggested innocently, cutting the pepperoni and red pepper pizza Kyle had made earlier. Kyle narrowed his gaze, giving his brother a little head shake, but Daniel just smirked at him.

"Oh, come on. I see Kyle every day," Philip said, oblivious.

"Every weekday," Kyle corrected, taking a sip of his ice water.

Philip ignored him. "I want to hear what's new with the rest of you. Mags, you go first."

"I finished a painting. An acrylic."

Kyle sat up straighter. He had one of her earliest works hanging in his bedroom upstairs: an oil painting of Mt. Jefferson. It was fairly basic, and she'd begged and pleaded for him to get rid of it, but he didn't want to. It was like the trading cards: it made his room right. It was the perfect balance of interesting and calming, minimalist though it was.

"You want to propose a trade?" he asked.

She shook her head. "Not this time, Grumpy."

"Can we see it, at least?" Winnie asked, bumping her shoulder against Maggie's. Maggie shyly pulled out her phone and brought up a picture, which they then passed around. He pinched the image to make it bigger on the screen. It was a forest of aspens in black and gold and white, and he could practically hear the wind rustling through the delicate leaves and feel the sun on his face.

"I like this one."

"You like all of them," she said, grabbing her phone back.

"What's wrong with that?" he asked, grabbing a slice of pizza.

"Nothing," Philip affirmed. "I like it, too. You should sell it on Etsy or something."

Maggie rolled her eyes. "Because something doesn't have value unless you get paid to do it, right?"

Kyle sat back, watching the soccer game on the TV. There was no point in arguing with her, but that didn't stop Daniel and Philip.

"Philip, would you be willing to look at a car for me?" Kyle asked.

Philip sipped his Coke. "Sure. You looking to buy a new one?"

Kyle shook his head. "This one belongs to Ainsley. Her door doesn't close correctly."

"What make and model is it?"

Kyle didn't know that was essential information; he looked to Daniel.

"It's a Ford truck of some kind, older," his brother supplied.

"Sure, I mean, I can at least look at it."

"Can you swing by the school tomorrow and look at it?" He knew Philip was off, and he could sacrifice some sleep to do this for her.

"Sure, man." Philip turned to Winnie and Daniel. "How about you guys? What's new with you?" he asked, looking at the couple, and Kyle felt himself grimace. Were they so joined at the hip now that he couldn't even ask them individually? They had to be a unit all the time? Even now, sitting on the couch, they were as close as close could be.

Daniel put down his orange pop bottle and rubbed his palms on his khaki pants. "We kind of have an announcement, actually." The TV was already muted, but Kyle had the impulse to turn it off. He had a feeling he wasn't going to like this. Everyone quieted, waiting.

"You guys know the old Foster place? Hattie told me it's going up for sale. We're going to put an offer on it."

"Hey, that's great, you guys!" Philip stood up to give Winnie a hug and shake Daniel's hand. Kyle stayed where he was, his eyes fixed on the screen again. Was it suddenly colder in here? That made no sense; there were more people here than usual. Their body heat should be contributing to the temperature of the room in a positive way, not the opposite . . .

"It's a little closer to the hospital, right?" Maggie asked. "You'd have plenty of room for kids, too." Kyle felt his body tightening, like someone was turning a key in his back, winding him tighter and tighter inside, the pressure growing unbearable.

"Scheming for more nieces and nephews already?" Daniel smirked, and she grinned at him as Winnie blushed a little.

"Yeah, what's wrong with my kids?" Philip asked, throwing his arms wide. Kyle couldn't take it anymore.

"Excuse me," Kyle said, jumping up and heading upstairs.

"Hey," Daniel called after him. "Where are you going?"

"I'll be right back," he called over his shoulder, fighting to keep his voice steady. And he would be. No matter how much he was freaking out inside, this was his house. He couldn't leave guests down there alone, even if they were his family. Kyle closed his door quietly and sat down on the edge of his bed, unable to keep himself from rocking forward and backward. It was better than jumping; they'd hear jumping on these old floors.

This was out of order. Daniel had said he was staying until their wedding in January. This was only the end of September. *September.* Even if the house took a while to close, he'd still be leaving early. He was breaking his promise. Kyle felt that two sides of him had drawn rapiers, masked and ready to fence with each other. The brotherly side, the side that cared about Daniel, had an offense prepared: *This is a good thing. Winnie is good for Daniel; you wanted to see your brother get married and have a family. A family you'll be part of.* That part insisted that he would still see Daniel, that this was the start of something and not the end.

But the other side, the scared side, parried back: *He's breaking his word. He doesn't care what he told you, because he doesn't care about you. He'll say that you'll see each other, but he's putting Winnie ahead of you. He's changing plans without even talking to you. He used to tell you stuff. Now he tells her.*

Still rocking because the stimulation felt necessary, Kyle snapped at his brain to shut up: he didn't believe that. They were still close. They would still be close. Change was just hard, it was always hard, hard, hard. It was hard when he went to college; he pushed back. Change was hard when he moved into this house, but he got through it. Change was hard with every new school year, every new soccer team, but every time, he found a new equilibrium, a new . . . A quiet knock at his bedroom door made him go still.

"What?"

"You okay in there?" Daniel asked, his voice muffled by the wood.

"Yes." He felt bad about the amount of disdain that leaked into his tone and tried to soften it. "I'm fine. I said I'll be down in a minute."

He could feel his brother hesitating, deciding if he believed him. "Okay. I know we both have to get to work soon, and Winnie just got called in for a birth if you want to say goodbye."

"I'll be down in a minute." He waited until his brother's footsteps faded before he took a deep breath and rolled his shoulders. *Oh, good. Something new to worry about.*

CHAPTER SEVENTEEN

COOPER WAS QUIET ALL morning. He didn't poke at Harmony during morning calendar. He didn't get up for five drinks of water during his small reading group. He didn't talk when she was giving directions. In other words, something was obviously very wrong. Ainsley pulled him aside as they went outside to morning recess.

"Hey, Coop. How are you?"

He shrugged, eyes on the carpet.

"You having a good day?"

He nodded, but he dug the toe of his sneaker into the thin pile, kicking at it. She knelt to see him better.

"Because if you weren't, we could talk about it. Might make you feel better." He launched himself at her so hard, he nearly knocked her over.

"She's gone," he sobbed. Ainsley rubbed his back, glancing around. They weren't supposed to have a lot of physical contact with the students; she understood why, on a legal and abuse-prevention level, but at times like this, the rules clearly did not apply.

"Who's gone, sweetheart?"

"O-O-Orangesicle. She ran away."

"Your kitty ran away? Oh, that's so sad. Honey, I'm so sorry." She squeezed him tighter as he cried. She didn't shush him. She whispered that it would be okay, that they would find her, that she was probably just exploring the woods and she'd be back in a day or two when she got hungry—all the things parents had been telling children about lost pets for hundreds of years.

His tears slowed, his breathing became more steady, and he wiped his face without shame. "I hope she comes back. I can't sleep without her."

"I hope so, too. I tell you what, if you want to make some posters during journal time, I'd be fine with that. I'll even make you some copies to hang up on the way home. How does that sound?"

"I'm gonna start now . . . Miss B, can I use your orange crayon? I lost mine."

"Sure, honey. My box is under my desk." It was too big to fit inside. She used it as a reward from time to time. Surely a lost kitty counted as trauma worthy of two hundred available colors.

She looked online for a lost cat poster they could print out and color, and it only took about thirty seconds. But Cooper insisted that those cats weren't a close enough facsimile of *his* cat, and his drawing would provide a better likeness of her. He worked quietly, dedicated to his task, right up until lunch. She made him take a break: even brokenhearted artists needed sustenance. But his sad moment had prompted a deeper ache inside her: Ainsley wanted to be a mother. She'd been denying it for some time now, telling herself that her students were enough for her, but it wasn't true. She wanted to be able to hug her kids without worrying about the legal ramifications or whether someone would take it the wrong way. She was staring off into space, still deep in thought, when Starla rapped on her classroom door.

"You okay?"

"Sure," she said, shaking herself back to the present. "Ready for lunch?"

"Been craving Annie's burgers all day . . ."

"Great. Let's go get it, girl. Grab that box for me, will you, Star?" Ainsley asked. "Just out to the car for me?"

"Sure." She rummaged through the top of its contents as they walked. "Spoons? Bowls?"

"We had a birthday," Ainsley explained. "I don't like to use the throw-away stuff, so I got some random ones at the thrift store, and it's easier to just stick it all in the dishwasher at home."

"Except then you have to drag it all the way home and all the way back . . ."

Ainsley grinned. "Nope, I got someone else to drag it for me."

Starla rolled her eyes, then stopped on the curb. "Where's your car?"

"It's in the back," Ainsley said, digging around in her purse for her keys. "I like to let the parents have the spots close up. I don't like kids wandering through the parking lot after . . ." She stopped. "Wait, where's my car?"

The women stood in the middle of the parking lot. They looked at each other. They looked at Ainsley's usual spot, empty. They looked at each other again.

"Could someone have borrowed it?" Starla asked, shifting the heavy box higher against her hip as if it were a child. That felt like something that would happen around here. Her dad had had quite a few calls as a cop where it ended up that a friend or relative had just borrowed a car because it was unlocked. But hers had been locked; she was sure of it.

"No, I don't . . . I don't think so."

"Who would steal your car right out of the school parking lot? That's fairly audacious," Starla said, turning back toward the building. "Do you have security cameras or anything?"

Ainsley followed, shaking her head. "Just on the front of the school. Intruder awareness and all that." She sighed. "Well, I guess I'll be eating candy for lunch and spending my free time on the phone with our beloved Officer Painter . . ." Their friend Lizzie was the newest member of the sheriff's office.

"Sorry," Starla said, and she looked like she meant it as she passed Ainsley the box. "Let's just take my car."

"No"—Ainsley waved away the offer—"I've got food. I'll be fine. You can give me a ride home tonight, though, if you want. I was going to walk your kids down anyway." She sighed again. "And I'll have to cancel all my meetings and stuff unless I can borrow Winnie's car, provided she's not working." Ainsley groaned. "So much for our lunch date."

"Bummer." Starla nodded somberly. "Why don't you call Kyle? I'm sure he'd run you around if he's off."

"I think he works tonight, so he might be asleep."

"Just text him. This is what partners are for, right?" *Are we partners, though?* There was a touch of irony in the statement, and Ainsley wasn't sure if Starla realized it.

"Here, I'll take the box back. Thanks, Star."

"Good luck," she said over her shoulder as she headed to her car.

Ainsley texted with her thumb as she lugged the box and her large bag back inside.

Ainsley: Some jerkface stole my car. Can you believe that?

Kyle: No, he just moved it where the ground was level.

Ainsley: What? Who did?

Kyle: My brother. I asked him to fix your door.

Kyle: You're welcome.

Annoyance didn't begin to describe it. Ainsley stalked back into her classroom and shoved the box behind her desk. Gretchen B. was digging around in her desk, her small face hidden behind the open top. Ainsley took a deep breath and tried to calm down before she spoke to her.

"You're supposed to be at lunch, kiddo," she gently chided.

"I know, but I just wanted to show Devin my new—"

"Whatever it is, it can wait until after lunch. Now scoot."

"But Miss B—"

"Gretchen!" she snapped. "Go. Now." The crestfallen look on the child's face told her that she'd gone too far, but the girl darted from the room before she could say anything more. Her phone dinged.

Kyle: I didn't think you used it during the day.

Kyle: You're not saying anything.

Kyle: I was doing a nice thing . . . and it was really easy to break into it with the door broken.

He added a smirk emoji. *That does it.* Ainsley calmly silenced her phone, opened her top desk drawer, dropped it inside, and slammed the drawer shut. She'd had enough of that conversation for one afternoon. She was officially over this day.

CHAPTER EIGHTEEN

SURE ENOUGH, AFTER school, her truck was right where it belonged, with a little something extra on the hood: a nervous doctor and his nephew. Kyle hopped down, tossing his keys to himself.

"I moved your car back."

Ainsley marched directly to the driver's side door, Aiden and Emily right behind her. She opened the door for them, watching them slide across; they could ride without boosters this one time. She vaulted herself into the driver's seat, tossing her bag at their feet. Her grading slipped out and fluttered to the floor of the truck, which was cleaner than usual. Come to think of it, the outside was cleaner, too. Did he detail her funky old truck? *You can't buy your way out of this one, Durand.*

"Did you have a good day?"

She breathed a humorless laugh. "No."

"Why not?"

"I had to miss lunch with my friend, we are concerned about the lost kitty situation, and I thought my car had been stolen. So my day su—" Her gaze fell to Cooper. "... uh, stunk."

"Got your truck door fixed, though. That's good, right?"

Ainsley shook her head slowly. He obviously was not getting what he'd done wrong, but she wasn't about to get into it with him in the school parking lot. Her silence seemed to upset him. His expression grew stormy, his eyebrows snapping together.

"You said the barrier to fixing your car was money; I got it done for free. What's the problem?"

Ainsley closed her eyes as her temper flared up like a grease fire. *Smother it. Just don't give it air.* "Dr. Durand, I am at work. This is not a discussion for my place of business."

"When, then?"

"Pardon?"

He shifted restlessly, his hands on his hips. "Coop, go wait in the car, bud." The boy trudged off as Ainsley watched to make sure he wasn't going to get hit, even though the parking lot was mostly empty. "When are we going to discuss it?" he repeated. "I'm headed to work soon."

"I know."

"So?"

She blew her bangs out of her eyes. "So I don't know when we're going to discuss it, because I don't know when I'll see you next." *And I'm still mad at you for messing with my car to prove a point.* "You guys buckled?" she asked the kids, and both nodded.

Kyle stared at her for a long moment. "No. That doesn't work for me. I need a date and time."

She started her engine. "Life's hard, then you die."

"Ainsley," he growled, but the noise of the engine drowned out whatever else he was going to say as she pulled out of the spot, satisfied at having the last word. Her feeling of superiority was short-lived, because Kyle pulled out of the parking lot directly behind her. Instead of turning right toward Philip's, he turned left to cross the bridge into the heart of town.

What the . . . Is he chasing *me?* She gave him two more blocks to do the sane thing and turn around. He didn't. She glared at him in her rearview mirror, then pulled into the library parking lot to let the Miller kids out, and he pulled up next to her. They both rolled down their windows.

"What the . . . heck, Kyle?" He still had Cooper in the back, who was watching them, wide-eyed. "Are you following me?"

"You said we couldn't talk about this at work. We're not at work now. Just tell me what I did wrong. Please."

Ainsley groaned and tipped forward to let her forehead hit the steering wheel. He was obviously not going to give up. "Come to my house. Go drop off Cooper and then come back."

"They feed me dinner . . ."

"I'll feed you. Just . . ."

"Okay." He backed out of his spot, and Ainsley sat there for a few moments, trying to figure out why she'd capitulated so easily. It wasn't like she enjoyed holding grudges, but she usually at least waited until her temper had cooled before she tried to talk it over. She heard the crunch of footsteps on gravel and turned her head to see Starla peering into the truck.

"Hey, you got your truck back."

"Kyle . . . borrowed it to get it fixed."

"I see." She pursed her lips like she was holding back a smile.

"What, Star? Just say it."

"That was rather possessive of him."

Ainsley snorted. "You can say that again."

"A hot, neurodiverse alpha hero is wooing you, hon. This probably won't be the last time he stomps on your boundaries without realizing it. Just explain it to him. Calmly, if possible. They don't love yelling." Starla's brother-in-law Jason had ADD and might be on the autism spectrum as well, and they hadn't always gotten along at first. Ainsley knew the advice was good.

"I don't, either." She sighed. "Okay. I'm off to make pancakes for my . . ." How did she want to finish that sentence? *Friend? Boyfriend? Best friend's brother? Trailer make-out construction buddy?* ". . . for my alpha hero."

But on the short drive home, she suddenly realized that wasn't quite right: Kyle wasn't a romance hero, Kyle was a *dragon*. She'd read, watched and listened to Lord of the Rings enough times that she should've seen it immediately. He was protective, intelligent, and often lacked commonly accepted manners. But when he found a treasure, he added it to his cache and let no one touch it. He certainly did seem concerned about her safety.

Ainsley had just put the bacon in the oven when there was a quiet knock at the door.

"Come in," she yelled, and Kyle's dark head poked into the room. "Hey."

He closed the door and silently slid onto a stool at the breakfast bar. Kyle drummed his fingers on the counter incessantly, watching her work.

"So about earlier," she started, but he held up a hand.

"I'm sorry."

She glanced up at him from the batter she was pouring onto the griddle. "For?"

"I talked to Philip, and he said I shouldn't have fixed your car without asking, which now that I reflect on it, does make sense. I just saw a problem, wanted it solved, and I had the means to do so. I didn't think about how it might inconvenience you or violate your sense of safety. And for that, I am sorry."

She crossed her arms playfully over her stomach and raised an eyebrow. "But not for actually fixing it?"

His gaze slid sideways, his dark eyes thoughtful, and his brow wrinkled. "No. I can't be sorry for that. You shouldn't drive around with a broken door. It's not—"

"Not safe." She smirked. "I know, I heard you the first time you told me." She was about to reveal her earlier revelation about his draconian nature, but she realized that his fantasy knowledge was so poor, he'd never be able to accept it for the huge compliment that it was. *I mean, he's never even read Lord of the Rings.* It was tragic, really. *Never laugh at live dragons . . .* The immortal words of Bilbo Baggins should be heeded.

Ainsley slid him a plate with a stack of golden-brown pancakes on it, then placed silverware, the butter, and the syrup next to it. Kyle carefully cut into them, sniffing them.

"It's a mix?"

"Duh," she said. "Who makes pancakes from scratch?"

"I do," he said, putting the first bite in his mouth. "Mmm. And mine are better, no offense."

"Good, then you can cook next time." She passed him the bacon.

"Good. I will." He glanced up at her from his plate shyly. "I'd like to cook for you."

Be still, my beating heart. He'd been here countless times. Sat right in that seat, but he'd never said anything like that before. She did not mind it. Not one bit. Ainsley started into her own dinner.

"I'm surprised you eat breakfast for dinner at all," she said, her mouth full.

"I admit that it's not my first preference," he said, still eating. "But I was trying to be nice."

"So you *do* know how to compromise. Interesting."

"Ha, ha," he deadpanned, and Ainsley laughed. Without thinking, she licked the butter and syrup off her knife.

Kyle looked aghast. "Did you just *lick a knife*?"

Ainsley shrugged. "Yes?"

He set down his knife and fork carefully on his plate. "Come here."

Warily, Ainsley made her way around the eat bar to his side of it, and he turned to tug her close to him, between his open knees.

"You should not be allowed to have sharp things," he whispered.

She snorted. "That's your opinion."

"Do you need someone to keep your mouth busy, is that it?" That made her stomach drop and her lips curve into a smile.

"Why?" she asked, sliding her arms over his shoulders. "Are you suggesting an activity?"

"Oh yeah." Kyle brought their foreheads together and kissed her.

She kissed him back harder, nipping at his lower lip . . . It was so pouty and sweet, she adored it. And, she thought as his kisses turned hungry, he even had a soft underbelly like most dragons. She'd seen his plenty of times: his way with Cooper, for one. As much as he complained about playing board games and having to wait for him after school, she knew he loved the kid. Maybe she was part of his weakness, too. Dragons didn't like weakness, and given his exhibition with her car door, he certainly didn't lack for physical strength. There was only one more test to do: look into his eyes. *Dragon-spell.* It was well known that dragons had hypnotic powers of suggestion.

Ainsley pulled back just enough to see into his eyes without making him look like a cyclops. His brown eyes poured into hers . . . She really couldn't liken them to anything. They were dark enough to be chocolate, but that just didn't feel right. It was more like they belonged to some kind of bear . . . a grizzly? She didn't know. But all food metaphors fell short. They captured her.

"Whatcha doing?" He'd lost his usual diction, his words slurring a bit like he was drunk. Drunk on her. Lord, she wanted that.

"Just checking."

He lifted an eyebrow and leaned forward to take her lips in another long kiss. "Checking what?"

"Your hypnotic powers."

He stroked her hips with his thumbs, then gave her a little squeeze as he chuckled quietly.

"Well, I don't have them that I've ever noticed. How would I have gained these powers?"

"Maybe you're like Medusa or something . . ."

"I don't have snakes for hair or anything . . . Also, I don't think Medusa hypnotized people so much as turned them to stone and ruined them completely."

"Okay, know-it-all."

"Me?" he asked, all innocence.

"Yes, you have an answer for absolutely everything. Please quit correcting people all the time. It's annoying."

"About Medusa?"

"About everything."

"Well, I think *you've* got them, the snake hair things . . ." He was kissing down her neck, his hands bracketing her ribs. "I feel ruined when I'm with you."

Ainsley smiled, but he must not have been able to tell, because he paused, tensing.

"Like, in a good way."

"I know. It's okay." *It's okay, dragon. Your treasure knows you mean well.* She kissed the end of his nose. "You want to watch part of Lord of the Rings with me?"

Kyle crinkled his nose in distaste. "No, thank you."

"Really? Why not?"

"That doesn't appeal to me whatsoever."

"But you like fantasy video games!"

"I don't do classics in any genre. They don't hold my attention. Video games have a medium that I find visually stimulating. So no. No Lord of the Rings."

She sighed with a smile. "So much for compromise . . ."

CHAPTER NINETEEN

AFTER THE PANCAKE DAY, Kyle started coming over after he dropped off Cooper. She cooked the first two nights, but after she apparently put too much garlic in the fried rice, he showed up the next night with a bag of groceries in each hand and made himself comfortable in her kitchen. Tonight he'd roasted a whole chicken. She was already making plans for the leftovers. She was going to make an epic sandwich tomorrow.

Ainsley watched Kyle over the top of her book. After dinner, he'd washed her dishes and pulled a book out of his bag. He started reading, eyes scanning the page quickly. A little wrinkle would appear between his eyebrows, he'd stare off into the distance, then he'd go back to reading again. He did that for thirty minutes solid without saying a word to her. She couldn't take it anymore.

"Kyle."

He kept reading.

"Kyle, honey."

His head lifted, but he didn't look up. "Mmm?"

"Are you just going to read until you have to go?"

He gave her his gaze then, frowning. "Did you not want me to?"

"I . . . I don't know?"

"You seem unhappy."

"More just . . . confused?" She scootched closer to him. "Why did you come over if you're just going to ignore me?"

"We talked during dinner and during its preparation. And I'm not ignoring you."

Now she was frowning. "You're not?"

"No! And I came over because I like being with you. I like having you around while I read."

"Don't you want to, I don't know, talk or something?" *Or something* was code, but she wasn't sure if he'd get it. She leaned into his body and the phrase at the same time, putting a light hand on the leg he had braced against the couch cushions.

"Like watch a show? We can do that if you want to."

Sexy code was apparently difficult for dragons. She sighed. "This makes you happy?"

"Oh, yes. Very. As an educator, I would think you'd be familiar with parallel play."

Ainsley bit her lip until the urge to snicker passed. "I'd say I'm more familiar with it than with zombie apocalypse preparations, but go on—how does this relate?"

"I can't handle a lot of face-to-face all the time, that's all. I get . . . peopled out. I'd rather be like this. You know, comfortable."

Comfortable? Not talking, reading in silence? She'd never spent a more uncomfortable evening with someone she was dating. Wait, were they dating?

"You're not saying anything," he pointed out.

"I'm just thinking," she said, caressing his leg absentmindedly. "I just don't . . . I don't get it."

"That's okay," he said, putting down his book. "It must be hard being neurotypical. I'll teach you." Kyle pulled her into his arms, tipping them back to hold her on the couch. "You know, secretly, I have always admired this shirt, but now that I've touched it and I know how scratchy it is, I don't know how you can wear this."

She chuckled into his cotton-clad shoulder: Cotton. Always cotton. She'd never seen him in anything else, come to think of it, when he wasn't at work. "I think it's polyester," she said, twisting and craning her neck to see the label.

"Ugh. That explains it."

Ainsley laughed. "What's wrong with polyester?"

"Besides feeling like fire? Itchy, terrible, caustic synthetics? Besides all that, you mean?"

"Naturally, I thought those things were a given," she said, tickling his ribs, and he jerked away from her.

"Hey!"

"Hey what?"

"Don't tickle me. That's not cool." To her mild surprise, he pulled her closer, laying her over his body. "You'll get used to it. Come on." With a little shifting and scootching, he made room for her on the couch. She lay with her back against his chest, her head on his shoulder. Kyle handed her back her book. "Now read." He put his arm around her, letting his hand rest on her belly, holding his e-reader with his other hand. Ainsley opened the book again and tried to figure out where she was . . . Five pages later, she was still distracted. But he wasn't wrong; she was getting used to it. Twenty pages in, she'd sunk into his warm embrace, her breathing slow and deep, her mind completely absorbed by the fantasy world she'd entered in the book, even as her body rested with Kyle. She'd never known reading could be a contact sport. When he stood up to leave, she was genuinely sad.

Ainsley's phone buzzed with a text, and she groaned.

"It's my mom. My dad must have told her about the . . . trailer thing."

Kyle grinned, and he was so good-looking, she wanted to take a picture of him, just like that and frame it. Put it on her mantel. Or even better, on her nightstand.

"She wants us to come over for dinner."

"Okay." He was putting on his jacket now, zipping it up to his neck. She'd really expected more resistance, and it threw her off for a moment. She really could not read him at all sometimes.

"Um, okay. How's Friday night?"

"Don't you have the town meeting Friday night?"

"Oh. Yes. Um, Saturday night, then. Are you coming to the build?"

"Yes, I'm looking forward to it." He dropped another sweet kiss on her lips. "Especially the cleanup." He kissed her again, like he couldn't help himself.

Ainsley grinned. "Me too. But let's try not to get locked in this time . . ."

"Best date I ever had," he returned as he shut the front door behind him.

"MY RELATIVES CAME OVER on the second voyage of the *Mayflower*," Nancy said, smiling broadly. "The Hanover line." It was Saturday night, and her mother was serving green beans at the formal dining room table, which was covered with the good white lace tablecloth. Ainsley really felt like her parents were taking this a little too seriously; it was so new. She'd expected pizza and beer, not a whole turkey, complete with oyster stuffing.

"That's fascinating." Kyle smiled, nodding, but Ainsley noticed his mouth twitching strangely. When the conversation shifted away from them, he pulled out his phone under the table. He typed something into it, smirked, and put the phone away.

"What's so funny?"

His smile fell immediately. "Nothing."

"No, really. What was it?"

"Nothing, Ains. Really."

She scowled. "Kyle . . ."

"Mrs. Buchanan, this turkey is so good," he said, pointedly ignoring her unhappiness. "I'd love to get the recipe." Her mother beamed.

"I hear you're quite the chef as well," Nancy said, and Ainsley knew her chance to find out what he'd been doing had gone . . . but it still nagged at her throughout dinner.

Her father was strangely quiet, sitting back with his arms crossed, answering questions with grunts and shrugs. "Stop it," she mouthed, and he smirked back at her. Dessert was appropriately disappointing: fruit salad. Ironically, her father didn't even partake.

As soon as they'd said their good nights and the car doors slammed, she turned to him.

"Okay. Now tell me."

Kyle looked confused as he started the car. "Your parents? They're great. I still get the feeling your dad's not my number-one fan, but really, anyone who's touching his daughter wouldn't be high on the list, right?"

Ainsley waved her hands spastically to stop his chatter; it was nice that he was being more open with his thoughts, but this was not what she wanted to talk about, and she only had a few minutes before he went to work. "Not my parents. What did you look up under the table?"

"Oh, that."

"Yes, that."

He turned onto Fourth. "Like I said, it was nothing."

"Kyle!"

He smirked, then sobered. "You told me to stop being such a know-it-all."

"What does that have to do with anything?"

Kyle said nothing.

"Kyle Howard Durand!"

He shot her a confused look. "That's not my middle name."

"You're right—because your middle name is IMPOSSI-BLE."

"Actually, it's Edward. But I wish it was impossible. I'd like that. I'd intimidate people even more."

Ainsley let her head fall forward, her chin resting on her chest, and sighed deeply. "Fine, don't tell me." They drove in silence until they reached her apartment. "Bye." She started to get out when she felt his hand on her thigh.

"I don't want you leaving mad at me. I'm not going to see you until Monday."

"Then tell me what you were laughing about!" she said, flapping her hands frantically. "When I told you to stop being a know-it-all, I meant with everyone else, not with me! I'm . . . I'm used to it!"

His eyes dropped to the gear shift, and she could tell he was considering this. "There was no second voyage of the *Mayflower*."

"What? Yes, there was. My relatives were on it."

He shrugged. "The internet seemed pretty sure of itself," he said, pulling out his phone. "I can send you a link . . ."

"Kyle, my grandmother has been telling that story for *years*."

"Well, then it sounds like she's been mistaken for years. I wonder how your relatives *actually* came to America?"

She stared at him for a moment, then opened the car door and got out.

"Ains, wait." His quick footfalls on the stairs told her that he was trying to catch up; she didn't slow down. She had the door open by the time he reached her. "Wait a minute," he said, catching her around the waist. "Come on, all families have a mythology."

"What does that mean, Kyle?" She turned to glare at him over her shoulder.

Jaw ticking, he nudged her into the apartment and shut the door behind them, pressing his palms to the door, caging her between his arms. "It means my uncle Buster tells everyone he's a Mensa candidate. My dad claims our grandpa Tank once delivered a baby on a moving train. My mom thinks I loved sweet pickles as a kid, and I definitely did not, since they are disgusting. Stories change over time, whether fish are involved or not. History is as fluid as the future. It's not a big deal."

Ainsley pressed herself flat against the door, trying to avoid his steady gaze. "It's embarrassing. Why would she say that if it wasn't true?"

"Because that's what her mother told her, and someone made it up at some point. The details got forgotten or conveniently ignored. I just thought her version was funny. I wasn't laughing at *them*, really," he said, snaking a hand into her hair, shuffling closer to her. "Not any more than I was laughing at human nature."

She looked up at him; he seemed so earnest, and she took a deep breath and let it out slowly. Being laughed at still stung after all these years . . . She pushed down memories of the Incident. High school was a long time ago. She should be over it by now . . . She wanted to focus on the present, on the hot guy in front of her, not the one who'd embarrassed her.

"Mythology?" she asked, bringing her hands to his belt loops to tug him closer, flush against her.

He nodded somberly. "Mythology. Your family mythology is adorable, just like you."

"I am pretty adorable."

"So adorable." His move toward her lips was slow, an implicit ask.

She lifted her chin. "I thought you had to get home."

Kyle's face fell. "I should," he said. "You're right. I've got vacuuming to do and—"

Ainsley pressed a finger to his lips. "Hon, I was kidding. It was sexy banter. You know. I'm playing with you. Teasing you."

"Sexy banter," he repeated softly, removing her hand to kiss her lips. "I like sexy banter."

"I know you do," she whispered back, leading him over to the couch. "And now I'm going to show you what most people think of when they use the term *parallel play* . . ."

CHAPTER TWENTY

ENOUGH WAS ENOUGH, Ainsley thought as she licked her ice cream cone. He'd driven her all the way into town to 22 Below, one of those specialty ice cream places in Salem. It was a good sign . . . Maybe he thought he needed to butter her up. He didn't. She'd have been fine with Dairy Queen; heck, she'd have been fine with skipping dessert and going straight back to her place. He'd taken her out three times: it was time. True, one of those dates was dinner at her parents', and once was being locked in a tool trailer together . . . Did that count? Was that not three? She was so ready for this, she'd been distracted all day at work. Their hot make-out session on Saturday night had given her a taste of how good this was going to be . . . It had been a while. She may or may not have shaved, exfoliated, and moisturized to excess in anticipation of where the night would go.

"Good?" Kyle licked a drip off the top of his waffle cone, and she realized she was staring at his tongue.

"Y-yeah. Yes," she stammered. Her own ice cream was dripping down her hand.

"Need a napkin?" She could read him well enough to know he thought she'd lost her mind. *Say something to restore confi-*

dence, Buchanan. Something that doesn't make you sound like a sex-addled horndog.

"Sure." Yeah, that was it. That'd do the trick. Kyle held out a brown recycled paper napkin to her.

"You okay?"

"It's our third date," she blurted out. She stopped herself before she got to the rest: *And I want you to show me what you were thinking about in the trailer.*

"Yeah, I guess so."

"So," she prompted, wiping her hand. "On the third date, a lot of people . . ." Ainsley gestured between them vaguely.

He looked at her blankly, then licked his darn cone again. "Plan a fourth date?"

If her hands had been even remotely clean, she would've smacked her own forehead in frustration.

"No, they don't plan a fourth date—"

"I'm sure some of them do." He bounced his gaze towards the high school couple who'd just walked in. His knee was shaking under the table; he had to be joking.

"Are you messing with me? Because if you're messing with me . . ."

He finally cracked a smile. "It's so easy. It's harder not to, really."

Ainsley threw her balled-up napkin at him, and he laughed, low and quiet. "You're a jerk."

"I'm sorry."

"No, you're not."

"No, I'm not really," he chuckled, grinning. "But I do think we should hold off a while yet."

"Stop, Kyle. Seriously."

"No, I am serious now." He took a swig of his water, and when he put down the glass, she scrutinized his face. He looked as determined as he had the time he'd won the Turkey Trot in '03. Daniel had bet him a month of laundry-doing that he couldn't win it all. She'd made a note then and there to never bet Kyle on anything . . . except now she kind of was. She was subjecting her future plans and her reputation to the whims of a Durand.

She leaned forward, lowering her voice. "Tell me you're joking. Please."

He shook his head, apparently calm. "Studies show that lots of millennials aren't having sex. They call it a sex recession. We wouldn't be alone."

"Yes, but *I want to be alone*. That's the point."

"I hear that, but I just don't think it's wise. If you became pregnant . . ."

She huffed. "I'm not going to get pregnant, Kyle. I'm on the pill."

"It's only 91 percent effective, adjusting for human factors. And you're pretty forgetful; I bet you don't take it properly. And condoms are no better, that's only 85 percent. Not great odds, really."

Her mouth fell open. She'd forgotten it just last night. It helped with her acne, so it didn't really matter for procreative purposes. Of course she'd take it correctly if it did . . . if it *mattered*. But she couldn't exactly deny his claim when she'd screwed it up just last night, and he saw the truth on her face.

Kyle laughed. "See? I'm not ready to have a kid. Are you?"

"Yes." The word jumped out before she could stuff it back down into her heart, and her face heated as she scrambled to explain. "I've always wanted kids." But what she didn't want was to trap someone who didn't love her into a lifelong relationship, whether that was co-parenting or marriage. She understood his reservations from that standpoint, but . . . her girl parts were blubbering as her brain tried to explain that this did make some sense.

"No surprise there," he said quietly. "But I'm not willing to take chances. Look at Starla and Charlie, Ains. Their relationship is so screwed up, they should be on *Dr. Phil*."

"Is that show still on?"

"Focus. They had a kid—a great kid, but still a kid they weren't ready for. I still have a lot on my plate with work. I'm helping Dr. Baker with the residency program, and they need a lot of supervision; and that's in addition to my emergency room shifts." He reached across to touch her hand, but she pulled it back just in time. She wasn't trying to punish him . . . She was just *so* disappointed. She couldn't take physical contact right now; she'd been primed for so much more than hand holding tonight, and her body was not taking the news well. It was then Ainsley noticed several other patrons were watching them, and, realizing they were caught, the eavesdroppers quickly went back to their own conversations.

He got up and motioned for her to scoot over. She gave him a hard look, and he hooked his mouth up in half a smile. "Please?" he said.

Begrudgingly, she let him into the booth and onto the seat next to her. He sat down without touching her, even though she could tell he wanted to. He played with his napkin under the table, twisting it. She'd thought he had more to say, but he just stared at her, pleading in his gaze.

"But before this, with other girlfriends, you . . . did, right?"

"No."

"Never?" she whispered, aghast. "But all those girls were always hanging around you . . ."

He shrugged. "I don't know what to tell you. It just wasn't right." That made her feel a little bit better. Maybe it wasn't personal, then. But she was still mad.

"You could've told me earlier."

"Yes. I should've. I'm sorry."

"Before I wasted all that time shaving everything. It's fall now. I don't have to, no one else is going to know."

His gaze heated, and he looked her up and down a little. "Everything?"

"You'll never know now, will you?"

"Oh, come on . . ."

"Nope. No one but me will get to appreciate my efforts tonight."

"That's just cruel."

"*You're* just cruel."

"I didn't say never. Just not . . ."

"Not yet." In the blink of an eye, she was seventeen again, sitting with Shane Burgess at Annie's, sharing a milkshake. He'd been showering attention on her for a few weeks, and he'd been touching her all night, making her crazy in the best way. Too bad he hadn't had the same reservations about being committed to each other before they hopped into bed . . . That had certainly aimed her high school social life in an awful direction. The fallout had been worse than she'd imagined was even possible.

"It's okay." It wasn't, really. It made her feel small. She felt like she'd shown up for a costume party in street clothes . . . relationships weren't supposed to make you feel out of place. She wanted to leave. "Let's go home."

"No, Ainsley, just—" Kyle growled.

"Now, please."

"I can see us together. In the future, I mean. Can't you?"

"I . . . I don't know. I guess so." Of course she could. Pushing their babies in a double stroller, going for morning runs. Him collapsing into bed after a long shift, still hungry to connect with her, making her pancakes in the morning. Her decorating her room for the next school year, making him do the heavy lifting. Him grumbling but loving it.

"Let's just give it a little more time, okay? Please?" He seemed so genuinely agitated, his leg shaking the whole bench.

She sighed, looking away. "Well, it doesn't seem like I have a choice, so . . ." She pushed on his hips, and he stood from the booth, gathering their coats. "Can't believe I painted my toenails for this dumb dragon."

"What did you say?"

Oops. "Nothing."

"Did you call me a dragon?"

"It's not an insult . . ." She held the door for him, trying to soften the blow with an act of consideration.

"Ainsley, you're calling me an animal! How am I supposed to take that as a compliment?"

"Because it's a really awesome animal! It's like calling someone a unicorn, right? Because they're so unusual and unique. You're unlike anyone I've ever known. I just . . . I just don't know how else to classify you sometimes."

He opened the car door for her, still clearly displeased. "Animalia, Chordata, Mammalia, Primates, Hominidae, *Homo sapiens*. Same as you." She climbed into the passenger seat and cringed when he slammed her door shut.

This is so *not how I imagined this date ending . . .*

CHAPTER TWENTY-ONE

THIS WAS THE LAST THING he wanted to be doing today. The woman handcuffed to the bed was shaking, and Kyle gave himself an unnecessary reminder to avoid meth at all costs. It held no interest for him, but it didn't hurt to remind himself from time to time. His curiosity could be stirred sometimes by unusual things, and then a passing interest could become an obsession. Getting obsessed with meth would be fatal.

He'd just broken the patient's skin, ignoring her moans, when he heard the whisper: "He's a machine." He was used to people likening him to some kind of mechanical creation. Robot. Android. It was all the same. Reductive.

"I'm not, actually." Kyle didn't look up from his work. "But if you pay attention to what I'm doing, you might learn something. Unless *you're* a machine, in which case you can only learn something if your subroutines will allow learning." He taped down the needle and moved to make a note in her chart. But the comment was still there, in his head, stuck like a piece of gum to his shoe. He wanted it off. It was as terrible and uncomfortable as the real thing; he'd never understood gum chewing as a pastime. The residents whispered with their heads together, then left as the woman began to fall unconscious. Kyle retreated to the on-call room, still feeling that comment. *Out, out, out.*

Daniel caught his arm. "Hey. Greg didn't mean it like that. He meant it like a compliment."

"How is being called a machine a compliment? Machines are built, made by someone. They're not capable of independent thought. I'm eminently capable. No one made me."

"Are you still confused about where babies come from? Do we need to have the sex talk again? Thank God you didn't become an OB/GYN." His brother grinned, but seeing that his joke didn't get the reaction he'd hoped for, he sobered. "He meant that he envies how you can set your emotions aside in situations like that. Seeing her like that was upsetting for Dr. Trout. That's all."

Kyle sat down heavily on the saggy couch. "I suppose that's an advantage sometimes."

"Sometimes," Daniel agreed, flopping down next to him. He let his head tip toward Kyle, and it fell hard on his shoulder. The weight felt nice, but he didn't want people seeing them snuggling, even if they were related.

"Get off me."

"No."

"I did feel bad for the girl."

"I know you did, bro."

"They don't. They think I don't feel anything, just because it doesn't show on the outside."

"Screw them. Who cares? You're a great doctor. Anyone who's seen you in action knows that. Your brain is just wired different."

"My brain gives me an advantage in many situations. I'm just not sure it . . ."

His brother sat up and looked at him. "Not sure it what?"

"Not sure it knows what to do with Ainsley."

Daniel smiled knowingly. "Because she pushes all your safety buttons."

Kyle dragged both his hands through his dark hair, letting out a deep sigh. "She pushes all my buttons, period."

"You could probably find someone else, you know."

"You give terrible advice. You're supposed to tell me to persevere, to hang in there. That's what I told you with Winnie."

"No, you told me I was shallow. You didn't even sugarcoat it, just laid it out there. 'You're shallow, Daniel.'"

"It's the same thing. I was motivating you, and I told you as nicely as I could. I was only pointing out your faults so you could work on them, to become the person Winnie needed you to be."

"I wish that didn't make sense." Daniel paused. "Do you want to make it work with Ainsley?"

"Of course I do. I love her."

His brother blinked at him rapidly.

"That surprises you?"

"Yeah, a little bit. I mean, I knew you liked her a lot, but you guys haven't . . ." Daniel must've seen the hard look in his eyes, because he backtracked quickly. "Haven't been together that long."

"That's not what you were going to say." Kyle stood up and crossed his arms, feeling caught. Feeling like he'd been outed. "She told you."

"No," Daniel said quickly, "she told Winnie; Ainsley and I don't talk about sex. She's just frustrated, bro. Cut her a little slack. She needed to talk to someone; she's trying to figure this out, too."

"Do you think I should . . ." Kyle's face burned. He didn't want to talk about this, even with Daniel. And he found it easier to talk to Daniel than any of his other siblings, even though Philip probably knew more about long-term relationships, and Maggie was a woman. Daniel just sat, hands folded over his belly, waiting. "Do you think I should have sex with her?"

"Do you want to?"

"Yes," he admitted. "But I've waited a long time for this. 'This' being a relationship that I really want to be in. And I don't want the physical aspect to screw things up. I don't know how that's going to go for me."

"Then wait."

"None of my previous girlfriends could accept my decision to limit our physical relationship. I don't want to lose her because she's frustrated. I don't want her angry with me."

"Then don't wait."

"You're being intentionally unhelpful," Kyle growled, and Daniel chuckled.

"No, I'm not, it's just not straightforward. But if Ainsley loves you, too, then she'll wait. It might help her to know that there are other factors involved. Let her know that you're attracted to her."

"I'm sure she already knows," he said dismissively. "She spends a lot of time close to my body. I'm sure she can feel it."

"Well," Daniel said slowly, "there's body attraction and there's heart attraction. Also, women like to hear things out loud. Share your thinking with her. It'll help. I promise."

"That's a pointless promise; if it turns out to be bad advice, it won't come back on you, it'll come back on me."

"It's an idiom, smarty." Daniel threw a pillow at him, and Kyle caught it and threw it back. Daniel picked up a couch cushion to defend himself, but they both froze when the door opened.

"There you are," Winnie said, smiling. "I should've known you'd be together. Your dad's here."

"Why?" Kyle asked.

"I'm not sure. Something about lunch?"

"Oh. Right. We're going out together."

"And you didn't invite me?" Kyle couldn't tell if Daniel was actually hurt by this; he employed a lot of sarcasm that was sometimes hard to distinguish from actual feelings.

"No, we didn't. He just wanted to spend time with me."

"Fine, then. See if I invite you the next time we go for a bike ride."

"Good, I don't want to be invited. I have no interest in bike riding."

"It's the helmets, isn't it?" Daniel asked, grinning.

"I've told you a thousand times that it's the helmets."

"So ride without one."

"You're so ridiculous. I can't even with you." Kyle grabbed his backpack from the lockers and slammed it shut, taking the time to check his Master lock briefly before leaving. He didn't want to give his brother any opportunity to mess with his stuff while he was gone. His father was waiting for him near the nurses' station by the front door.

"Hey, son."

Kyle grunted an appropriate greeting.

"Ready to go?"

"Yes. Nurse Harper, please inform anyone who asks for me that I've gone out to lunch and will be back shortly."

"Will do." He saluted. "Nice to see you, Dr. Durand Senior."

"Nice to see you, too," his father said, giving a friendly wave. "So, where to?"

"You choose. It's been a taxing day."

"No, that's April fifteenth." His dad laughed at his own joke, and Kyle rolled his eyes. "Lighten up, son. Let's walk to Mashita; it's such a nice day out. I gotta soak up the sun while I can."

"That's fine." They walked three blocks in silence. Kyle's brain began to ease its death grip on analyzing his conversation with his brother and the situation with Ainsley. Walking did feel good; it was proven to release endorphins and boost one's mood. It probably helped that it wasn't raining.

"Daniel still giving you trouble at home?"

Kyle snorted. "When hasn't he given me trouble? All he does is make messes and hog the living room furniture." *And help me with personal problems and give me someone to talk to at dinner and share a pot of coffee with.*

"I bet you're glad he's moving out then, eh?"

Kyle didn't answer. Surely it was obvious. He let his heels strike the concrete more forcefully with sharp, staccato steps.

"How are things going with Ainsley?"

"Fine. How are things going with Mom?"

Evan grinned. "Things with Mom are fine, thanks for asking. The rest of them seem to assume that Mom and I are fine no matter what."

Kyle grimaced. "Relationships are a lot of work. I wouldn't take that for granted." He hadn't meant to go there in his conversation with his dad . . . Maybe it was too weird. But Evan wouldn't tell anyone, and he did have thirty plus years of marriage experience. "Did you and Mom ever have . . . relationship issues?"

"You mean like arguments? Oh, definitely. Just last weekend, she wanted to go to Sisters to check out an antique—"

"No, that's not what I meant. I mean like . . . sex issues."

His father turned his head toward him slowly. "Yeah. All relationships are bumpy in some ways. I wouldn't say they were big problems. But right after you were born especially, we weren't on the same page. She was exhausted and insecure about the weight she'd gained, and I was lonely and resented you and Philip getting all her attention. And of course, being autistic, you hated being a baby and basically never slept. But we worked through it. I started helping out more at home, cut back my hours."

"I can't apply that to my situation."

"What's your situation?"

"Ainsley wants to have sex with me. Daniel recommended that I explain my reservations. I'm considering that advice."

"Communication is usually a good thing. Good practice for marriage, anyway."

"I don't relish explaining myself. I don't usually come off looking like a hero. Especially when I can't explain exactly why."

"Why can't you?"

"Because I don't know!" he boomed. An older couple passing them on the street sped up, and Kyle frowned. "Maybe we should talk about this later."

"No, it's okay. Look, are you attracted to her?"

"That's a stupid question. She's objectively very beautiful. She's the most beautiful woman in Timber Falls. Maybe in the whole state."

"Well, as long as it's not a symptom of deeper issues between you . . . just make sure she doesn't get the wrong impression."

"I'm fairly sure she's already *got* the wrong impression. She had third-date expectations. She was . . . unhappy with me."

"So set her straight. She's known you a long time. Surely you two won't let something like this come between you."

Kyle gave him a curt nod. "No, you're right. We shouldn't."

CHAPTER
TWENTY-TWO

KYLE FIDGETED ON AINSLEY'S couch. He played with his keys. Anything would be better than sitting on her uncomfortable gray IKEA monstrosity, his knee bouncing uncontrollably. All it was doing was giving him time to reconsider, to doubt his decision. *No.* He wasn't going to lose her over this. If this was what she needed, that's what they'd do. She did lots of things that he needed. She hadn't used garlic once since he'd mentioned it. Even her shirts seemed to be cotton more often on nights when they were going to be close, though that could be a coincidence. *It's not,* his mind insisted. *You love her. Just do this for her and get it over with.* Maybe he should put on music . . . Which John was it that she liked? Was it John Legend or John Mayer? How could he have allowed this important detail to slip his mind? It was usually so faithful to trap all her little left-behind bits, all the little things she mentioned that she loved. The sound of footsteps on the stairs jerked him out of his thoughts and had him jumping to his feet.

The front door opened, and Ainsley came in, her head down, digging through her purse for something.

"Hey."

Her head snapped up, and she grinned with delight upon seeing him. "What are you doing here?"

"Winnie let me in. I hope that's okay."

"Of course it is." She dropped her bag and hurried over to him, giving him her signature greeting of her arms around his neck. She jumped, and he caught her against him, giving her a sweet kiss. Her eyes were sparkling. "What a nice surprise." *So far, so good.*

"I made you dinner." He led her over to the kitchen, where a steaming silver pot of red minestrone soup and fresh French bread waited. He'd thought to keep it light; he'd thought about including a salad, knowing how they both felt about the importance of vegetables, but opted to keep it simple. Who knew how their bodies would react to so much fiber; he didn't want to be embarrassed in the throes of . . .

"And the surprises keep coming . . ." She sniffed it. "Smells delicious, babe."

"My mom's recipe."

Ainsley gave a gasp. "Your mom shared *the* minestrone soup recipe with you? The top-secret, not-outside-the-family recipe?"

"No, I found it in her kitchen."

"So you *stole* us the recipe." She tapped her chin thoughtfully. "I see. Are we going to have to go on the lam now?"

He shook his head, pulling out silverware. "On the lam?" he asked with disdain.

She ignored him. "I can have my hair cut and dyed in an hour. We'll travel light, set up a little roadside stand near the beach, and sell our illicit soup to weary travelers . . ."

"Stop." She was just making him more nervous, and their food was getting cold. The sooner they ate, the sooner they could get on with it. Or rather, get it on. "First of all, everyone knows people at the beach mostly want clam chowder from Mo's."

"True." She snagged a piece of bread and took a bite. "You think we should go farther inland?"

"Secondly, we're not going anywhere," he said, steering her toward the table. "Let's eat."

"Right." She rubbed her hands together greedily. "Let's fuel up. We'll need the calories for our life on the run."

"I just said we're not going anywhere!" he said gruffly. "Now sit down."

"What's got you in a mood today?" she asked, sinking into her seat at the table. "Rough day of sleep?" She looked at her phone, frowning. "Wait, shouldn't you be at work right now?"

"I'm transitioning back to days."

Ainsley clapped her hands excitedly. "Are you serious?"

"I'm usually serious."

"This is so great! Now we can actually *do* stuff together!"

Speaking of which . . . He cleared his throat. "Yes. It's good news. Now let's eat, your food is getting cold." *My feet, too.*

She put down her bread. "Kiss me first," she murmured. "When we get good news, we kiss. It's a thing."

Since they were both sitting, it was easier than it sometimes was. In fact, it was so easy that he kissed her a bit longer than he might've otherwise. Touched her a bit more, too, since he wasn't tired from a long night of work. Being with her was a comfort; he'd spent all day thinking about her. He relished the sweet little noises she was making now, as she climbed into his lap. *Wait, no. We have to eat first.* She wasn't sticking to the script . . . which was probably unfair, because she hadn't *seen* the script. Next time, maybe he would email her a copy of the night's agenda with time for amendments. That would prevent misunderstandings like this.

"Did Winnie say when she'd be back?" she murmured as she kissed his neck.

"Out all night," he breathed. Kyle nuzzled her with his nose, searching for her lips against his again, pressed her harder, and their tongues tangled like two salmon he'd once seen spawning. They were just as wet, too. Kissing was really weird; good, but weird.

God, she was really going after him . . . It felt good. Really good. Her hands skimmed over his chest, moving restlessly. He could taste her desperation on his tongue, and guilt gnawed at him. He should've done this earlier. No matter. He'd do it now. Ainsley squeaked as he stood up, supporting her under her legs. She wouldn't see the rose petals he'd scattered in the hallway if he was carrying her, but he didn't dare stop her now. He crushed them under his socked feet as he marched down the hallway toward her bedroom. Things were moving in the right direction, and objects in motion tended to stay in motion . . . Did sex have its own physics, or did it mirror the rest of the natural world? If he stopped her now, he was fairly sure it would require some friction . . . but not the kind she was looking for. Not the kind he'd committed to if he wanted to keep her. And he wanted to keep her very, very badly.

He'd scattered more rose petals on her denim down comforter; he'd had to make the bed first, but then he'd scattered them. He didn't love what a slob she was, but maybe when he lived with her, he could reform her. It hadn't worked with any other facet of her personality, but he would try nonetheless. She was clawing at his shirt as he laid her gently on the bed, and he shucked it off for her. Her hands against his skin were hot, and it ratcheted up his desire another notch. Her mouth never stopped moving against his; she probably didn't even realize she was groaning. *Poor girl.* Well, she'd feel better in a few minutes, hopefully. He'd done significant research and was confident he could help her. He moved to unbutton her jeans (thank God for casual Friday; she could've been wearing something much more complicated), and she stopped him with a hand on his wrist. Her gaze was hazy and heated when it met his, her lips redder than usual from his kisses. He loved seeing her like that, and it spurred him on.

"What are you doing?" she breathed.

That didn't, though.

Isn't it obvious? Kyle didn't answer; he'd already decided that since he knew she wanted this very much, he didn't need to stop unless she asked him to. Flipping her shirt up, he kissed her stomach, and she sighed, threading her fingers into his hair, gently scratching his scalp. She felt good, tasted good, even. That surprised him a little. Maybe this wouldn't be as hard as he'd thought.

"Kyle, honey? What's happening here?" Now that her mouth wasn't occupied, her brain seemed to have re-engaged as well. *Crap.* "Are these . . . rose petals? When did you light candles?"

"They're electric. Real is a hazard," he murmured against her skin as he came back up to kiss her neck. Apparently, it had been a mistake to leave her top half unattended. If she was distracted enough, she wouldn't ask questions or make him remember or recant what he'd said before about this. His own words slammed back into him like a battering ram: *91 percent effective. Look at Starla and Charlie. I can see us together. Can't you?* That future was what had given him pause: When his father had explained sex to him as a kid, he'd told him that he should wait until he was married. It didn't matter now that he knew other people did things differently; an order had been established in his mind. And he found that very difficult to subvert in any context.

"Kyle?"

"I changed my mind," he said, kissing back toward her mouth. "I want you." Technically true. "I want to have sex with you. Now." He tried to go in for another sultry kiss, but she turned her face away. *Uh-oh.*

"Did you?" she asked lightly, scratching his back with her fingernails gently. "Talk me through that decision, will you?"

"Sure," he said, resting his body against hers, hoping to distract her again. "I thought about it, and you're right. There's no reason to wait." He kissed her again, and she let him, but the heat wasn't there. *Damn it.* He felt sweaty and panicky; this wasn't going at all how he'd planned it. He wasn't sure he could work himself up again like this anytime soon if it wasn't going to happen tonight. And her roommate was out tonight. The pressure felt like a vise on his skull. *This is it, this is the perfect time. It has to be now.*

"What about contraception? You had concerns . . ."

"No, it's fine. It'll be fine." His brain thundered at him like cannon fire at his blatant disregard for the facts. *91 percent effective. Nine in a hundred couples will become parents. Aiden was a surprise.* He wanted to cover his ears against the thoughts, but he tugged at her shirt instead, losing patience. "Take this off. Come on."

"Okay," she said gently, putting her hand over his. "Okay, I will take it off. But first, I want to hear that you're ready to be a parent."

He tried. He tried to force out the words that he knew were a lie, but his lips just twitched and twisted, remaining firmly shut. Ainsley smiled at him, the blush on her cheeks still high.

"Oh, honey," she whispered, pulling him down to rest his head on her chest. He lay on top of her lush body, and she held him against her. The tension he'd felt began to retreat; their hearts and their breaths synchronized, both slowing.

"You need this. You need me," he mumbled into her shirt. "And I want you to be happy."

"I am happy," she said, stroking his hair. "I'm so very happy with you, sweetheart. I've never laughed so much or been fussed over with such care. Your grumpy butt is my favorite."

"But sex . . ."

"'But sex' nothing, babe." Her voice was quiet, but firm. "You're not doing this just because I want it. That's manipulative and cold. I don't want that, okay? I don't want it. Don't want you walking around worrying that we've made a person too soon, stressing out over it."

"Not just that," he muttered. "It's out of order."

She was silent for a moment, and he heard the uncertainty in her voice. "Because we should get married first?"

"Yes." He sat up, propped up on one elbow. "I'm sorry. Once I establish an order in my mind, it's very hard to erase it."

"I understand," she said, bringing his palm to her lips for a soft kiss. "It's fine. Really."

He collapsed onto her again, burying his face into her neck. How had he lucked out, getting a partner like her? Tears stung his eyes, and he sniffled.

"Kyle, honey?"

"Our evening is ruined," he announced, his voice thick with emotion, and he tried to clear his throat. "I'll just go home." He felt her cheek curve as she broke into a grin.

"Oh, don't worry. I know how to salvage it." That teasing lilt in her voice . . . what was she thinking? What could she possibly—oh. Wait.

"No," he said, sitting up, looking around for his shirt.

"Oh, come on. Please?" She put her hand on his arm, fluttering her eyelashes.

"No."

"Not all three. Just one, just the first one. You said you wanted me to be happy. This would make me very, very happy . . ."

"Why? Watching tiny, hairy men carry a dumb ring through mortal peril? How is that entertaining in the least?"

"Not all of them are tiny. Some of them are human-sized." Ainsley sat up, her hands together in a prayer pose. "Please? Please? Please?" She modulated each repetition to a different pitch, as if trying to find a frequency he could hear. "You kind of owe me."

Kyle pulled on his shirt and ran a hand through his hair to straighten it again. "Fine. *One* movie." Ainsley tackled him back to the bed, squealing her happiness, and even though his heart warmed to see her joy, the squealing seemed excessive.

She took his face in her hands and gave him a loud smack on the cheek. "Kyle, you *are* going to lose your virginity tonight. Your Lord of the Rings cherry is about to be popped."

CHAPTER TWENTY-THREE

ON WEDNESDAY, AFTER school, Ainsley dropped by Bilqiis's apartment to hang out. She hadn't seen her much since the grocery store incident, and she wanted to find out if anything like that had happened again. She had connections in the community; she could do something about it. She set her bag on Bilqiis's couch, then dropped herself into a chair at the kitchen table. It was quiet. Too quiet.

"Where's Fawzia?"

"Oh." Bilqiis carried a ceramic pot of tea to the table and set it on a folded towel. "Today, she learned some sad news. She wanted to be alone."

"Oh? What happened?"

"One of the children in her class will have a birthday party this weekend. She invited all the class except Fawzia."

Anger sparked hot in Ainsley's chest. "Do the parents know? Surely they don't condone that kind of . . ."

Bilqiis looked at her sadly, still smiling. "It is the hardest thing for me," she said softly. "Mr. Zane is difficult, too, but this kind of hurt, exclusion . . . people she thought were her friends proving otherwise. It is harder. Hard to see her suffer. I know how she feels."

Ainsley did a little bit, too. Not to the same extreme; her own exclusion was due to her own social stupidity . . . but Fawzia? What had she done? This sweet, energetic girl who loved to just run? What could she possibly have done to deserve being the only one not invited? She wanted to invent excuses for these parents . . . perhaps they thought their food wouldn't be something Fawzia would like or be allowed to eat, knowing that Islam had certain dietary conventions. But really, if they'd just asked, they'd have learned that nothing they planned to serve would likely cause a problem. They just didn't want her there. And they didn't care if she found out that she wasn't invited.

"May I talk to her?"

Bilqiis nodded, sipping her tea, gesturing with her head toward the hallway with the bedrooms. "Please, go ahead."

Ainsley quietly crept down the hall and knocked on the young girl's door.

"What, Hooyo?"

"It's Ainsley," she said, then remembered Bilqiis's rules about addressing adults. "It's Miss Buchanan."

"Come in."

Light from the hall flooded the floor of the dark room as she opened the door. A poster of a young Black woman wrapped in an American flag and holding an Olympic medal featured prominently above her bed. The rest of the furnishings and the plain brown sheets didn't seem to fit Fawzia's rainbow sense of style whatsoever, and the country-style log cabin quilt felt more appropriate for an eighty-year-old than an eight-year-old. Fawzia sat tucked in the corner of the room, clutching a unicorn pillow, her eyes puffy and red.

Ainsley sat on the edge of the bed. "Who's that on your poster?"

Fawzia's mouth dropped open. "Allyson Felix. You don't know Allyson Felix, Miss Buchanan?"

"I guess not. Can you tell me about her?" Ainsley surveyed the wall; there were other pictures—some in hijab, some not, all black, all women, all athletes.

The girl hopped up, the pillow forgotten. "She went to the Olympics at eighteen and won second in the 200 meters. That's what I want to do."

"You want to take second?" Ainsley teased gently, and Fawzia shook her head, holding back a smile.

"I want to represent Somalia in the Olympics, even if I do it as an American. I want to be like Samia Yusuf Omar. She was sixteen."

"That's a big dream," she replied, not adding *for a refugee.* It was a big dream for anyone, frankly. But if anyone could pull it off, she believed Fawzia could. She'd made the mistake of challenging her to a footrace at the beach and been soundly trounced; the kid was like nothing she'd ever seen, even barefoot on the sand. It was like her legs took on a different state of matter when she ran; she was liquid. She flew. "I didn't know Somalia had ever had athletes participate in the Olympics."

Fawzia tipped her head. "Many people go to other countries, where it's safer. That's what Samia was trying to do when she died. Al-Shabaab, they threatened her, and she drowned trying to get to Italy."

"I'm sorry," Ainsley murmured, and she truly was. Oppression was everywhere. What the Sadiqs had experienced in Somalia was far beyond her high school experience. It was almost too big and too sad to think about. Fawzia must have seen her countenance fall, because she went back to a happier subject.

"Allyson beat Usain Bolt's record for most gold medals, too."

Ainsley felt her eyebrows lift in surprise. "She did? That's awesome."

"Yes, and she'd just had a baby less than a year before."

"Holy hobbits," Ainsley said, taking a harder look at the woman in the poster. "That's really something, Fawzia."

"Yeah, I know. She's my hero."

"Well, you have good taste."

"Thank you." The girl smiled, but it quickly fell when her gaze dropped to her book bag, and she sighed. "Why didn't they invite me?"

"I don't know, sweetheart. I'm sorry. I bet that feels pretty bad." She pulled the girl to her side, giving her shoulders a squeeze. "Maybe we could go shopping for some stuff for your new room that weekend? My treat."

"Really?"

Ainsley nodded, and Fawzia flung her arms around her. Ainsley loved being the recipient of such ardent affection, even if it was motivated by the idea of getting free stuff. Kid love was like that sometimes. "If nothing else, you need a new quilt, girl. This one's not our style at all, is it?"

Fawzia shook her head violently, and they both laughed.

FRIDAY NIGHT, AINSLEY went to the town meeting. She needed to talk to Councilman Rogers about the fall festival again; it was coming up fast, and lots of people still hadn't paid for their booths. If he made an announcement about it, surely a few would cough up the money, and then she wouldn't have as many phone calls to make tomorrow. She put her coat across two seats at the front on the left. She knew Daniel was busy with Winnie tonight, signing the offer on the house they were interested in. It was a gorgeous Craftsman with a big yard backing up to the river. The house itself wasn't in great shape, but it had good bones. Winnie was nervous about the inspection, she knew, but Daniel had his heart set on it, so they'd probably buy it regardless. Mrs. Foster's kids didn't have the money to make repairs, and they both had homes elsewhere in the area, so they didn't want the property. Chances were good that they could get a deal on it.

Ainsley managed to track down two people she needed to talk to, Mr. Braverman and Mr. Jacobs, about the route for the fun run for the fall festival; several people had complained last year that the route blocked the road to the falls, and some out-of-towners hadn't been able to get to the state park. By the time they wrapped up their conversation, the meeting had started, and Ainsley slid into her seat quietly. *No Kyle?* Maybe he hadn't been able to make it after all; she knew it was tight for him to come and still make it to work on time.

She turned her attention to Councilman Park, who was plugging her mother's giving tree project again. She'd meant to sign up for a family, but she'd forgotten again. Lately, it felt like she was being pulled in so many directions, her attention was even more scattered than usual. Also, she should really ask her mother for a family whose kids had never been in her class, lest she appear to be showing favoritism.

"Dr. Durand, did you have an announcement?"

Her head whipped to the right, in direction of his gaze. Kyle stood up.

"Yes, I'm looking for someone to help me in the medical tent for the fall festival. No medical background is necessary."

"Okay, yes. Good. If someone could please step up and fill that need, we'd all appreciate it. Always good to have another set of hands in case we have another hypothermia incident like in '98." Mr. Park's gaze fell on her, and she felt her face heat as his eyes narrowed in confusion. "Wasn't Ainsley going to help?"

"After further discussion, that's not going to work out." Kyle sat down, never looking in her direction, never giving any indication that he even knew she was there.

"I see. Well, see Dr. Kyle Durand if you want to volunteer. I know Ainsley is also still waiting on some booth payments, so please see her tonight if you've got the cash in hand. It's for a good cause, people. Let's not forget that." Ainsley couldn't even be happy that Councilman Park had remembered her announcement. Had Kyle not seen her coat there, saving him a seat? She sat in the same place every week, it wasn't like it was hard to find her. And his announcement, however well intentioned, had come off like he was trying to get rid of her. She struggled to focus on the rest of the meeting, and when they broke for refreshments, she tried to make her way over to Kyle as quickly as possible without looking like that was what she was doing. But she was too late; cookie in his mouth, he was already pulling on his jacket, heading out the door.

Ainsley: Where are you off to?

Kyle: Work.

Ainsley: Didn't you see me? I saved you a seat.

Kyle: I saw you.

Ainsley: And?

The recipient of your message is currently driving and cannot send or receive messages at this time. Your message will be delivered upon their arrival.

Not good. She blew her bangs out of her face and helped herself to three peanut butter cookies, her insecurities raging in the back of her mind. Not good. Not good at all.

CHAPTER TWENTY-FOUR

"ALL RIGHT, LET'S SEE if we can get this sod done real quick," said Ainsley, clapping her hands. "Grab a rake and we'll get to work." Things between them had been tense; their text messages were short, in all senses of the word. Being face-to-face didn't seem to be helping matters, either.

"Don't we need a soil test first?" he asked.

"Nope. This is the soil, that's the sod. It's a match made in heaven."

Kyle scrolled through his phone, frowning. "Look, this article says we should pull all the weeds first, too, and it strongly recommends the soil test."

"And yet," she said, leaning on her rake, "I've been doing this a while, and I happen to know that it'll be fine."

"But the directions . . ."

Fed up, she threw down the rake and turned her back on Kyle. "Dad?" Ainsley called. "You ready to go? I'm starved. We should've left an hour ago."

He called back something that Ainsley couldn't really make out over the circular saw's whine, and she spun around to face Kyle. "Do it however you want. I'm out. I can always fix it next week if you screw it up."

His spine went straight like she'd electrocuted him. "Wow. That's harsh."

"I'm just saying, Kyle, you're new at this."

"Which is why, Ainsley, I want to follow the directions to the—" He stopped speaking abruptly, his gaze cutting across the yard. "What's your dad doing?"

She turned to look. He was taking fawn-like steps across the dirt, rubbing at his mouth, mopping at his sweaty brow with his arm.

"How should I know from all the way over—"

Kyle pushed past Ainsley, and she lost her balance and fell, sitting down hard on her backside in the soft dirt.

"What the . . . ?" She turned to watch Kyle sprint across the yard and driveway to reach her father just before he started seizing. He caught Gary under the armpits and gently lowered him to the dirt.

"Dad!" Ainsley scrambled to her feet and ran over to them. "Dad, are you okay?" She couldn't keep the panic out of her voice.

"Ainsley, go get some juice," Kyle commanded. "Mr. Buchanan, I've got you. You're going to be okay, sir." He had her father's head cradled in his lap, keeping it from banging against the ground. She stood there, tears in her eyes, watching his arms jerk and convulse.

"Shouldn't we call 911?" someone asked.

"Ainsley," Kyle snapped. "Juice. *Now.*"

Through the haze of her fear, she stumbled toward the street. There would be juice in his truck somewhere; her mother would've made sure of that. *Should I call her?* Ainsley threw open the driver's side door and looked under the seat. Sure enough, a six-pack of orange juice boxes was stuffed under there, dusty and probably expired, but it would work. She slammed the door and hurried back across the yard, pushing through the crowd that had formed around him, hands shaking as she tried to poke the plastic straw into the pre-perforated hole.

Kyle took the juice box without a word, ripped out the straw and began to squirt it directly into his mouth. Her dad had stopped shaking, but his skin looked terrible, and when she knelt next to him and grabbed his hand, it was clammy and cold.

"Dad?" she whispered, squeezing his hand. "I'm here. It'll be okay, Kyle's taking good care of you."

Kyle looked at the ingredients on the side of the juice box, then his watch. "All right, Mr. Buchanan. I'm going to ask you some simple questions, and I'd like you to try to answer them by nodding or shaking your head, okay?"

Gary nodded.

"Before you fell, did you feel confused, dizzy, or nauseous?"

He nodded again, and Ainsley covered the hand she was already holding with her other hand.

"Are you feeling shaky, anxious, or irritable?"

He nodded again.

"We usually eat at 12:15," she put in. "He said he just wanted to finish up with the . . ." A sob came out of nowhere, and she covered her mouth with the back of her hand.

Kyle's hold on her arm was gentle but firm. "Ainsley, I think he's going to be okay, but he's probably hypoglycemic. I need you to stay calm so you can help me. Can you do that for me?"

She nodded frantically, wiping at her leaking eyes, and he gave her a warm smile. "I know you can. Deep, slow breaths, okay? I don't need two people passing out."

It was sort of a joke, but she didn't laugh. She couldn't. Not while her dad was still lying on the ground, looking like death warmed over.

"Mr. Buchanan, in about ten minutes, we're going to test your blood sugar, and if it's too low, you and me are going to take a little ride up to Santiam, all right?" Kyle put two fingers to her father's neck, still looking at his watch. "Your heart rate is starting to come down. That's good."

Gary nodded, and he seemed to be getting some color back. Ainsley rubbed his hand, the hairy, age-spotted skin feeling more dear to her than ever before. The minutes ticked by so slowly, Ainsley felt an hour had passed before Kyle turned to her. "Ainsley, could you please go get his testing supplies?"

"Glove box," said Gary, trying to sit up. Kyle helped him, supporting him from behind in case he went down again.

"I'll get it," Ralph said, hurrying toward the truck. *These old guys can move when it suits them,* she thought, grateful that she didn't have to leave her father's side.

Someone had brought Kyle the first aid kit, and he expertly wiped Gary's fingertip with an alcohol wipe before waving it dry. Ralph came back with the glucometer, and Ainsley held her breath as the machine calculated his blood sugar.

"That's acceptable," said Kyle, and he patted Gary on the shoulder. "Tell your body it's doing good work, Mr. Buchanan."

"Good work," he murmured, but Ainsley didn't think he was talking to his body.

"The next order of business is a meal. I'd rather you didn't drive far . . ."

"Will you come with us?" Ainsley blurted out, and she felt her cheeks burn as everyone looked at her.

Kyle gave her a crooked smile. "If you want me to," he said softly, "but really, he's going to be fine . . ."

"I want you to. Please."

"Okay." He touched her hand. "I'm sorry I knocked you down, I didn't mean to. Are you okay?"

She wiggled in place. "My tail bone's a little sore, but I'll be fine." She felt a deep sigh welling up in her, and she let it out, her lips purring like a motorboat. Her dad imitated her, then gave her a small grin.

"You," she said, pointing at him, "are in *big trouble*, old man."

"What happens at the site stays at the site," he replied, shrugging.

"Nice try. Let's go get lunch, and you can keep trying to fruitlessly bribe me and Kyle not to tell Mom."

"There's no reason your mother needs to hear about this, is there?"

They stood up, and she immediately put a protective arm around his back, stabilizing him. Kyle quietly got on the other side, and they started toward the truck.

"You know she checks your supplies, don't you?"

He groaned. "The juice."

"Yes, the juice. She's going to know whether I tell her or not. You should just come clean."

"What's your vote, Doc? Should I tell the missus or risk her wrath?"

"Well," Kyle said slowly, "I don't think a husband and wife should keep secrets unless they're poker-related." He glanced at Ainsley, who managed to smile back at him.

"Good answer, Doc," said Gary, angling for the driver's seat.

"Uh, Pop? We can take your car, but I'm driving," said Ainsley.

"What, you don't trust me?" he asked, grinning, as he dug his keys out of his front pocket and handed them over. Her own hands were shaking as she took them, and she helped her dad into the middle seat. Kyle caught her before she climbed in.

"How about you let me drive? Give yourself a few minutes to come down off the event before we put your concentration to the test . . . It's not far." She looked past him toward her dad, whose eyes were closed, his shoulders sagging. Mutely, she nodded and passed him the keys. He walked around to the other side and opened her door before getting behind the wheel.

"Seat belts," said Kyle in his doctor voice. "Where to? My treat."

"Steak sounds good to me," Gary said, stretching an arm around his daughter's shoulders and giving her a kiss on the temple.

"You're a riot, Pop. He just saved your life and now you're going to stick him for a steak lunch while he's still paying off medical school?"

Gary pulled his lips to the side, considering this. "Muchas Gracias would be fine."

"I don't think I saved his life, Ains."

"Shut up, Kyle."

"Okay."

CHAPTER TWENTY-FIVE

AINSLEY'S INSIDES JUST wouldn't settle down all through lunch. The men chatted about sports and politics and strange news articles, having one of those circular "Did you hear about that weird thing up in Portland?" conversations where each person keeps trying to one-up the other good-naturedly. She picked at her empanadas, but just couldn't get much down. She made sure her dad ate, then they went back to the site and got Kyle's car so he could drive her home after they dropped off her dad.

"You okay, darlin'?" Gary asked as she pulled into his driveway.

"Of course," she said, giving him a bright smile. "Are you?"

"Yup. All this has happened before."

"Well, it better not happen again," she said, twisting the *Battlestar Galactica* quote as she reached over to give him a hug. "Say hi to Mom for me."

"You're not coming in?"

"No, I'm tired. I think I'm just going to let Kyle take me home."

"Okay, darlin'. Well, thank the doc for me again. Even if he did break my mailbox."

"Pop," she sighed. "I told you, it wasn't him."

Taking her head in his hands, he kissed her forehead. "Love you."

"Love you, too." They got out and slammed their doors.

"Don't worry about cleanup at the site. Ralph texted me. He did it."

"Okay." Ainsley hugged him one more time before she walked to where Kyle's truck waited on the street. "Take care of yourself tonight."

He held up one hand with the other over his heart, grinning at her.

Kyle got out and opened the door for her again, and she slid inside with a murmured "Thanks."

She looked out the window as he got back on Highway 22, not really paying attention, watching the trees fly by and the river roar past, even in the waning afternoon sun. He pulled to a stop, and she looked around.

"This isn't my apartment . . ."

"You just noticed that? Man, you'd be an easy target for a crime."

Ainsley crossed her arms over her stomach. "If you want to dump my body somewhere, you should drive a lot deeper into the woods. The water's shallow here."

Kyle chuckled, then got out of the truck and walked around to her side. He opened her door and held out his hand expectantly. Warily, she put her hand in his and jumped down, finally looking around better.

"We're at Manfield Park."

"Yes," he said quietly, tugging her forward toward the rust-red wooden covered bridge that spanned the fast-moving river.

They walked through the aspens that edged the parking lot and down the path to the bridge, which only cyclists and pedestrians were allowed to cross now. It was a nice evening; she was surprised to see the park so empty. Kyle led her onto the bridge, then turned her toward the river and put his arms around her from behind.

"Okay," he said. "You can let go now."

"Let go of what?" she asked, afraid she knew the answer.

"I asked you to hold it together for me during your dad's diabetic emergency. And you did; you did a great job. But now you need to let it out."

"I'm fine," she said, squirming uncomfortably. "Can you just take me home?"

Kyle made no motion to leave, still gently pressing her against the railing of the antique bridge with his hips. "Doesn't the river look beautiful?"

"I guess so."

"You're not even looking. Just look at the water for a minute," he said, moving his hands to her shoulders, running his strong thumbs across them with just the right amount of pressure. "Then we can go."

"This is silly, really," she huffed, leaning into the massage. "It's not like he even went to the hospital . . ."

Uh-oh. She'd said the *h* word. That word had feelings attached, dragging them along like a ball and chain behind them. She pursed her lips as the tears sprung to her eyes.

"Would you be more upset if he'd gone to the hospital?"

"Of course," she said, trying to act like she had something in her eye.

"Why?"

"Because last time he . . ." *Kyle.* Curse him; he'd done this to her. Made her cry in public. Made her relive one of the worst days of her life. She let out a shaky breath, the tears unstoppable now. "Because last time he was in the hospital, they said he might not survive another episode like that. They said his heart is weak."

"Mmm." Kyle kept rubbing her shoulders as she recounted that awful day. The text message she'd gotten during her microeconomics class: *Come home. Dad collapsed.* How she'd never broken as many traffic laws as she did that day. How they'd taken turns staying the night on the lounge-chair-turned-bed in his room, making sure he was okay.

"It's just that he's my *dad*, you know? I grew up thinking my dad was the strongest man in the universe, only to find out . . ."

"He's just a man?" Kyle turned her gently and wrapped her in his arms.

She nodded, and her sorrow broke like a flood. She pressed her face into his neck to muffle the sound but made no attempt to hug him back, instead curling herself into his chest, letting him stroke her hair, rub her back until her sadness was just a trickle, a running nose, and a hiccup.

He tried to pull back to see her face, but she covered it with both hands.

"No, I'm a mess. Don't look at me."

Kyle pulled her hands away, his face serious. "Grief is not ugly, Ainsley."

"I'm not grieving, I'm just . . . sad."

"Is there a difference? You miss the dad you used to have, the carefree one who could delay his lunch an hour without consequences. You miss being the daughter instead of the care-taker. You miss baking for him, spoiling him. Sounds like grief to me."

"Why are you doing this?" Ainsley whispered, looping her arms around Kyle's neck to pull him tighter to her. "Why did you bring me here?"

"Because you needed it. And I was worried if I took you to your apartment, you wouldn't let me inside. I didn't want you to push me away. You need me now."

She looked around. "I think this is the bridge we made the T-shirts for."

"It is," he confirmed.

"Is it safe to stand here?"

"Yes, their complaint was that it's not safe for vehicles. I checked."

"Of course you did."

"You say that like it's a bad thing. I can't take you to a bridge that might be structurally unsound. That's irresponsible." He kissed her temple. "Come on. I'll take you home."

She let out a shaky sigh and let him lead her back to the car. He opened her door and helped her inside. Ainsley scooted over to the middle seat so they were shoulder to shoulder and couldn't help but notice that he seemed pleased. They were driving up Franklin when he slammed on the brakes. She threw out her hands instinctively, protecting her face from smashing into the dash, but Kyle had his seat belt off and was out of the car before she knew what was happening.

"What do you think you're doing?" he yelled. He disappeared as he knelt down in the street, and Ainsley craned her neck to see what was going on. Kyle stood up, holding an orange-and-white striped kitten in his arms. He held it up so they were nose to nose, still raising his voice sternly. "Orangesicle, this is a terrible place to take a nap. Cooper's been worried sick about you. You're coming home with me." As he marched back to the driver's side door, Ainsley felt like a rabbit who only realizes too late that the cage with the nice carrots inside isn't a coincidence. She didn't just like this strange, grumpy man who practically set off the airbags to retrieve his nephew's kitten. She loved him. At some point, she'd signed her heart over to him. Though she had no idea how to get it back, she didn't think she wanted to; if he cared for it half as well as he cared for kittens and his patients, she'd be just fine. He passed the frightened creature to Ainsley, who snuggled against her chest.

"Don't yell at her, babe, you're scaring her."

"She's being reckless. She could've been killed. We'll stop by my brother's and take her home first, okay?"

Ainsley nodded. She'd not only caught feelings, she was downright infected with them. They were taking over her whole system. She stayed in the car when he ran in with the cat, who was greeted with more chiding at the front door by Claire, then Cooper's delighted yells. It took her brain back to his midmorning breakdown over the matter, and how her maternal yearnings had been stoked by the event. Having now witnessed Kyle's stern cat-parenting techniques, her curiosity was piqued.

Kyle got back in the car and began to back out of the driveway, still muttering under his breath.

"Do you want kids?" she asked.

"Two. A boy and a girl." Of course he'd thought it through. It was difficult to imagine a subject he hadn't already pondered. She couldn't help but tease him.

"What if you have two boys?"

"Then I'll be disappointed forever."

"That's a horrible thing to say. It's not his fault he wasn't a girl."

"I'd still love the kid, I'd just be disappointed in general."

"That seems like a theme for you."

He snorted. He was quiet for a moment, then he grabbed her hand and brought it to his lips. He pressed a kiss to her knuckles for a long moment, then put her hand on his leg so he could shift. She warred between resentment and tenderness at the gesture. He was often doing that: finding little ways to connect them physically when they were alone. But he hadn't so much as high-fived her at the town meeting, he'd barely looked in her direction and ignored the seat she'd saved him, but now he wanted that touch? *Is he hiding us? He took us to a park out of town when I was upset. He comes to the build in Stayton. He went to the beach with us, out of town. He took me to ice cream in Salem. Does he not want people in Timber Falls to know we're together?* He pulled up in front of her building.

"Want to come in for a minute?" she asked, trying to act more casual than she felt.

"I can't, I have to get home." He sounded tired; it was probably true, but her mind, poisoned by her fears, took it in another direction. *Now he doesn't even want to be alone with me, either?* It was happening again. It was just like with Shane: she'd shown up to cheer him on, thinking she knew where they stood, but then the ground shifted suddenly under her feet.

Embarrassment burned her cheeks, and she couldn't get out of the car fast enough.

"Okay. Bye."

"See you tomorrow?"

"Right."

He didn't pull out of the parking spot until she got inside. She shook out her hair, giving it a break, and rolled her shoulders. All this tension was getting to her. She'd just gotten into her pajamas when a text came through.

Kyle: and this is the wonder that's keeping the stars apart

Ainsley smiled as she completed the couplet, the small reassurance of his feelings calming her like a hug.

Ainsley: i carry your heart(I carry it in my heart)

CHAPTER
TWENTY-SIX

THURSDAY MORNING, KYLE woke up early. He'd put in too many hours this week, helping the resident group, and he was out of time, legally, to be able to work. He lay in bed, looking at the ceiling for about ten seconds before he decided to forget about sleep. Tonight, he had to help Ainsley set up for the fall festival, but he wanted to see her before then. He shot off a text to her.

Kyle: You up?

Ainsley: Yeah.

He smiled. She wasn't exactly a morning person.

Kyle: Want to go for a run?

Ainsley: Can't. Too tired. Stayed up late baking.

Kyle: Why?

Ainsley: I promised Starla I'd bring cupcakes for the bake sale.

Kyle: So why didn't you do them earlier in the day?

Ainsley: Because I had other responsibilities earlier in the day.

Kyle: You're overcommitted.

Kyle: What are you trying to prove?

She didn't respond. That was strange. Kyle stretched and scratched his belly for a minute, then decided to go empty his bladder. She'd probably have responded when he came back.

Huh. Still nothing. Well, he could still go running without her; he changed into his nylon shorts and a sweatshirt. He was admittedly confused about why she'd abruptly stopped their conversation as he thundered down the stairs.

He started toward the kitchen in search of coffee, only to find Daniel and his fiancée at the center of a mild chaos of boxes. Brown cardboard boxes, liquor store boxes. *Moving boxes.* He froze. *This isn't supposed to happen yet.* His heart started beating hard, thumps he could hear in his ears and feel behind his eyes.

"What's going on?"

Daniel and Winnie both looked up sharply, guilt painting his brother's face.

"I thought you were at work."

"Well, I'm not. So what's going on, what are you doing?"

"We're just gathering up a few things in case our offer gets accepted . . ."

"Gathering? You're not gathering, you're *packing*," he accused. When Daniel said nothing, Kyle decided to lob another cannonball across his bow. "You don't even have a place to live yet. Why are you wasting time packing?"

"Take a deep breath, man," Daniel said, putting down the wide, clear tape he was holding, coming over to where Kyle stood.

"You said you were staying until you got married." Kyle stepped back so he couldn't touch him.

"I am," he said, holding up his hands in a show of innocence. "I'm staying until January. Okay? I promise. I won't move out until January."

"I'm depending on that income. And your lease dictates that you have to give a month's notice. It's only October now."

"I realize that . . ." Daniel was fidgeting, Kyle noticed. He'd made him uncomfortable. He felt momentarily sorry for yelling at him, until his brother spoke again, softly. "It's gonna be okay, Kyle."

"Don't talk to me like a child!" he snapped. "I don't even want you here, okay? I was doing you a favor by letting you stay, not the other way around. I'm happier by myself. Leave whenever the hell you want. And take your stupid mess with you!"

Kyle stormed out the front door, grabbing his running shoes on the way, ignoring his brother calling his name behind him.

AINSLEY WAS POURING coffee into her travel mug when a knock at her door startled her badly enough to give herself third-degree burns. *Who on earth could that be?* she wondered, trying to wipe the coffee off her blouse. Hoping it wasn't Starla with a marriage trouble emergency, she wandered over to the peephole and peeked through. It was Kyle; his hair was damp and adorably mussed, and he was breathing hard. She opened the door, but the smile she ordered her face to produce didn't arrive in time.

"What are you doing here?" Things had been a bit weird between them since last weekend. He stepped forward and kissed her. It helped a little, like when moms kiss a kid's skinned knee. But the wound was still there.

"Hi."

"Hi," she said, softening. "Kyle, what are you doing here? I need to go to work."

"Just checking in."

She picked up her heavy bag with a sigh. "And you didn't think to call?"

"No, I left my house unexpectedly without my phone." He wiped the sweat off his forehead with his sleeve. "I'll pick you up at five thirty tonight, okay?"

"No," she said quickly. "I have to . . . I'll take my own car." Man, this was going to be tricky. She just couldn't handle going together tonight; she had too much going on . . . inside and out. "I have stuff to drop off." She gestured to the two big boxes of food and paper plates and cups and plastic utensils.

"Okay." He paused. "But I'll see you there, right? We're going to sit together at dinner?"

"Uh . . ." She needed to stall for time. "I don't know, babe, it's gonna be really busy. I'll try, okay?" She swiped a thumb over the corner of her mouth, and his eyes narrowed.

"You're not going to sit with me?"

"What?" she scoffed, turning so he couldn't see her face. "I just said I'd try."

"Ainsley." He circled her slowly to see her better; it was not helping her trapped feeling. "Do you want to sit with me?"

"Yes," she said, enunciating for emphasis, feeling her panic rise. "Of course I do."

"Then why did you just lie to me?" He straightened. "I know your tells."

"I saved you a seat at the town meeting, but you didn't sit with me," she pointed out.

"You sat right in front! I didn't want the speakers blasting my eardrums!"

She sighed. "Can we talk about this later?"

"No. Why don't you want to sit with me?"

How could she begin to explain it to him? Daniel wouldn't be there tonight to cast reasonable doubt on why she was sitting with Kyle Durand. He was already gone when the town rumor mill crushed her last time, pulverized her like grain into flour over what happened with Shane. Daniel had never tuned in to such things, so he probably never told his brother because he didn't know himself.

Kyle sucked his teeth. "Fine." He stepped forward and picked up both boxes. "Can you get the door?" he grunted, avoiding her gaze. Silently, she opened the door and let him go first, edging by him on the landing when he stopped to make sure she was behind him. She opened the trunk.

"Kyle . . ."

"I'll see you later," he said, starting off at a jog.

She did see him later . . . between the columns outside the gym as he helped Mrs. Miller with a crate of apples. Getting up on a ladder to help hang orange and black crepe paper streamers. Sticking to the edges, and yet somehow in the midst of it all. And at the thank-you dinner for all those who'd come to help set up, he pulled out a chair for his mom and sat down next to her, pointedly avoiding Ainsley's tortured gaze. *Guess I deserve that. At least he's not sitting with Jennie.* In her head, she reminded herself that she'd never seen him show more than po-lite interest in any other woman in town since he moved back . . . but that didn't mean it wouldn't have bothered her.

She'd been pondering his question all day . . . what *was* she trying to prove? It wasn't that she found it hard to say no, exactly; she liked being busy. But she did wonder if the busy-ness wasn't covering for something else, some deeper need that she didn't want to examine. Ignoring her personal trauma had worked quite well for a long time. Hadn't it?

If you want him, come and claim him. Arwen's immortal words, said to her enemies, somehow still rang true. He was hers for the taking, by all outward appearances . . . but hadn't Shane been, too? It wasn't that she needed to hear an "I love you" before they could go to town functions together, but . . . how could she know he was serious? He ate his ham and pota-toes and salad, mostly ignoring the people around him, and never looked at her once. She knew because she stared at him all night.

How he knew when she was ready to leave, then, was un-clear. But when she came back from the bathroom, he was gone, and when she got to her truck in the corner of the dark parking lot, he was leaning against it, thumbs in his belt loops, head down, eyes trained on the asphalt.

"Going home?"

She nodded.

"Text me when you get there?"

She laughed a little. "What's going to happen in Timber Falls between the school and my apartment?"

"It doesn't hurt to be cautious. Just like it doesn't hurt to park under a streetlight when you know you'll be coming out to the parking lot alone in the dark." He gave her a pointed look, and she rolled her eyes.

"Yes," she said, slipping her arms around his waist, "but I'm not alone, am I?" He let his arms drop to her waist, too, and she turned her head to lay it against his chest, listening to his heart, silently willing him to understand her motivations over the last few weeks without having to explain herself . . . even though she knew it was impossible. He held her for a few minutes, then kissed the top of her head and pulled away from her.

"Just text when you get home, please. See you at pickup." The coldness of his words didn't match his body's warmth and welcome whatsoever, and Ainsley tried not to let it sting, but she found herself rubbing her chest to ease the ache there.

"Kyle?"

He was already across the parking lot, spinning his keys on his fingers, vanishing into the darkness.

CHAPTER
TWENTY-SEVEN

SHARP POUNDING ON HER door startled her. She finished tying her shoe, then went to peek through the peephole. It was Kyle. His hair stood on end like he'd been plowing his fingers through it all night. Based on how he was glowering at her door, too little sleep had apparently not helped his disposition. She was not ready to talk to Grumpy Kyle yet. She tiptoed away from the door as quietly as she could. Just as she reached the kitchen, her cell started to ring: "Po-tay-toes! Po-tay-toes! Po-tay-toes!" yelled Sam Gamgee, and she cursed herself for her whimsical sense of humor.

"Ainsley Buchanan, I know you're in there! No one else has that goofy hobbit ringtone. Open the damn door."

He was still holding his phone to his ear when she whipped the door open.

"Pipe down, will you? I've got neighbors, for heaven's sake!" She whisper-yelled, pulling him inside by his T-shirt.

"Well, I wouldn't want to wake your *neighbors*," he snarled.

"What is your problem?"

He threw out his arms. "My problem is that you're avoiding me! And I have no idea why!"

Standing there, seeing him so livid, so incensed, she asked herself what she'd been thinking. Her whole life was out there in the community . . . and if her whole life was destined to meld with his, then obviously, they were going to have to be seen together. It shouldn't feel like a risk, sitting with someone at the setup dinner. But it did. It felt like walking a tightrope sans balance pole.

"Come with me on my run."

He gave her a quizzical look, then gestured to his clothing. He was in a T-shirt and jeans.

"So go home and change."

"And you won't leave without me?"

"No."

"And you'll open the door again when I get back?"

She scowled. "Yes."

He held up his hands in innocence. "Hey, when someone is avoiding you for unknown reasons, these questions must be asked." He put his hand on the door. "I'll see you in twenty."

He managed it in seventeen. He must've barely even paused to hydrate . . . maybe he didn't believe that she'd be here, she thought, ashamed. She should've just talked to him before now, but . . . it hurt.

Kyle paused next to her. "Well?"

"Stop being a jerk, Kyle," she said, as she began to jog down the street. He caught up with her quickly.

"*I'm* being a jerk?"

"Yes," she puffed, "you are." She was quiet for a minute, then turned into the park. "Nine years ago, I was in a relationship. At least, I thought I was. Apparently, he had other thoughts on the matter."

"Who are you talking about? Not Daniel?"

She huffed out a laugh. "Heck no, not Daniel. I love your brother, but he's . . ."

"Goofy."

"Yes."

She paused again. It was a little easier, not having to see his face. She tried to take a deep breath, but her breaths were already deep as her body eased into its running rhythm. "I thought we were dating, but apparently, Shane didn't."

"Shane Burgess? The All-State defensive back?"

"Yes. And when I showed up to support him at a football game with a sign that said 'That's my boyfriend,' I found out just how wrong I'd been. Complete with memes and assorted internet bullying." They called it pulling an Ainsley . . . The meme said "TFW he's not actually" with a picture of her crestfallen face still holding her sign. She hadn't seen it around lately, but it still circulated occasionally.

Kyle was silent.

"So going public with a relationship is not easy for me." She cleared her throat. "I wish it was. I wish I could just parade around town with Timber Falls' most eligible bachelor and not care what anyone thinks, but . . ."

"But you do care."

"Yes." She panted. "I do care. I don't want that to happen again, ever. And you and me, it just makes no sense. I'm not ragging on myself, I think I'm reasonably attractive. We just run in different circles, and there's so many other girls who'd be a better fit for someone like you . . ."

"Someone like me." He said the words flatly.

"Yes. You're a doctor. I don't think I act like a doctor's wife." Her heart, which was already beating out of her chest, began flailing around like a firefly trapped in a jar. "Kyle . . . do you get what I'm saying at all?"

Their synced footfalls quieted as they transitioned to the thick yellow fallen pine needles on the trail, and she put on more speed to stay with him as they ascended the steepest part of the path. At the top, breathing hard, but not as hard as she was, he stopped. He clasped his hands together behind his head, walking in a circle.

"That's messed up, Ains. And it's even more messed up that you didn't just talk to me about it." For someone who usually communicated in quips and grunts, he seemed to have found some vault of angry words to cash out. "How could you think I would do that to you? How could you think I'm that kind of person? I've been as overt as I can be about how much I like you, Ainsley. I've practically tattooed it on my forehead, and it's not good enough for you."

She felt her chin quivering. "Well, not *as* overt . . ."

He stopped pacing. "What?"

Her mind knew what needed to be said, but her lips balked, hating the taste of the words on her tongue.

"You've never called me your girlfriend. You've never said . . ."

His face reddened with barely controlled rage. "So you won't be seen with me in public because I haven't said *I love you*? Is that—is that what I'm supposed to take away from this?"

"No! I mean . . ." She felt her lip quivering, and she bit it. "I don't know. I was wrong before, with Shane. I just don't want to get ahead of myself again."

"Wow." He pressed his fingers into his closed eyes, then wiped down his face. "I should not have done this now. I'm going home."

"Will I see you tonight?"

"I don't know."

Her stomach tightened. "Tomorrow night?"

"I don't know." He turned and headed back down the hill before she could say anything more.

DRIP, DRIP, DRIP. The gutters were leaking again outside her classroom. Her kids were outside for their afternoon recess, and without the urgency of eager young minds in front of her, she couldn't focus on anything. As it was, she'd had enough trouble getting through the morning: she put up the wrong date, she misspelled *terrible* when Rio asked her during reading time (teribble? It hadn't seemed right, but . . .). And of course, today happened to be one of her principal's "drop in and observe you teaching when you don't know I'm coming" days. She'd need her endorsement if she went for her national certificate. It was just another trophy, really. She would never leave Timber Falls, not even for love. *Especially when the person I love loves it here as much as I do.* Maybe she'd just assumed that; Kyle didn't show up to a lot of town events. But he cared about the town—she knew he did. Didn't his plans to stay say it all? Rural medicine was not for the faint of heart.

I screwed this up, she thought as she stared out the window at the flowering plum trees outside her window. *I should've just been upfront with Kyle about it. More than that, I should've shown him.* Well, it wasn't too late, certainly. Slowly, she turned to her computer and opened an incognito browser. She couldn't have it coming back to anyone by any means that she was googling herself. Into the search bar, she typed "TFW your boyfriend isn't after all." There it was. Her blonde hair in pigtails, Timber Falls Football face paint not masking her horrified expression. Her shoulders slumped, her sign that said "That's my boyfriend" drooping. Ainsley's finger hovered over the "Share" button, hesitating. Was it necessary, really? And did she want him to see her that way? As an object of ridicule?

Ainsley had always thought that if she were bullied, it'd happen nemesis-style, more like her problems with Ranger. You know, one big, bad enemy who she'd rubbed the wrong way with a flippant comment about their physical appearance. Someone she'd tripped by accident in the hall or whose french fries she dumped in the cafeteria while showing off her dance moves. She never expected it to be such a group effort, to be so virulently singled out by so many people. To be whispered about and dragged through the mud so publicly, yet so anonymously. It was like trying to fight a ghost; she'd reported the first few posts to the school, but after the bullies started using fake profiles, there was nothing to do but block them and move on with her life. Which wasn't easy when the messages they sent kept coming . . . "So pathetic." "If I were you, I'd kill myself." "That guy? Your boyfriend? What were you thinking?"

Notes stuffed in the crack of her locker, videos of her running from the field posted for all to see, taunting emails sent from throwaway accounts. That word, *throwaway*; it made it all sound more innocent than it was. Because while they might have thrown those words out, laughing, when they landed, they scalded her. Being an object of mockery changed her. And there was just so much of it. They'd piled on her, relieved that it wasn't them who'd made the mistake, happy to have someone else look like a fool.

She closed the window without sending him anything; he could google it if he wanted to see. Kyle would come back around. Probably. Ainsley put her head down on her desk, trying to let the cold of the classroom seep deeper into her. Maybe she wouldn't feel so much then. Just go numb to all of it. She'd never found a way to dull the pain, actually. She'd tried drinking briefly, but she hated vomiting and seemed to have a very low tolerance . . . another short-girl problem, maybe. With a sigh, she stood and ambled down the hall to pick up her kids at the doors to the playground. They seemed more subdued than usual, and she wondered if they'd caught her gloomy mood. She'd never understood why people bothered to try to hide things like that from kids; they weren't stupid. In fact, sometimes, they were more in tune with the world around them, and that included people. Then again, sometimes they just wanted to color *Frozen* pictures without being interrupted.

Annabeth slipped a hand into hers and smiled up at her. Ainsley smiled back.

But inside? Inside, she was broken thinking about how she'd rejected Kyle because of her own insecurities. Hadn't she put him through the same kind of rejection she'd felt, all those years ago?

CHAPTER
TWENTY-EIGHT

MUCH TO AINSLEY'S DELIGHT, Bilqiis and Fawzia agreed to come to the fall festival in Timber Falls. And the atmosphere did not disappoint: all of downtown had orange and purple lights leading to the high school gym, and outside, the weather was nice enough to have booths and stalls set up for all kinds of activities: apple bobbing, popcorn, a pie contest, and even a dunk tank despite the chill in the air. Ainsley was torn away as soon as she arrived, her help needed with several booths that hadn't been set up yet, so she encouraged them to wander around and take it all in, shoving a few tickets in their hands. She was bent over, trying to get an extension cord connected, when she heard Ranger's voice.

"What are you hiding under that head covering, anyway? Why don't you take it off for us?" She looked up in time to see Bilqiis dodge his hand as he reached for her scarf, and Ainsley could see that her fingers were shaking hard as she touched it to make sure it hadn't shifted. Ranger's back was to her. It wasn't a fair fight in any way if she started when his back was turned, and her dad had taught her to always start a fight to someone's face; you could do more damage and have less liability.

"Hey! Toilet paper brain!" Okay, maybe the kids' insults were rubbing off on her a tiny bit. "Why don't you leave her alone? There's lots of candy around for good boys and girls. If you walk away now, you can have some, too." This was not active bystander behavior, she thought as he turned to her, his gaze livid. He kept himself between her and Bilqiis, and it was really messed up how badly Ainsley just wanted to knock him down to get to her. But he was basically a less handsome Mr. Clean, so she thought she'd better not try.

"Stay out of this, Buchanan."

"Can't. Sorry. I was in it the moment you started to pick on my friend. It's a solidarity thing. You understand." With the hand still at her side, she motioned for Bilqiis to take off, but her friend hesitated. *Go. Go, Bilqiis. Slip away while his back is turned.*

"It's just hair. Does she not realize that *hair* isn't private?" he sneered.

"First of all, you don't need to talk about her like she isn't here. And secondly, I know *you've* got hair in places I don't want to see, so maybe we just can just agree that *some* hair is private." Behind him, she saw Bilqiis laugh a little, then push back her shoulders and tap Ranger on the shoulder.

He turned back to Bilqiis slowly. "What?"

"I am not hiding anything. In fact, I am putting on display the beautiful culture that I come from. I am showing you that being a Muslim does not mean I am a terrorist, that most Muslim people are peaceful. I am showing you what it means to be a woman in a different way. If it makes you uncomfortable, I am sorry, but it is my right. It is my right."

Fawzia's eyes were huge as she listened to her mother's speech, and Ainsley wondered what was happening in her head. Would she understand later on what her mother had done? Would she look back and draw strength from this moment when she was grown? Bilqiis took her daughter's hand and dragged her toward the kettle corn, Fawzia still looking at Ranger and Ainsley in slack-jawed wonder. Ranger seemed pretty shocked himself, and with Bilqiis now at a safe distance, he rounded on Ainsley.

"Of course you'd take their side." With two giant steps, they were nose to nose, and Ainsley's heart was beating so hard, she could hear it in her own ears. Many people have a little voice in their heads that in this situation would tell them to run or retreat. Ainsley did not have that voice.

"Get out of my face, Zane. I'm warning you." She must have looked like a hobbit to him: a foot shorter, staring up at him with ire in her gaze. "My dad's a cop. He made me take self-defense classes from the time I could talk."

"And yet you've been mouthing off ever since." He pushed on her shoulder, and it took her a second to regain her balance. Sweat broke out on her forehead despite the cool fall weather. "Always putting your nose where it doesn't belong. Maybe I should do something about it."

She pushed on his chest with both hands as hard as she could, and only managed to send him one step backward. "You're welcome to that opinion. Just stay away from me and my friend, and we won't have a problem."

His nostrils flared, his shoulders came up, and he took another step as if to push her back, but she was ready for him this time. She lifted her running shoe and brought it down hard on the bridge of his foot. Ranger let out a string of curses and doubled over. That move did really hurt: she knew because she'd tried it on her brother, Travis, once, and he couldn't wear tennis shoes for a week because of the bruising. Had to wear flip-flops in forty-degree weather. Served him right for stealing her authentic Lord of the Rings elven pin off her backpack.

"What's going on here?" Officer Painter was striding over with Kyle hot on her heels.

"She assaulted me!" Ranger shouted, sitting down hard, and Ainsley rolled her eyes.

"He's been harassing women in the community for months, and he was doing it again today. Got right in my face and shoved my shoulder, so I used a nonlethal self-defense technique."

Lizzie eyed them both as Ranger continued to curse softly and hold his foot. "Yes, it certainly seems nonlethal."

"He threatened her, too, I heard him!" piped up Mrs. Renfro. "Said maybe he'd do something about her, Officer! That's a threat!"

Lizzie held up her hands for quiet. "All right, both of you, come on over to the squad car, and I'll get your statements. Mrs. Renfro, you too, please, since you were a witness. The rest of you, go back to your festivities."

Everyone obeyed; they'd seen her take Chase Carpenter down last year when he was tripping on drugs at the town's centennial celebration. The cute freckles sprinkled on her nose camouflaged a lady who excelled at her chosen profession.

Ainsley followed Lizzie across the street and Ranger limped along behind. Kyle was just behind her; if his scowl got any deeper, he was going to dent his face. His voice was low, but he articulated his thoughts just fine.

"I can't believe you. That was the stupidest, most foolhardy, reckless thing I've ever seen you do, and that's saying something, because you have done some insanely stupid things. But this takes the cake, Ainsley. You just picked a fight with a man with a history of violence who's twice your size." The adrenaline was starting to wane, and it left her feeling shaky and nauseated. Kyle's lectures were the last thing she needed right now.

"You can go back to your tent now." There was no fight in the statement, just a quiet refusal to engage.

He stared at her, hands on his hips, eyes burning with frustration. "Go back to my—so I'm dismissed, is that it? I saved you from getting pounded, and now I'm excused? Damn it, Ainsley, you're the most infuriating person I've ever met. When are you going to get it through your head that you're important to me? Important to lots of people who don't want to see your skull bashed in? I can't be the first person to tell you this. When are you going to wake up and see that I actually care about you?"

"I don't know, it'd probably help if you actually said the words from time to time," she retorted.

"Are you kidding me right now? Are you fu—"

Lizzie cleared her throat, and based on her clipboard and pen, she was ready to take Ainsley's statement. "Maybe I'll start with Ranger . . ."

"No. Start with her. If you don't, she'll probably run out into traffic. But don't worry, she'll think she has a good reason, and she'll do it alone." He started to stride away, and something inside Ainsley just . . . snapped. Like a clothesline piled too heavy with wet clothes, worn from being in the sun, picked at by birds. She'd known she was holding on by a thread for a while, feeling frayed inside, but the snap still came as a surprise to her brain, which could not stop the angry words that tumbled out.

"You know what?" she yelled at his back. "*No one* is going to bully me or my friends. *No one.*" She felt hot tears on her cheeks, and she wiped them off with the cuff of her long-sleeve T-shirt. "I lived in silence while my peers"—she gestured to the other festival-goers around them— "destroyed my confidence over a simple miscommunication between me and Shane. They tore me down and hurt me, and I said nothing—*nothing*—because I thought it would make it worse, and I literally couldn't live with that."

Kyle had turned back, and he was staring at her, wide-eyed, his mouth agape. *Kyle hates yelling. Stop yelling, especially since this has ceased to be about him.* Her mouth, having seceded summarily from the rest of her body, continued to ignore the pleas of her brain for calm.

"And do you know who would've helped me, if I'd asked? My parents, my friends, my counselor, my teachers. All of them. All of them would've helped me. Even if they couldn't have stopped the messages and the trolling and the memes, they would've hugged me and told me that it would be okay. They would've listened to me and believed me and assured me that I wasn't crazy. Told me it was okay to be furious and sad and embarrassed." She swiped at the tears again, hating them, hating that she was turning a fun town event into a drama fest. But she couldn't let him walk away like that. "Instead, I was virtually alone, not knowing who was on my side and who was against me."

She stalked over to him until they were toe to toe, then stared up at him with her head thrown back. The anger in his gaze had tempered, but it was still there. "If you can't live with someone who is willing to lay it on the line for her friends, then just break up with me now. Because I'll be damned if I'm going to stand here and let Ranger bully Bilqiis for one more second. Not only because it's wrong, but because I would've given *anything* to have someone do that for me. No one is going to silence me anymore. Especially not—" She choked on the words, but her heart demanded they be said out loud. "Someone I love."

His chest was rising and falling fast, and she knew he was upset despite his stony expression. Kyle hesitated, then swiftly turned and walked away. She watched him go, and the crowd around them started to disperse. Parents suddenly realized their children were listening to a lover's quarrel, and hurried them toward a more kid-friendly activity, like ax-throwing. Ainsley walked back to the patrol car and sat down hard on the curb. She put her arms on her knees and let her forehead rest against them, her hair cutting off every worried glance and aghast stare. Someone sat down next to her on the curb, and she knew it was her dad without looking up; that stupid cologne.

"Kiddo?"

"Yes?" She didn't lift her head, couldn't meet his gaze right now.

"You're right. We would've done all those things for you." His big, warm hand came to her back, hesitantly, then he rubbed up and down, his calluses catching on the cotton of her shirt. Ainsley released a shaky sigh, snuffling into her shirt sleeve as she lifted her head just a little bit. The crowd was all gone now; even Ranger was sitting quietly nearby.

"I know, Daddy."

"Sorry it isn't working out with him. Even if he did break my mailbox."

Ainsley sighed again, and in spite of it all, she laughed.

CHAPTER
TWENTY-NINE

KYLE DIDN'T GO TO AINSLEY'S that night. He needed to do some thinking about what she'd said. It wasn't that she was all wrong, but she also wasn't all right. He felt they both had a tendency to value their own opinions too highly, and he wasn't sure how to communicate that to her without hurting her even more. He didn't want to hurt her any more. She loved him, after all.

Also, he had something important to do at home, and it was overdue. As expected, Winnie and Daniel were snuggled on the couch, her reading, him watching Netflix.

"Hey, Kyle," his brother greeted him.

"Pause, please." There was no point in beating around the bush.

Daniel groped around a little, found the remote, and paused the show.

"I just wanted to say that it's okay if you move out early."

"Oh. Okay. Thanks."

"It doesn't make sense for you to pay for two places, and I'm glad you found a house." He felt like he was vibrating inside; the urge to jump up and down was strong, but it was incongruous with what he wanted to say. He made his feet stay on the ground and settled for swaying in place a little.

"You're not going to charge me a penalty for breaking my lease?" Daniel asked, one eyebrow cocked. Humor? Yes, humor. Brothers were weird.

"No. Though I should, because I'll miss the rent that you would've paid. Not that you ever paid on time, anyway."

Daniel stood from the couch and slowly came in for a tight hug. "I'll miss you, too, bro."

Kyle felt tears stinging his eyes, and he blinked them away. But he squeezed Daniel back hard, putting into the hug everything he couldn't figure out how to say. He knew he wasn't losing his brother on a head level, but his heart? It wasn't convinced. He hated change. This kind was the worst of all. Even when he saw it coming, he wasn't ready for it.

Kyle cleared his throat. "I'm sure we'll still see each other regularly."

"Definitely." Daniel swiped just under his eye. "I'll make sure of it."

"And we still have Sibling Night."

"Yep."

At the sound of a teary snuffle behind Daniel, both men turned to look at Winnie.

"I know why we're crying, but why is *she* crying?"

"Because I'm taking him away from you," she sniffled, wiping her wet cheeks with her pink sweatshirt sleeve.

Kyle considered this for a moment. "No. If it wasn't you, it would've been something else. He had to grow up sometime. Everyone does. You shouldn't feel responsible." He paused. "Would you like a hug?"

Daniel and Winnie both laughed in a watery way.

"Sure," she said, unfolding her legs and standing from the couch. Kyle made sure the embrace was gentler than the one he'd given Daniel, but still firm enough to convey comfort. Wimpy hugs were good for nothing.

"I know you'll take very good care of him," Kyle commented as he set her away from him. "Which is good, because he needs it."

"Who's going to take care of you, though?" Daniel teased. "I'm not just a liability, you know. I do stuff."

"I've designated Ainsley to take over your responsibilities. I'll be proposing to her shortly."

Both their mouths fell open, and it took them a minute before they said anything.

"I see," Daniel said, nodding slowly. "Maybe don't put it that way when you ask her, though."

Kyle scowled. "I'm not an idiot. I watch movies. I know I have to say romantic things. But I was hoping you'd look over a draft for me . . ."

"Of course, bro. Gladly."

"Can I see the ring?" Winnie asked, bouncing a little with excitement.

"I haven't procured one yet; I'd value your input on styles."

As she beamed, he knew he'd said the right thing for once.

"This is really helpful, actually, Kyle," Winnie said. "Starla Miller just called, and she's starting to make plans to leave Charlie. If we move to the new house, she can stay with Ainsley, where the kids are already comfortable."

"Oh." Selfishly, he didn't want Starla and her brood moving into his girlfriend's apartment; it was going to make date night a lot more crowded. But the larger part of him was relieved to hear that she wouldn't be living with a man who treated her so poorly. No one deserved that, least of all Starla, who always saved him the quietest carrel in the library. And despite his earlier reservations, maybe it proved that some mistakes were more fixable than they first appeared.

"Oh, and Kyle?" Daniel said. Kyle exited his own thoughts and gave his brother his full attention. "The Starla thing? That's a secret."

He gave him a knowing nod, then aside to Winnie, he explained, "I'm very good at secrets, but I have to *know* that it's a secret. Remember that come Christmas."

"Will do," she replied with a grin.

CHAPTER THIRTY

MONDAY WAS AS AWKWARD as she knew it would be. After spending the weekend strategizing with Starla about what she'd need to do to leave Charlie, she was already tired. The teachers who didn't give her looks of sympathy either avoided her gaze entirely or appeared ashamed of themselves; maybe they'd been involved? She hadn't meant to call out anyone specifically except Ranger. There had been so many memes and shares back then, she really couldn't remember who'd been party to the bullying. It wasn't like she'd kept an enemies list carved into the back of her yearbook, crossing out their pictures.

She'd started to forget about the incident until circle time at the end of the day. They had a few minutes to kill; she'd just finished reading *Ferdinand*, a classic picture book about a bull, who ironically also stood up to bullying, too. Defied expectations, refused to fight in the bullfights in Madrid, preferring instead to smell the flowers. Pacifism was its own kind of rebellion, and she didn't mind putting that in her students' heads one bit. "Does anyone have any questions?"

Harmony raised her hand. "Why were you yelling at Cooper's uncle?"

Ainsley felt her eyebrows go high on her forehead. Well, it was a valid question. She swallowed, but before she could respond, Denver piped up. "She got arrested, dummy."

"Denver, we don't call names," she chided gently. "And I didn't get arrested. Officer Painter just wanted to talk about what happened between me and Mr. Zane." Thankfully, she didn't have any of his kids or nieces or nephews this year, or this could be *really* awkward.

"Why, what happened?" asked Heaven, her big brown eyes wide.

"You weren't there?" Cooper said, disbelieving. "It was so awesome. Miss Buchanan was all 'nobody pushes my friends around' and then she like karate kicked Mr. Zane so she could help that lady with the hat . . ."

"Her name is Mrs. Sadiq, and it's not a hat, it's a hijab. She told me once that covering her hair is a way to remember where she comes from and show respect to herself and the people around her."

"A *hat* shows respect?" asked Verity. "My dad says we're not supposed to wear hats in church . . . Does she take hers off in church?"

"Again, not a hat. And she doesn't go to church, actually." The gasp the children released was loud; you would've thought she'd just told them Santa Claus wasn't real.

"Where does she go on Sundays, then?"

"Does that mean she can watch football? Dad has to watch his later. He hates that. He says he gets spoiled on Twitter."

"She doesn't go on Christmas and Easter? My uncle Randy goes on Christmas and Easter, and he says that's just as good . . ."

Ainsley stammered, a little overwhelmed by their chatter, "I-I don't know, guys." Their volume increased, and she had to hold up her hands for quiet. "Would you like her to come visit our classroom? I'm sure she could answer these questions better herself." The children agreed in a vote of fifteen to six that it would be best if they got their information from the source. But Ainsley wasn't off the hook yet.

"Miss B, you said we're not allowed to hit, but you hit that man." The other small heads nodded insistently in agreement.

"That's true, I did. That was wrong, wasn't it? What do you think I should've done differently? What would you have done?" She stood up and turned to the whiteboard, but her heart stuttered as she noticed Kyle in her doorway, leaning casually against the frame. She blinked, staring at him for a moment too long, so that the children noticed. They hadn't spoken since the fall festival, and she'd missed him. Every text message she'd gotten had been a huge disappointment simply because it wasn't from him. She could've won the Publisher's Clearing House, and if he wasn't with the prize patrol when they opened the door, she'd have slammed it in their faces.

"Uncle Kyle!" Cooper jumped up and ran to him, giving him a bear hug around his middle. Kyle bent and whispered something to him, and Cooper nodded, then ran back over to the rug and sat back down. Ainsley turned to the whiteboard again, and they brainstormed other ways she could've solved her problem . . . They all agreed that she would've been much better off going to get Officer Painter right away, rather than trying to solve the problem on her own.

"He was a big man, Teacher," said Harmony. "You shouldn't fight such a big man."

The bell rang, and Ainsley's gaze shot to the clock. *Shoot, we should be lined up by now.*

"Everyone, quick, get your stuff. Blue table, you go first . . . No, not everyone at once, okay? Blue table first, then green table . . ." There was mild chaos as the kids got their stuff together, swapped back pencils and books and water bottles and all the other things they'd traded or borrowed during the day, and lined up. Kyle disappeared into the hall while they were getting sorted, and she could see him through the windows. Cooper ran to him again, and Ainsley mentally checked the boy off her list. Kyle still hadn't said a word, and she wasn't sure if he was just here to get his nephew or for something more. She thought she'd seen something in his face that seemed like regret or humility, but it was so hard to tell with him . . . Dragons often weren't big on broadcasting their feelings, she supposed. It came with the territory of being a badass.

She hurried them out, but theirs was the last class, despite their efforts to be speedy. She'd let that last lesson get away from her . . . but it was so important. Modeling reflection and courage . . . these things mattered just as much as math and science in her mind, whether the standardized tests measured them or not. She would spend time on them. When she sent the last group off to bus number 8, she hurried back into the building, pulling at the lanyard around her neck nervously. If he wasn't there, she wasn't going to get upset . . . If he wasn't there, it might not mean anything. Maybe he just wasn't ready to talk yet. She rounded the corner into the early elementary wing, and her heart sank. No Cooper. No Kyle. They'd left. He'd left without saying a word.

"Hey." She turned. Starla was just coming out of the library.

"Hey. What are you doing here?"

"Kyle called me. He asked if I could pick up Aiden and Em today."

"He did?"

Starla grinned at her, then nodded. "And it was a good opportunity to switch back a few picture books that got into the wrong drop box." She slapped Ainsley lightly on the backside. "Go kiss and make up. I think he's waiting in your room."

Kyle was sitting in the Think It Over Chair, facing the wall. Ainsley hesitantly picked her way through the desks toward the corner with the bulletin board of paper jack-o-lanterns the kids had done during a lesson about symmetry as her friend made herself scarce. "What are you doing here?"

"Thinking." He didn't turn around. "Cooper said this is a good place to do it."

"You know, the kids call it the Naughty Chair."

"That works for me." He paused. "Are you still mad at me?"

"That depends." She let her hands fall to his shoulders. "Are you sorry?"

He nodded. Ainsley started to massage his shoulders; she felt the tension began to drain from them, and his head dropped forward. Kyle sighed.

"I don't regret what I said. But the way I said it maybe wasn't right."

"Okay." She wasn't sold on that apology, but she wanted to listen. She wasn't sure she'd been a great listener lately.

"I was scared." He swallowed. "I thought he was going to hurt you, Ainsley. I thought . . ." He sighed again and caught her hands, pulling her around to see him. "I am sorry I called you stupid. Will you forgive me?"

Pursing her lips, she gestured for him to sit up in the tiny chair. Ainsley slid onto his lap sideways.

"I think I need a little time in this chair, too."

"No complaints here . . ." He leaned back to see her face better, stroking her hair down her back. "No one's trying to silence you, least of all me. But confronting Ranger by yourself was a really dumb thing to do."

"Yeah, I guess so . . ."

"You *guess*? Are you kidding me, Ains?" He pointed insistently to the whiteboard she'd just filled with nonviolent conflict-resolution ideas, and she laughed a little. His breath was coming faster, and she was fairly sure he was holding back more angry words. She held up her hands in surrender.

"Okay, it was a really dumb thing—"

"I don't want to break up with you, Ains. I just want to be in all your foolish plots together. I want to be in everything with you. You're sunshine," he blurted out, his face reddening. "You're sunshine, babe, and I'm the rain on your parade, but together, we're a rainbow. I love you. I love you, and I can't lose that."

"That's really, really corny," she whispered.

"I know," he whispered back, bringing their foreheads together. "But you loved it."

"I did."

He swallowed hard. "You've got to take better care of yourself. I can't imagine if I hadn't seen what was happening and called over Officer Painter . . ."

She put a hand on his shoulder. "It's okay. It's okay, Kyle. I'm sorry, all right? I'll do better. I'll try to start looking before I leap."

"Just let me have your back, okay? I'm not saying you shouldn't defend Mrs. Sadiq; of course, you should. But I was fifty feet away. Anyone around you would've helped if you'd just told us what was happening." He put his hand over hers, lifted her hand to his lips to kiss her knuckles.

"Don't do that. Kiss my lips."

Kyle blinked at her, then chuckled. "Okay, bossy."

"Stop bantering and do it."

He glared. "I don't think I'm *bantering*, I'm just—"

"So you can kiss me in a dark trailer, but not in my classroom? That makes no sense."

"Why do I have to be the one who starts it?"

"The man starts the kiss. This is known."

"And here I thought you were a feminist . . ."

That did it. Ainsley brought her other hand up to his face and pulled him forward, touching their lips together in the barest of grazes. She brushed his cheek with her thumb, feeling his stubble under her fingers. "More?"

He nodded. "More."

She pressed into him more fully for a longer one, sucking lightly at his lips, coming just shy of biting him with her teeth. Ainsley felt his hand slide up her shoulder to her neck, and when he gently squeezed the back of it, she felt her face heat.

"More?" Her own voice was hardly recognizable.

"How about I just tell you when I've had enough?"

Ainsley laughed softly, but Kyle tugged her forward again, his kiss more insistent, deep with longing and excitement at the same time. She felt his happiness as his chest vibrated with a grumbly groan, and she giggled.

"I officially love this chair," he said.

"I'm at work, Dr. Durand. Maybe slow down a little . . ."

"It's educational. The children have to find out sometime."

"Yeah, in fifth grade, though, not first."

"I know." He kissed her again. "*Someone* volunteered me to help with the boys' talk this year."

"We're short on male teachers up there. It's good for the community . . ." Her train of thought derailed as his stubbled cheek rubbed against her smooth one.

"You know what else is good for the community?" he asked, kissing down her neck to her pulse point, turning her insides to jelly.

Ainsley made a noise that she could only assume was her brain disconnecting from the rest of her body. *Brain offline. Backup instincts now engaging.*

"Come on, do the sexy banter with me."

"Wh-what?" Her heart was racing.

He kept talking between lingering kisses. "You're supposed to say, 'What is, Kyle?' and then I'd say, 'A happy Ainsley, because she's on every committee that this town has.'"

"Uh-huh," she breathed, tipping her head back as he kissed behind her ear.

Someone in the doorway cleared their throat, and they both froze.

"Miss Buchanan, might I have a moment of your time?"

Kyle scowled. "I knew I shouldn't have brought you."

Daniel chuckled. "Glad to see you two are making up. Where's the grown-up-sized bathrooms? Cooper didn't know, and my bladder is about to burst."

"They're by the principal's office," she said as Kyle continued to kiss down her neck.

"Dude, get a room."

"Dude, we did. Now get out. And shut the door behind you." Daniel chuckled as he left, but left the door open. Kyle wasn't letting up; he caressed her arms, drawing her in for more kisses.

"I should probably get back to work . . ."

He sighed. "So much for compromise," he said, throwing her own words back at her, and she smacked him with the back of her hand, laughing.

CHAPTER
THIRTY-ONE

WINNIE AND DANIEL'S big day was finally here, and Kyle couldn't wait for it to be over. Everyone was rushing around, too many women were wearing perfume, and he couldn't find Ainsley. Daniel was already standing at the altar, and they were supposed to be starting the procession. He was supposed to walk her down the aisle, and she'd gone off looking for a safety pin for one of the other bridesmaids who was having an issue with her dress. Every room he ducked his head into made him more anxious . . . He started whistling just to calm his nerves as he opened the door to the nursery when he heard her voice behind him.

"There you are!"

He turned, and all the upset words he'd been cueing up died on his lips. Her long hair was curled in large rings, her fingernails were painted in ombré hues of pink, both courtesy of his mom. Her dress was asymmetrical, only over one shoulder, but for once, he didn't think about how she must be cold or how things should be even. He thought about the long slit up the side of the dusty-pink dress. He thought about her perfect lips, painted in a slightly darker shade.

"Kyle!" She snapped her fingers, as if to break his trance. "Come on, honey, we gotta get this party started! Winnie's mom is freaking out." She grabbed his hand and dragged him back toward the doors to the sanctuary. It only gave him the opportunity to examine the dress's fit from behind (very nice), and he couldn't help but think that maybe he should let her lead him around more often. Had he been going about this all wrong, all this time? He'd been trying to push in all these directions, but maybe the trick was just to let yourself be dragged along once in a while.

They got in line at the doors, and Ainsley was fussing with her dress and hair, touching her face self-consciously, picking at her bouquet.

"Hey."

She looked up at him, her blue eyes wide.

"You're the most beautiful woman here."

Ainsley gave him a small smile. "You're supposed to tell the bride that."

"The statement stands for itself."

She grinned at him, and he wanted to bottle her up for drearier days. He'd meant what he said in her classroom; she was his sunshine, today and every day. She tipped her face up like she wanted a kiss, and he bent his head down obediently; it was going to be easier than normal since she was wearing such tall shoes . . .

"Hey!" Dr. Baker hissed. "None of that. Get going down the aisle. Right, together, left, together."

Kyle straightened, his face hot at having been caught in a moment of indulgence by the mother of the bride and his colleague. He offered his arm to Ainsley, who took it, giggling.

"Never seen you blush before," she whispered as they slowly moved down the aisle.

"Your fault," he mumbled, and she giggled again, squeezing his arm.

They parted ways at the foot of the steps to the stage, but he didn't take his eyes off her the whole ceremony. He couldn't. He had Daniel and Winnie's rings on his little finger, as the wedding coordinator had commanded, but in his inside jacket pocket, he had one more. One that had been burning a hole in his pocket for weeks . . . He just couldn't seem to find the right time to ask her. Her apartment was too mundane. There were too many people at school and at the build site. He wasn't one for audiences for landmark moments in life, but given their history, he felt she needed a grand gesture.

Listening to the pastor's classic platitudes on marriage, an idea formed in his mind. He'd need some help . . . but he was getting better at asking for it. The community loved her; they'd love to be involved in his proposal. He'd almost worked it out when the ceremony ended, and Daniel and Winnie were retreating down the aisle again. He picked up Ainsley, trying to ignore how loud the music was.

"You okay?"

"Yes." He squeezed her hand. "Never been better."

Daniel had made him promise to stay until the toasts, so he was standing around watching Maggie cut cake when Mr. Buchanan appeared at his elbow.

"Hey, Doc. Good wedding."

"Yes, sir."

"Congrats to your brother, they seem like a nice couple. Known him a long time."

"Yes, I agree." They stood in silence for a minute before Gary cleared his throat.

"Look, Doc, I want to declare a truce." He was being too formal; if this man was going to be his father-in-law, he needed to try to loosen up around him.

"Please, call me Kyle."

Gary adjusted his tie, as if it were too tight. "I know I haven't exactly been real friendly, Kyle, but all you did for me in the scare the other day at the site, and then the way you defended Ainsley at the fall festival . . . well, I just wanted to extend a hand in friendship. That flap about the mailbox is all but forgotten."

Kyle reached out and shook Gary's offered hand firmly. "Thank you, Mr. Buchanan, I appreciate that, but . . . what mailbox?"

Gary paused for a moment, unsure. Then he groaned. "You've got to be kidding me."

"I'm afraid not. I have no idea what you're talking about."

"Bet I know who would," Gary muttered, pivoting to look around the narthex.

"Just a minute, sir. While I've got you, I did have something I wanted to ask you . . ."

SHE KNEW THEY WERE standing behind her even before she turned . . . Her boyfriend and her father wore twin expressions of ire, arms crossed over their chests.

"Can I . . . help you?" she asked, cognizant that she was definitely the source of their upset.

"That depends," her father replied. "It seems Kyle here doesn't know a thing about what happened to my mailbox."

"Oh, really?" Her voice was small and squeaky, mouse-like. Even she wasn't buying her innocent act. It was beyond pathetic. She cleared her throat. "Well, I guess we'll never know what happened."

"I think someone does know," Gary said. His voice might appear casual to those ignorant of his ways, but Ainsley knew better. "I think she knows exactly what happened, and yet, she's been letting me hold a grudge against her boyfriend for no good reason."

"Okay, look," she said forcefully, "it was right when all that happened with Shane and I was under a lot of pressure at school and was backing out of the driveway while I checked my phone because it dinged with a notification, and I hit your stupid, ugly mailbox and then you assumed it was Kyle and I just didn't correct you and all this time I've kept trying to find a good time to tell you and it just didn't want to be found, and I'm sorry to both of you." She sucked in a shuddering breath. That felt good to get off her chest.

"Ainsley." Kyle was still glaring at her. "Would you like a hug?"

"Yes, please." He shuffled forward and gathered her tight in his arms.

"How many more of these traumatic past events are we going to uncover, do you think?"

"Oh, I don't know . . . not too many more, I don't think."

He squeezed her tighter.

CHAPTER
THIRTY-TWO

THE BIG DAY HAD FINALLY come. Most of Timber Falls had come out despite the rain. It was one already, time to get things underway, but she hadn't seen her father yet. Ainsley wove her way through the groups of people standing around, feeling anxious. Where was he? Had something happened? In all the excitement, had he forgotten breakfast? She tried to open her phone, but the screen was dappled with rain and wouldn't recognize her thumbprint.

"Ainsley!" It was Bilqiis, Abshir, and Fawzia, cutting toward her through the throng. Bilqiis wore a bright-red hijab over a red, gold, and brown striped dress, the fabric crisscrossing over her chest. Ainsley felt a twinge of jealousy at how amazing she looked.

"Bilqiis! You're here! Have you seen my dad?"

"He is inside, in the kitchen with your husband."

Ainsley sighed. "He's not my husband, Bilqiis." *Not even close.* They had only been dating a few months, she reminded herself. There was time. There was time for all of it. No rush. She was getting used to the way things were. And things were good.

239

She stuck her head into the house. "Dad! Come on, people are getting wet out here."

"Coming, kiddo!"

She heard Kyle's voice say something in a low tone, and her father chuckled. Those two were thick as thieves ever since they'd figured out her mailbox omission. She didn't trust them . . . They were cooking something up.

"All right," her dad boomed, coming out onto the front porch, clapping his hands. "All right, attention, please! We'll try to keep this short." The crowd quieted, straining to hear him over the drops of rain trickling through the gutters and onto the front yard. "The Sadiq family—all of them—have put an enormous amount of time and energy into this home. And this is their *home*. By coming here, you are welcoming them into the community wholeheartedly. They've asked me to thank everyone for the hours they spent building, their instructors for their financial education and home ownership classes, and those who donated furnishings for the house, especially my daughter, Ainsley Buchanan." She blushed at that, shooting a glare at Bilqiis, who smiled back at her. "Please join me in welcoming this family home."

Abshir produced scissors and cut the ribbon they'd placed across the door. The whoops, yells, and applause that went up from the assembled group brought other neighbors out of their houses. Abshir held up his hands for quiet. The soft-spoken man shouted, "You can all come inside, but take off your shoes first!" The crowd laughed, and they shuffled forward. For the next hour, Ainsley chatted, laughed, and hugged her building cohorts. She would see them again in the spring for another build, but she'd miss them in the meantime.

The party was winding down when Fawzia came up to her, hands behind her back.

"Put your hands out, Miss Buchanan." Ainsley obeyed, but Fawzia added, "And close your eyes."

Ainsley scowled at her. "I'm not going to get anything alive in my hands, am I?"

"No, miss. Please, miss?"

Begrudgingly, she did as she was asked, and felt cold cardboard in her hands.

"Okay, open them!" She held a small box the size of a CD case in robin's egg blue.

"Okay, what now?" she asked, and Fawzia laughed.

"Now open it, silly!"

Cautiously, still unsure whether this was a trick, she pried open the lid gently. Inside, in Kyle's square handwriting, was an index card which read

"But the strong base and building of my love is as the very centre of the earth, drawing all things to it."
—William Shakespeare

This house is where we started building a relationship, but where did it all start? Go to the place I used to drop you off after school.

What? What was this? She looked around, but didn't see his dark head anywhere nearby.

"Where is he, Fawzia?"

"Follow the directions. That's all I can tell you." She giggled, bouncing on her toes. The girl mimed locking her lips and throwing away the key, and Ainsley laughed. She pulled out her phone.

Ainsley: What are you doing?

Kyle: ☺

Ainsley: Kyle?

Kyle: Follow the directions, Ainsley.

Ainsley: Is this because I said we never do stuff in Timber Falls? Because I'm over that.

Ainsley: I know you love me, babe.

No response? Huh. No response. Well. Confused, but curious, she said goodbye to a grinning Bilqiis, then grabbed her purse and keys and hurried out to her car. She drove back to Timber Falls, straight to her parents' house, as fast as the law would allow, but there were no more text messages from him when she arrived. The man himself was nowhere to be seen. Apparently, as usual, he intended to be a man of mystery. Her mom met her at the door, grinning from ear to ear.

"It's in the mailbox."

She rolled her eyes. Of course it was. She found the same blue box. Inside, another note:

> *"Oh, you've got the future in your hand. / Signed, sealed, delivered, I'm yours."* —Stevie Wonder

> *You lied about the fate of this mailbox's predecessor, which was very naughty. Go to the chair with this name for your next clue.*

Her mouth dropped open, and she looked at her mother with wide eyes. *The future? Is he . . . ? No. He couldn't mean that, he probably didn't realize how it sounded. Just a fun date.* "Did he break into the school on a Sunday?"

Nancy grinned. "Now, does that sound like something Kyle would do, or something *you* would do?"

"Point taken. I just can't believe he inconvenienced someone to—" Ainsley said, heading back to her car, then noticed that her mother was getting on her trench coat and walking shoes. "Where are you going?"

"I have somewhere to be." Her mother grinned, shrugging her shoulders, and gave her a quick hug.

Shaking her head, Ainsley got back into her truck and headed for the school. All the lights were already on, and the front door was propped open, which was handy, since she hadn't stopped by her apartment to pick up her ID badge. She was so flustered that she hadn't even thought of it. She ran through the halls to her classroom, hoping he'd be there, only to find Daniel waiting with the next box. She didn't bother with pleasantries and ripped into it without reservation this time.

> *"The giving of love is an education in itself." —Eleanor Roosevelt*

> *You do so much good for the community on the PTA and all your other committees . . . Go to the place where we'll be sitting together at town meetings from now on.*

Those last three words had tears and laughter bubbling up out of her, and she looked at Daniel in disbelief. "Did you help him with this?"

"Just a little bit," he said, winking. "This part? This was all him." He put his hands on her shoulders. "Now if you'll excuse me, I have somewhere to be."

"Wait," she called. She didn't want to ask him, but she needed to know. She'd never asked Daniel's opinion on the two of them. He turned back to her. "You never pushed us together. Did you not . . ."

"Oh, no," he said, hurrying back over to grip her shoulders. "It just . . . Kyle's got to do things his own way. When I tried to talk to him about you, he'd just shut down. So I decided to stay out of it and let nature take its course. Or rather, let our nephew's misunderstanding light a fire under his grumpy butt."

She choked out a laugh, wiping away another tear. "I know, right? So grumpy."

"The grumpiest," he agreed.

"Okay. But just so you know, I think I finally picked a favorite Durand."

Daniel grinned as he pulled her into a long, best-friend-sized hug, which she ardently returned. He put his jacket back on. "I'll see you later." He hurried out of the classroom, and she took the time to turn off the lights and lock her door before she followed him. The VA hall wasn't far. And given the situation at the school, she was fairly sure she'd be able to get inside.

"Hey," Starla greeted her softly, looking up from her novel, then tipped her head toward Ainsley's normal seat in the fifth row, where her next box was waiting.

> *"Love is something sent from heaven to worry the hell out of you." —Dolly Parton*

*When I was worried about your car door, this is who I
asked to fix it.*

Ainsley paused, perplexed. She'd only been to Philip's
house once, when they dropped off Orangesicle. She knew it
was on Coral Street, but she wasn't 100 percent sure which one
was his . . . Seeing her hesitation, Starla silently produced a second index card from her back pocket.

*Philip's address is 103 W. Coral. Blue house, red front
door, white shutters. Can't miss it.*

Ainsley threw back her head and laughed, then gave her
helper a big kiss on the cheek. "Thanks, Star." She paused. "Is
this really happening?"

"It really is." Starla smiled back. "And it's about time."

"Looks like we're both making big life changes..."

Her smile didn't dim. "I guess so."

Ainsley shot out the doors as her friend chuckled. *How
many people are going to be at this thing, anyway?* She couldn't
use the word *proposal*. Not yet. Her mind crackled trying to figure out what spot he'd pick for the culmination. Not that she
was going to try to skip to the end; she wasn't going to miss a
moment of the adventure he'd planned for her. Full of nervous
energy, she decided to just run to Philip's . . . It was only half a
mile. She arrived on his doorstep, damp and sweaty, hand out.

"Did something happen to your car?" he asked, concerned,
but she shook her head, gasping for breath. Cooper bounced
in front of her like he was on a trampoline, and she gratefully
took the box from him.

"Thanks, kiddo."

"I love her and it is the beginning of everything." –F. Scott Fitzgerald

You're getting close now! Find the place we first shared a piece of wedding cake.

"Do you want a ride back to your truck?" Philip asked, putting on his shoes.

"Let me guess, you've got somewhere important to be, but you can drop me on your way?"

Philip grinned, bouncing his eyebrows. "Coop, get your shoes on, dude! You're not going to want to miss this."

Ainsley climbed into Philip's minivan in the passenger seat, and he dropped her off at the VA with a wave. She climbed back into her truck; the church was on the edge of town, by the river, up toward the falls. It would take a few minutes to get there. All the way there, she gripped the steering wheel tight, hoping like crazy this was her last stop.

Her heart fell a little when she saw Hattie, her hat dripping from the drizzle.

"Hello, Miss Ainsley," she called. "Got something for you!"

"Am I getting close?" Ainsley called back, starting to despair.

Hattie chuckled. "This is the last one. Promise."

"I'm going to hold you to that," Ainsley muttered, pulling off the lid.

"Love makes your soul crawl out from its hiding place."
—Zora Neale Hurston

*What happened here hurt you. Find me where the
memes were made.*

"Why?" she sniffled, wiping her cold nose, searching Hattie's face. "Why did he pick the football field?"

"I spoke to him about that at length," she said, shaking her head slowly. "But he was adamant. He said he wants to help you put the past behind you. He wants to make the place of your greatest humiliation a place of joy instead, seeing all your friends and family cheering the both of you on."

So it wasn't just a date . . . He was really going to do this, in front of everyone, in that place. It wasn't like Ainsley hadn't been back there; she'd been many times since then. She'd cheered on the Timber Falls Loggers on Fridays during football season for years. But it felt different this time. She was getting rid of her own ghosts, choosing to make new memories, choosing to trust a new partner. And she did trust him.

"You want a ride?" Ainsley asked her.

"Truth be told, yes, I do. I walked for fear there would be no parking."

"How many people are coming to the end?" she asked.

"Well," Hattie said slowly, as she climbed into the truck, "there was an email that went around to just about everybody. So I'd say a couple hundred, easy."

"But surely they didn't all . . ." Ainsley's words cut off when she turned onto the street: Hattie's fears had not been unjustified. It was full. Cars were parked up and down the street, leading up to the actual parking lot, which was also full.

"Go ahead and pull up to the front doors," Hattie directed. "I happen to know there'll be a spot for you up there." In the spot designated for the teacher of the month stood Gary Buchanan, arms crossed, looking imposing. He moved aside for her, then opened her door.

"Took your sweet time, kiddo. I had to fight them off with a stick."

She laughed and gave him a quick squeeze. "Is this legal?"

"My buddies at the station assure me that it is. Well, saving the spot is legal. I don't know about some of the parking jobs of these people. I think that Tahoe might be blocking a fire hydrant . . ."

"Let's get inside," she said, starting into the gym, when he caught her arm.

"He's on the field."

"Still? In this weather?"

Gary shrugged. "He said it had to be on the field. Told everyone to dress warmly. Everyone except you, apparently."

Her face hurt. It hurt, twisted hard by too many emotions. Grief, peace, delight, amusement, acceptance, love. So much love for this man. Without waiting for Hattie and her dad, she took off running for the football field; she couldn't wait anymore. Kyle was pacing on the fifty-yard line, looking tense even from such a distance.

When the people filling the stands caught sight of her, they started cheering, and Kyle's head snapped up, searching for her. She pounded across the field at a dead run to him, mud flicking up the back of her jeans, trying not to fall on the slick turf.

"You could've let them go into the gym," she panted as she approached, but Kyle just took her in his arms and kissed her like he hadn't seen her in a week instead of a few hours.

"Did you like my surprise?" he asked, nervously searching her gaze, and Ainsley laughed.

"Of course I did, I loved it." She kissed him again. "Are you going to get down on one knee in the mud?"

He grimaced. "I think they'll revolt if I don't," he said, casting a quick glance toward the hundreds of people in the stands, waving signs. "I regret inviting them."

"No, you don't," she said, pulling him close by his jacket, her breath warming the space between them. "I know you don't."

"You're right, I don't. I wanted you to see how many people love you, Ainsley. It's not just me, it's all of us. I'm the one asking you to marry me today, but I'm also asking you to really see how much you mean to us. To all of us."

He did drop to his left knee, making a face that the crowd was thankfully too far away to see clearly. Their noise ratcheted up another ten decibels. He pulled a ring off his pinky finger: a diamond solitaire.

"Ainsley Rose Buchanan, I love you. I know there are plenty of reasons you thought me getting closer to you was a mistake—we're not all that alike, really. But you know what's important in life, and you teach me new things every time we're together." He paused. "And you're really, really beautiful. Like, anyone you see on TV? Garbage. That's nothing compared to you. I really want to marry you and keep you right next to me forever and try to procreate together. So will you?"

She took a beat just to soak it all in, look around at all the love that was being poured out on her right at that second. Then she got down on her knees in the mud with him and nodded. Kyle slipped the ring on her hand with a grin, then kissed her again as the spectators rushed the field. Before she knew it, their "private" moment was gone, and they were being hauled up, slapped on the back, and handed a thermos of hot cocoa and a wool blanket. Kyle did allow the party to move inside now that she'd said yes, but he couldn't stay long because of the noise. Ainsley left with him; that's just where she wanted to be. With Kyle, from now on.

CHAPTER
THIRTY-THREE

THE NEXT FRIDAY, KYLE picked her up for the town meeting as promised. They were still in the parking lot when the well-wishers started up.

"Ainsley!" She turned to see Councilman Park striding toward her, his hand out. She shook his hand as he grinned at her. "Heard your big news. Congratulations!"

"Oh." She blushed. "Thank you, Councilman Park."

"I'm sure you'll have a lot to do for your wedding, but I was wondering if you'd consider heading up the town's birthday celebration this year. It shouldn't be too much work . . . Cindy Mellerman left all her notes from last year, but we really want to make it a special event . . ."

She opened her mouth to say yes, but caught Kyle's grimace out of the corner of her eye. She turned toward him. He'd erased the displeasure from his face, which was back to a stony neutral, but it was too late. She'd already seen it. *And he's right. I've got nothing to prove. Not anymore.* She turned back to Councilman Park.

"Oh, I'm sorry, but I just don't have time. I hope it's a wonderful event, and I'll look forward to attending."

His posture wilted. "Oh no. The other committee members will be so disappointed. I told them they'd have a ringer to help them; they're all new at this, they've never even been to the event before. You've been such a pillar in the life of the town all these years, I was just sure you'd say yes . . ."

Ainsley bristled a little at that, but she smoothed her emotions down before she replied. "Yes, well, I'm going to be a pillar from the sidelines for a little while. It's a needed change. Self-care and all that."

"We need to go inside now," Kyle said, taking her hand, giving it an affectionate squeeze. "Nice to see you, Councilman Park."

"Yes, well, congratulations again. Hope to be invited to the big day!"

"We'll be sending out invitations later this month," he said. "It's likely that you'll receive one."

The short man beamed, nodding, then hurried away.

"We may need a bigger venue," Kyle mused as he watched him go. "There are more people who want to attend than I anticipated. You're a very popular person. I gave your parents a budget estimate based on the preliminary research that I'd done, but if we want this many people to attend, we may need to—"

Ainsley tugged his head down to her level and kissed him. It wasn't much, just a moment of closeness, an implied thank-you. "Don't worry about the budget," she murmured. "My dad's got it covered."

"We don't want to bankrupt him."

"We won't." She kissed him again. "But thank you for the thought you've put into it." Her words pleased him, she could tell. "Do we really need to go inside?"

"No. I was just proud of you for saying no, and it seemed like a good moment to slip away before you changed your mind."

"Smart man." She let him stand up straight, grinning, biting her lip. "Also, when you weren't here, I agree to make Maggie a bridesmaid to make your mom happy."

He threw up his hands. "But that throws off the numbers, because I only have three groomsmen! You agreed, you said that you'd ask Starla, Winnie, and your sister!"

"But then I added one more." She shrugged. "It doesn't have to be even."

Kyle stared at her, mouth gaping, then finally snapped it shut. "We have very different expectations."

"So it would seem." She nodded. "If you want to explain to your mom why Maggie can't be a bridesmaid, that's fine with me."

His shoulders slumped. "No. I don't. But I know Maggie doesn't want to be involved in that way. She doesn't like dressing up. What if we made her an usher or something? We already made Coop the ring bearer, and Philip and Daniel are groomsmen. Does *everyone* in my family need to be in the wedding party?"

"It's nice to be loved, isn't it?"

"I can be loved from a distance. In fact, it's my preferred method."

"Even with me?" She grinned at him, and he gave her a begrudging smile.

"No. Not with you. You, I want to keep right next to me, not only so that you'll quit messing up my wedding. But you're the only one."

She put her hands on her hips in mock consternation. "Messing up *your* wedding?"

"Did I stutter?"

"No," she laughed. "But isn't it mine, too?"

"You are essential, but I have dibs. I've been thinking about it much longer."

"I see," she said. "Well, in that case, I get to plan the honeymoon."

His eyes flared with interest. "No. I should have *some* input . . ."

"Nope. This is great, this is perfect. You plan the wedding, I'll show up for the dress fitting, just let me know when. And I'll plan the honeymoon, don't worry about it. Even division of labor."

"Someone told me life isn't about fairness."

"She sounds smart. Pack a swimsuit. There will be a water park."

"What? No, Ainsley. I don't want to get dragged up and down the coast on our honeymoon; all I want to do is stay in and . . ." His voice trailed off, and he glanced around to see who was listening.

"Yes?" she prompted. "You want to stay in and what? Do puzzles? Play chess? Good, I already put that stuff on the list, too."

"Oh, for Pete's sake," he grumped. "You're impossible. You cannot manipulate me with sex."

"Pretty sure I can, actually." She licked her bottom lip suggestively, and he pressed closer into her. "Let Maggie be in the wedding, or you'll have to go down a water slide inside a defunct airplane in McMinnville. It's approximately two hours from where we're staying. Each way." Ainsley relished the ensuing staring contest. It was the only time she really got his full gaze, when he was trying to change her mind. It was lucky for her that her dragon only used his powers for good, because his pretty brown eyes were certainly mesmerizing her.

Shaking his head, he pulled out his phone. "I guess I could ask Greg Trout in order to even up the numbers. But we're not really that close . . . Maybe my cousin Jack would do it."

"Or we could ask Sawyer."

"Sawyer?"

"Yeah, you know, my cousin, Sawyer. Tall, blond, flannel, muscles."

"Oh, right. I know him." His gaze went distant as he thought. "Yes. That would be fine. He has a family connection, and I find his company very tolerable."

"He hardly says anything."

"Exactly. He'll be fine. I approve."

"And my mother and my aunt Rhea will be happy, because he won't be able to find an excuse not to come." She squeezed him around the waist. "Are you sure we can't elope?"

"Positive. This is how it's done. Rituals are important."

"You're right. About this. Not about everything."

He kissed her again. "Now, speaking of rituals, about this honeymoon . . ."

EPILOGUE

THREE YEARS LATER

"Are you ready? Are you pumped? Are you jazzed? Are your muscles warm? Do you want me to rub your shoulders? I think that's a thing people do before races. Do you want me to hold your sweatshirt? Is your number on securely enough?" Ainsley peppered Fawzia with questions, and the eleven-year-old girl made eye contact with her husband meaningfully.

"I know," Kyle said. "I'm sorry. She has a lot of energy these days. Please be patient with her." His own patience had been stretched thin the last few weeks, ever since school had let out. Now that they were done turning Daniel's old room into the nursery, it seemed his wife had nothing to do. His impression had been that pregnancy made women tired and lethargic. He should've known that would not apply to his favorite go-getter. Starla had suggested that she do a daily summer story time, and he owed her big time for that. He was half-tempted to go back to working nights, just until the babies were born . . .

Ainsley rubbed her seven-month pregnant belly resentfully. "Excuse you, I'm just being supportive. Unlike you."

"How am I not being supportive?" Kyle adjusted his red Stanford baseball hat. "I'm here, standing in the sun, ready to watch. That's supportive."

"You're squelching my enthusiasm," Ainsley announced too loudly, and several people around them chuckled. Kyle rolled his eyes.

"Back up, Miss B," Fawzia instructed, shooing her away from the starting line. "I'll be fine."

Kyle gently urged her back into the stands. They sat on the metal bleachers of the high school. Their engagement here seemed like ages ago. So much had happened since then. Twins. He still couldn't quite get over the shock; they didn't know yet if they were identical or fraternal, but they were both boys. Now he'd have to get her pregnant again to get a girl as well—not that that was a hardship. However protective he'd felt of Ainsley before they were married was nothing compared to now, with her pregnant with their boys. He would soon have three lives to care for. The very idea had his leg bouncing rapidly again, shaking the metal bench.

Ainsley put a hand on his knee. "Are you nervous for her? I know it's her first race, but I think she'll do great."

He took a deep breath and let it out slow, trying to calm himself down.

"I'm sure she will," he agreed. Ainsley had set all this up, as usual. A kids' run had never been part of the Fourth of July before, but now it would be. *See? Not all change is bad. Not all unexpected things are unwelcome. Twins will be fine. We'll all be fine. If I can live with Ainsley's mess and unpredictability, I can be a father. I can do this.*

"Why aren't Bilqiis and Abshir here yet? They're going to miss it!"

Kyle scanned the crowd with her; two dark heads, one covered, were down front. "There they are." Ainsley stood up to see better just as the starting gun went off.

She squealed, bouncing up and down, holding up her sign, which read "That's my friend!" He'd rolled his eyes last night when she'd explained to him that it had to be appropriately "rainbow-fied" when he was trying to get her to come to bed at a decent time. But now, he had to begrudgingly agree: it certainly stood out. Kyle hugged her just to keep her from jumping. He was far more used to PDA now, but it was still mostly utilitarian out here. Behind closed doors was another story . . .

"Go, Fawzia! Run, run, run!" There was no reason for her to shout so loudly. The girl had a significant lead, and she was definitely going to win. When she crossed the finish line, Kyle braced himself for Ainsley to go nuts, screaming and clapping. When she was silent, he turned to her; she was crying, fat tears running down her beautiful cheeks. He took her face in both hands.

"Are you in pain? Did your water break? What's happening?"

"Kyle, relax," she laughed, choking out the words. "I'm just happy for Fawzia."

He sighed in relief, tipping his hat up to bring their foreheads together. "Pregnancy hormones."

"Could be," she agreed, and as she pressed her sun-warmed lips to his, Kyle couldn't help but be glad that his nephew was such a bad listener.

"Love you, Ains."

"I love you, too." She grinned. "Now, celebratory ice cream at 22 Below. We promised." She bounced her eyebrows at him. "Are my chances of getting lucky any better this time?"

He dropped his voice so as not to be heard by the people around them, who were rushing toward the track to congratulate Fawzia. "I've been researching better positions for late pregnancy, so definitely. Yes."

She tossed back her head and laughed, the sun shining off her golden hair. "You, Dr. Durand, were so worth the wait."

Would you write a
review?

Kyle and Ainsley, they make quite a pair.
If you agree, do you think you could share
on Goodreads or Amazon, wherever you lurk?
I'll tell you a secret: it so helps my work.
And getting to hear that you loved them, too?
Well, it makes my whole week. Believe me. It's true.

There's a reason why I'm a novelist and not a poet, but in all seriousness, I would be so appreciative if you could spread the word about this series! It's a huge help to my business. Thanks!

Don't miss a moment of Timber Falls fun!

Could Be Something Good (Daniel and Winnie)
Must be a Mistake (Kyle and Ainsley)
Right Back Where We Started (Martina and Crash—keep
reading for a sneak peek!)

Coming Winter 2020...

More Than We Bargained For (Starla and Sawyer)
Never Say Never (Lizzie and Chase)
Maybe It's Just Me (Maggie and R.J.)

Also by Fiona West

The Borderline Chronicles (sweet fantasy romance)

The Ex-Princess: a chronically-ill princess who fled from her responsibilities is forced to face the fiancé she abandoned and journey across a magically-unpredictable continent. Can she keep the life she's given up everything to build?

The Un-Queen: a king caught between love and legality...can Abbie and Edward's relationship survive engagement and the opposition who wants to tear them apart again?

The Jinxed Journalist: a single mother gets her dream job as a journalist, only to find herself caught in royal scandal, opposing her son's new mentor. When forced to choose between love and her career, can she still come out a winner?

The Semi-Royal: a doctor takes an expedition with her brother's best friend that has life-changing results. Can she resist the underlying attraction that's been there for years?

The Almost-Widow: a security professional finds herself paired with a shy, sensory-sensitive man on the night watch. Can their friendship blossom into something more?

Right Back Where
We Started, coming
July 24th, 2020!

Read on for a sneak peek!

CARTER PACED IN THE foyer, his bare feet wearing a track in the red Persian rug. She would be here any minute. Martina. The one who got away, she was coming. He wasn't ready. Well, he *was* ready; he'd told his mom and the other people who needed to know and the house was clean and he was nicely dressed. But when Cindy called, she'd said Martina wanted to meet with him and his mom before she accepted the job, and he sure as heck wasn't ready for *that*. Every time he made another lap, his stomach twisted tighter and tighter, like an alarm clock being wound.

Tires on the driveway gravel. *They're here, they're here. Don't freak out.* He pulled back the curtains to see them. Martina wore a pale blue polo shirt with the company logo, her hair pulled back in a thick ponytail. She'd obviously straightened it first, then curled the ends. Her height was more obvious next to her boss, who wasn't exactly short. She was still beautifully curvy, and she kept tugging at the hem of the shirt, like she felt it was too short. Maybe she was just nervous. Of course she was nervous. The real question was what had changed her mind. She hadn't even looked at him the last time she came here; now she was here preparing to accept his job offer.

They rang the bell, and he waited two seconds before opening the door. "Hello again."

Cindy smiled brightly. "Hello, Mr. Carpenter, I'm Cindy Hewes. It's so good to see you again." She stepped into the foyer, and Carter could see the way she appreciated the understated opulence. Some people needed to have a flashy house, a place that proved they'd made it. That wasn't Harrison and Willow Carpenter. Their wealth showed, of course: bamboo floors, paintings that had to be worth millions on the walls, the household staff standing by, the room by room environmental and stereo controls. No random statues or fountains here, no marble. But he'd always found their house very comfortable, very lived-in. He and his brothers Chase and Christopher had left their soccer stuff by the front door like regular teenagers, and their mother hadn't let the staff pick it up for them.

Then he turned his attention to Martina; there was a challenge there, in her gaze.

She stuck out her right hand. "Mr. Carpenter. Nice to see you again."

Crash cringed internally at her formal greeting, but he accepted her firm handshake, gesturing her inside. "Mom," he called, up the stairs. "Your new helper is here."

Willow appeared at the top of the stairs. Her hair was thrown up into a haphazard bun, and she wore thick glasses. Her yoga pants and t-shirt from last year's Turkey Trot were clean, but until she started having problems, he'd rarely seen her in anything but Chanel, Dolce and Gabbana, Versace. Certainly never in tennis shoes, unless she was actually running, and even then... He glanced at Martina for a reaction, but her face was carefully pleasant.

Willow's face lit when she saw Martina. "Darling! They didn't tell me you were coming." Carter wished he could sit down; every time she said something like that, he wanted to bang his head against something.

"Hello, Mrs. Carpenter," Martina smiled. "How are you?"

Willow came barreling down the stairs so fast, Carter was surprised she didn't face-plant. "What have you been up to? I want to hear everything." It lifted his spirits a little to see her enthusiastic response to the person he'd like to hire to care for her. It made him feel like maybe he was doing something right after all.

"Yes, I'd love to get caught up," she said, then glanced at Carter. "Let's all go sit in the library," he suggested, and Willow started in that direction, then stopped.

"Who's *she*?" There was an ice to her words that Carter still wasn't used to. She was staring daggers at Cindy, who just smiled kindly.

"Oh, I'm a friend of Martina's," she said, extending a hand. "I'm Cindy." *Sort of true.* She must work with clients like this all the time; she probably had lots of tricks up her sleeve. Keeping a wary eye on Cindy, Willow shook her hand, then gestured them toward the library, as if she was in charge of this meeting. She'd always had that air about her; every party, every benefit Carter had ever attended that Willow had had a hand in, she was the one people turned to with questions. And she always knew. Always. It was one of the things he'd been most sure of.

Martina settled into a deep burgundy, high-backed wing chair near the window while the rest of them took the couches. This was the room where he'd introduced her to his parents, and he tried not to get lost in the memory...squeezing her hand, the polite pleasure on his mother's face, the unabashed rejection by his father.

"Mrs. Sanchez," Willow called, and the slender woman, dark-haired with gray highlights, appeared in the doorway. "Could you bring us some tea, please?" She nodded, then winked at Martina as she turned to go. That was a relief, at least; Mrs. Sanchez had always approved of her.

"So, tell us, darling, what have you been up to the last few years?" Willow asked.

"Well, I've been working as a nurse for a few years—"

"Have you really? That's what you always wanted to do, wasn't it? Do you remember, Carter?"

He nodded, his gaze on the unlit fireplace. He couldn't bear to see how she was reacting to all this. *Please, Martina. Please help us. Please don't walk away. I don't deserve it, but I need your help.*

"And now I've just gotten my degree in acute care to become a nurse practitioner."

Mom sat back hard in her chair, as if the news floored her. "Isn't that wonderful? I'm just so pleased for you, honey. Are you working with kids or adults or..."

"Adult Gerontology, actually," she said, and there was a strange note of apology in her tone.

"I see. Well, that's wonderful, honey." She hadn't used her name yet, and Carter wondered if she remembered it. She knew who she was, knew they were acquainted. Given how much time she'd spent here in high school, that wasn't surprising, but Carter was grateful. She was blowing up at him a lot. She knew she was forgetting. It would get easier once she didn't know, the internet and Dr. Rose had both promised. Carter wondered how long that would be. At any rate, this wouldn't be a quick assignment. This would be years. Did that change things?

"How about you, Mrs. Carpenter? What have you been up to lately?"

"Oh," she waved away the question, "you know. This and that. I haven't done many events lately. All the groups have gone all to seed, those women were impossible to work with. So I've stepped back to let others take the lead for a while. I'm sure they'll realize that my way is better, eventually."

"You were always a huge asset for the Ladies' Auxiliary, I remember that. No one planned events like yours."

Willow blushed, and Martina smiled at her. Mrs. Sanchez came back in with a silver tray and four steaming cups of tea. She stopped first near Willow's chair, offering her one.

"Who's that for?" Willow asked.

Mrs. Sanchez's face stayed calm, like she'd been expecting the response. She probably did at this point. "You asked for tea, Mrs. Carpenter."

"Who, me? No, I didn't. You need a vacation, Mrs. Sanchez," she giggled, making a face at Martina that said, 'can you believe her?' Mrs. Sanchez shot Martina a pained look at that, a silent plea. *Help us*, her eyes said. *We don't know what to do with her anymore. Help us, please.* At least he wasn't the only one begging. Silently, she moved on to Carter, who also silently refused it, rubbing his forehead. He lifted his head and took Willow's hand.

"Mom," he said gently, "Martina's going to be here with you during the day while I'm at work."

His mother brushed imaginary crumbs from her pants. "Why, is she shadowing me for an internship or something?"

"You know she's not."

Willow's lip trembled. "Is it because I fell? I won't get on the rolling chair again."

"No, no, it's nothing you did wrong. Remember how we talked about your memory issues? It's because of that. That's all, that's the only reason. Martina's a professional, and she can take really excellent care of you. I just don't want you to be in need when I'm not here."

"What was the diagnosis?" Willow asked, fiddling with the edge of her shirt.

"Early-onset Alzheimer's. When you hurt your wrist, Dr. Durand, he referred us to a neurologist, remember?"

"Doctor..." She swallowed hard. "Dr. Rose."

Carter felt as proud as if she were a child who'd just written her name for the first time. "That's right, Dr. Rose. And she'll help you remember to take your medications."

"And we can get caught up," she said, casting a shy glance at Martina.

"That's right," Martina said, smiling. "It's been too long, anyway. We always had a wonderful time together, didn't we?" They did; it wasn't manipulative to say so. It was the absolute truth.

Willow's eyes filled with tears. "I'm sorry," she whispered. "I'm sorry that I'm such trouble. I'm not trying to be." He pulled her toward him and squeezed her tight into his side on the couch. She cried into his shoulder, and he pinched his eyes shut so tight, his whole face screwed shut, trying not to cry, letting her wipe her face on his nice shirt. As Willow began to wind down, Martina moved over to the couch, sitting next to him.

"Willow, it would be my honor to take care of you. Will you let me? I want to make this as painless as possible for you. For all of you." His heart swelled with relief, and he took the first deep breath he'd taken in days, but the tears were threatening to fall more than ever now.

Cindy piped up. "Our company has been providing this kind of care for many years. Our employees are always professional and have the best training available. Ms. Lopez will be no different."

"Well," Willow said with a watery smile, lifting her head, "if it's necessary, I'm glad it's this one." This one; she couldn't remember her name. "I know you," she said, reaching out a hand, and Martina took it immediately, letting their joined hands rest on his knees. He felt the irony of being caught between them acutely.

"Yes, you know me," Martina smiled, and a single tear slid down her cheek. That had all his self-control eroding like a mudslide. "And I know you. I'll make sure we get you dressed to your usual standards. No more slumming for you, lady."

Willow looked down at her clothes, then laughed. "I do look a little casual, don't I?"

Martina hummed her agreement. "I'll have you back in Chanel in no time, if you want. We'll fix your makeup and your hair. Get you right again."

"Maybe we could go to the Ladies Auxiliary meeting...I don't know when it is, but..."

"We'll find out," Martina agreed, squeezing her hand. "It would be good to go. Familiar things are good right now. They'll help you feel calm."

Carter stared at her, needing to connect with her, thank her, get on his knees and kiss her beautiful feet. She, on the other hand, seemed to be pointedly avoiding his gaze. The ladies chatted for a few minutes longer, then Cindy gave them a subtle nod toward the door.

"We'll work out an official work schedule and use the pay contract we already established," Cindy said, standing from the wing back chair. "We'll be in touch, Mr. Carpenter."

"Please, call me Carter. Thank you so much, Cindy. Thank you both," he said, walking them to the door. Cindy was out the door already when he reached out to touch Martina's elbow.

"Don't," she said, her voice low. *Right.* He felt her coldness like a slap. Apparently, all the warmth she still had for Willow didn't extend to him. It shouldn't have surprised him...but it still hurt. But he couldn't afford to tick her off.

"I'm sorry," he said quickly, shoving his hands in his pants pockets. "I won't—I'm sorry."

"What do you want?"

"Can we talk? Tonight, once she's in bed?"

"I'm not coming here at night." Martina turned back toward the car.

"Annie's then. Please, Tini." She visibly straightened at the nickname, and he winced. *Don't overplay your hand, Carpenter.* "I just want to clear the air before you start work. Please."

She sighed, her breath fogging in the October cold. "Annie's. 9:00. Don't be late."

"I won't be late. Thank you."

"You're welcome, Mr. Carpenter." She hurried down the steps like she couldn't get away from him fast enough.

ANNIE'S WAS QUIET WHEN she walked in at 8:35. She'd wanted to get to pick their spot, giving him no opportunity to choose their former favorite booth. He was already there. He still looked very nervous, and she reminded herself that his emotional state was no longer her concern. That heart was off-limits. Big ol' "do not enter" sign there. Maybe she could get him to wear a t-shirt to that effect. She breathed a quiet sigh of thanks that he hadn't picked their old booth. She slid onto a stool at the bar and signaled Annie. The middle-aged white woman came over, wary.

"This is a familiar scene..." she said, drying a pint glass.

"No, it's not. A ginger ale, please."

"Get whatever you want, I'm buying." Carter pulled out his wallet.

"No." She put her hand over his, and he stilled, not looking at her. "Let's establish some ground rules, right now."

He slowly put his wallet away, nodding. "Okay."

"First of all, unless I am working at your house, I will provide my own food and drinks. This will not be a weekly or even monthly occurrence. I know there are times when we need to discuss things about your mother's care; those meetings should occur at the house during work hours. There will be no cutsie nicknames," she said, ticking the items off on her fingers, "there will be no incidental touching. There will be no discussion of the past unless it benefits your mother. What happened between us is ancient history."

Crash was spinning slightly on his stool, a power move that showed his abs off against his shirt, but his voice was small. "So I'm not allowed to call you Tini?"

"No. You may call me Ms. Lopez at work. And I'll call you Mr. Carpenter."

"Can I say something?"

She gestured for him to go ahead as she accepted her drink and took a sip.

"I just...I just really appreciate you doing this for me. I should've talked to you about it before I requested you through the agency. I was just afraid you'd say no."

"A heads up would have been nice," she agreed. "But having seen her in the grocery store...I understand."

"I needed you. She knows you, likes you. And I know we can both trust you completely." He lifted his ice-blue gaze to hers, and she saw how sincere he was. It was quite the switch from the brash, bossy young man she'd known before.

"How do you know I won't exact my revenge for our breakup?" She drew circles in the condensation on her glass with her thumb, letting it trickle down the glass.

"Because I know you, Ms. Lopez. You're a professional. You wouldn't do anything to my mom."

"True." She kicked a foot gently against his stool. "Do you have any conditions?"

Was that surprise on his face? Why shouldn't this go both ways? She shouldn't be the only one who got to dictate how things would be.

"I...I'm just so relieved you agreed to take the job, I don't think I deserve to put any conditions on it."

She lifted her hand to place it over his, then remember her own rule: *no incidental touching.* Harder than it looked, really.

"Of course you do," she said, flipping her part to the other side of her head with her one hand. "Come on. There must be something you want or don't want."

"Honestly, I...I don't know. I don't think so." He was staring down into his lager, which bubbled quietly. "I'm fine with whatever."

Crash's easy smile was missing. She realized she hadn't heard him laugh even once since she'd seen him at his house. "It's been a hard few months for you, hasn't it?" Damn it, they'd been together twenty minutes, and she was already plowing through the caution signs she'd set up for herself. *Stop it. Stick to the plan. Stop...caring.*

"I can't talk about this with you."

"You can if it's part of your mother's care."

"Ms. Lopez, I asked for you because it would comfort my mother." God, that sounded awful in his mouth. When someone's lips have kissed you, your professional name suddenly became repulsive falling from them. "I need your help, I do. And I knew you would want to help us if you could, because that's the kind of person you are. But honestly, I don't think I need to draw a lot of boundaries around our professional relationship, because I won't be around much. I'll pay you on time, through the agency. I know that the relationship that we had is gone now. I don't like it, but I know it." He took a long pull on his beer. "My therapist says it's good to accept things as they are, not as you want them to be. So I'm not trying to trick you or mislead you; I just need your help. And lucky for me, I can afford it." He turned to her more fully. "But if this is going to make you uncomfortable, I understand if you want to turn the job down."

"No..." He'd never been a bad guy; they'd just wanted different things. Different things that he hadn't bothered to clarify when she was talking about their future together...had he been selfish? Yes. He was still being selfish, really. Only a selfish person would ask their ex for such a personal favor. "No, it's all right. I'll take the job." At the same time, it was a job, not a favor. What was the worst case? He'd make a pass at her, and she'd have every right to tell Cindy that she wanted a new assignment.

No, her mind commented loudly, *the worst case is that he makes a pass at you, and you don't stop him, because you're lonely and you're still in love with him.* A new boyfriend would be essential, she'd already decided, just so that she had more incentive not to cheat with Crash. She'd never been unfaithful to a boyfriend. She wasn't going to start now. But ending up back in a relationship with him, as her employer? Cindy had already made it clear that was not an option. So she'd find another outlet for her romantic intentions...just a fling. Something to keep her mind off him.

"Here's the thing," he said, reaching for his wallet. "I want someone with real medical knowledge; lots of people can make sure she doesn't fall in the bath and wipe her mouth. I want someone who can make medical decisions, treatment decisions. I don't want her going back to the hospital; I mean, she can go see her neurologist when needed. But people are much more likely to die from a secondary infection during a hospital stay, and I don't want her to have to be hospitalized. So your role is going to be preventative as well."

"Well, I do have my Master's—"

"I know. And here's the last thing: I'm going to pay you what you're worth."

She sat up straighter. Her debts weren't drowning her, but she was treading water a little. Her father had paid for her undergrad, but she'd refused him for her master's out of pride. It was a decision she was proud of, looking back. But the way he was talking now made her nervous.

"What does that mean?"

"It means Cindy and I came up with a number, and you're not going to argue about it."

"But I don't have any real experience yet..."

"I don't care. You have the experience I care about, and that's a relationship with my mom that has positive associations for her. And your education makes you very valuable to me as an employee."

"I see. And what number is this?"

He did smile then, just half of one, just a hint of it, really, the left side of his mouth hitching up. "You'll find out when you get paid." He drained the rest of his drink and dropped a twenty on the bar. "Thanks, Annie," he called, then turned to Martina. "Can I walk you to your car?"

"No, I think I'll stay for a while."

Crash frowned a little, then shrugged. "Suit yourself. See you Monday."

"Okay." As she watched him walk away, she couldn't help but shake her head. She'd walked in here so ready to lay down the law with him...and now, all that fire was gone. Dust. Cold. Crash was broken. And if there was anything Martina couldn't stand, it was watching someone she cared about be broken.

"Didn't think I'd ever see you two back here together again..." Annie said, her voice low under the chatter of the game on the TV.

"Me neither." Martina wiped her mouth. "But it wasn't a date. This is just business."

"Uh-huh. Is that why he paid Gray and Booker $20 to move somewhere else?"

She sighed, letting her head fall to her arms. "This is a mistake, isn't it?" Martina was all about learning from experience, she just preferred that it be someone else's experience. Making her own mistakes wasn't her first choice, or even her fourth or fifth choice. *Too bad Crash was the biggest mistake I ever made.*

"Couldn't say," Annie mused. "Though I do see a lot of people make mistakes here. You'd think I'd be an expert by now."

Martina snickered. She'd take a distraction right now, and her imagination was sent spinning with that thought in mind. "What's the most romantic thing that ever happened here?"

The barmaid dried her hands, her gaze thoughtful. "I don't know that romance is really happening around here. Not like you mean it, anyway."

"Oh, come on," Martina pressed. "No engagements because they had their first date here? No long-lost loves finding each other again?"

"You read too much People magazine," Annie said, grinning. "Well, I take that back..."

"Yes?" She pressed forward, putting her chin in her hands and her elbows on the bar like Annie was about to tell a fairy tale.

"I'm pretty sure Darby Ferris and Shane Billingham hooked up in the back of her four runner a few months ago."

Martina stuck out her tongue. "That's old news, she delivered their baby a year ago."

Annie's eyebrows shot up. "Oh, really? Last I heard, we didn't know who the daddy was..."

Martina pulled her lips to the side. Her friend Winnie had delivered the baby, which is the only way she knew Shane had been there.

"Well, let me rephrase that: he was there when Bailey was born. I guess I don't for sure she's his."

"Seems pretty likely, though."

"Don't tell anybody, okay?"

"Tell them what?" Annie asked innocently, then gave Martina a wink as she moved down to the other side of the bar where Gray was signaling her. Martina brushed away the guilt she felt about spreading gossip; it wasn't a HIPAA violation or anything, but she should know better. Sometimes the news was just too good: it was just too tempting to let secrets spill out. And even this bit of juicy gossip had her thinking...she didn't know Darby was still seeing Shane. Last she knew, she was trying to do the single mom thing all by her lonesome, and it wasn't going all that well. She had moved back in with her mom a few weeks ago. Martina felt her gaze drifting to the TV.

"Oh, come on," she yelled in unison with half the bar as a 49ers defender took down a Browns cornerback in what was clearly a flagrant horse collar. "*That's* a no call? Seriously? You've got to be kidding me..." She wouldn't mind if the Browns won, since it would weaken the 49er's record against the Seahawks in November. Then again, they were going to meet the Browns next week in Cleveland, so it wouldn't hurt for them to be demoralized. The Seahawks historically didn't do as well on the road.

Right now, any distraction was welcome. Anything so that she didn't have to think about what working for her ex was going to be like.

Order *Right Back Where We Started* now!

Need a little more Timber Falls right now? Newsletter subscribers get the exclusive short story, How It All Began, which tells us how Evan and Farrah met (that's Daniel and Kyle's mom and dad). Sign up now at https://www.subscribepage.com/timberfalls.

Acknowledgments

TO MY EDITORIAL TEAM at Salt and Sage: you all rock. I can't say it enough: your professionalism, straight-up knowledge of your genres, and kindness make this so much easier.

To my critique partner, Angela Boord: thanks for 'getting' my work and assuring me that I can make it as good as it can be.

To my copy editor, Jessica Gardner: Thank you for sharing your expertise with me! I'm still floored by all the rules you know. All those tiny corrections take my diamond in the rough and polish it up!

To my cover artist, Erin O'Neill-Jones: Wow. Just wow. I still can't get over how you've captured these characters! Thanks for all your hard work on this.

Gratitude also to Michael McCreary for his book *Funny, You Don't Look Autistic* for giving me insight into an autistic person's mind.

And last, but certainly not least, thank you to my CFO, Mr. West. You are the peanut butter to my jelly.

Connect with Fiona!

Thanks so much for taking the time to sample my work. I hope you enjoyed reading it even more than I enjoyed writing it, though I doubt that's possible. Being an author is a dream come true, and getting to share my books with delightful, thoughtful readers like you just adds to the sweetness. Drop me a line and let me know what you thought or leave a review on Goodreads!

Sign up for my bi-monthly newsletter, The West Wind, for freebies, deleted scenes, book reviews, and insight into my writing process at https://www.subscribepage.com/timber-falls.

On Twitter as @FionaWestAuthor

On Facebook as @authorfionawest

On Instagram as fionawestauthor

On Goodreads as Fiona West

Or email me at fiona@fionawest.net.

I love talking to fans!

www.ingramcontent.com/pod-product-compliance
Lightning Source LLC
Chambersburg PA
CBHW051652180726
48284CB00006B/1972